Heir of Illaria

Dyan Chick

For my husband, who put up with my single-minded focus on writing while making this book a reality

CONTENTS

CHAPTER 1

Leaves rustled behind me. I pulled my dagger from its sheath on my wrist and held my breath, frozen in place. The rustling stopped, everything was quiet. I let out a breath and replaced my dagger. *Must have been a squirrel. I'm starting to be as paranoid as my grandmother.* A pang of guilt rose through me for sneaking out again. *Hopefully she'll forgive me when she sees the basket of berries I'm bringing back.*

Reaching for my neck, I made sure the pendant I wore hadn't come loose. As usual, it was safely hidden under my clothes. I sighed. *I really am becoming as paranoid as my grandmother.* The necklace had been a tenth birthday gift, a keepsake left behind by my dead mother. The circular snake eating its own tail, the Ouroboros, wasn't a symbol I saw anywhere except for my pendant, and I had been instructed to keep it that way.

Grandmother wouldn't talk about my mother. I always figured it made her too sad, but I felt like something was missing. Like somehow, I wasn't complete. When I was a child, I liked to imagine that one day, somebody with the same pendant would find me. They would explain everything, and I'd fill the hole inside me with the answers to the questions I couldn't put into words. I shook my head. My parents were dead. Nobody was coming to find me. *You're too old for those fantasies.*

I weaved around the trees to find my way back to the dirt road that cut through the woods. Low hanging branches caught in my hair, and I stopped to pull the leaves out. The

1

birdsong above me shifted. The musical notes changed into warning cries. My heart rate quickened and I looked around, expecting to see a predator. Instead, hoof beats punctuated the silence. Somebody was riding through the woods. I was steps away from the road, and peered through the trees to see who was coming. Two men riding formidable black horses were headed in my direction. An uncomfortable feeling crept into me, as if warning me to avoid these travelers. I sank back into the trees, hoping they'd pass without seeing me.

As they got closer, I could see that they were wearing the king's crest. A human skull embraced by the wings of a fiery phoenix. A chill ran down my spine at the sight of that skull. His crest was a reminder about his powers as a necromancer. My breath caught in my chest as they rode by and I clenched my basket tightly. All my life, I'd managed to avoid interacting with anybody who worked for the king. Today wasn't the day I was going to break that streak.

I took another step back into the trees as they drew nearer, hoping to further conceal myself. A dry branch snapped under my feet. I cursed silently. The horses swung their heads in my direction and the riders pulled back on the reigns to look around. My heart beat wildly in my chest. I closed my eyes and stood frozen in place. *If I don't move, maybe they won't see me.*

The horses started moving again and I opened my eyes. They were right in front of me.

"You there, girl!" shouted the first rider from atop his horse. "Step out here where we can see you."

My stomach jumped into my throat. I stepped onto the trail next to the large black steeds.

"What are you doing in the King's woods?" he asked me.

I lifted the basket I was holding. "Picking berries."

His tangled dark hair and thick stubble made him look more like a beast than a man. His dark eyes studied my blue ones. His irises were almost as dark as his pupils, making it seem like he could look right through me. I could practically feel the pendant burning into my skin and fought against the urge to check that it was still hidden. A shiver of fear ran up my spine, and I turned my gaze to the ground.

He dismounted and took a few steps toward me. My whole body tensed. *What does he want from me?* He reached his hand out and scooped a handful of berries from my basket. My hands began to tremble.

"What kind of berries are these?" He tossed them into his mouth.

"Blueberries." I took a step back, but the ground was uneven and I stumbled, almost losing my basket. He grabbed my wrist to steady me. That's when he found my dagger. I froze. *Is he going to think I'm a threat? Is he going to hurt me?* I'd started carrying a dagger after a villager had been attacked by a puma, though I'd never learned how to actually use it.

He pulled me closer to him, turning my arm. "What's this?"

The other rider climbed off of his horse and walked over to us. He was smaller than the first man and had a stocky build. His red hair and red beard matched his ruddy complexion. The sleeves of his tunic were pushed up to his elbows, revealing several tattoos on his forearms.

"Everything okay here?" he asked.

"This girl looks to be hunting in the King's woods." The first man pulled my arm toward his friend, showing my dagger.

I struggled to keep my balance as he pulled me to him. The basket around my other wrist tipped, sending berries all over the ground.

"You know hunting in the King's woods is punishable by death," the second man said.

The beast turned to his friend. "We haven't had a good hanging in a while in this part of the kingdom."

I'd seen a hanging when I was younger. My throat tightened as if I had a rope around my neck. It was getting hard to breathe. I reached my hand up around my neck and swallowed, trying to shake the image of the twitching body from my mind.

"I'm not hunting," I pleaded. "I just have it in case of a puma or bear."

The men looked at each other.

The second man started laughing. "You think you could take down a puma or bear with your dagger?"

"I don't know, but I'd at least try."

The first man smiled and threw my wrist away from him as if he found it disgusting.

I stumbled again.

"What's your name, girl?" he asked me.

I cleared my throat, trying to find my voice through the fear. "Wilona."

They looked at each other again.

Nervous butterflies flooded my stomach. *I said too much.* I needed to get out of here. Yet I stood there, glued to the spot. I was afraid to move. The King's Guard had too much unquestioned power for me to risk upsetting them. I pulled the basket back up my arm and crossed my arms over my chest.

"You live in the village nearby?" The beast lifted his chin toward my village.

"Yes." My hands were starting to tremble. I looked around, wondering if I should make a run for the woods. Find a place to hide.

"No doubt with your parents and a brood of siblings?"

I ignored him for a moment, still glancing around. Warning bells were ringing in my head. My grandmother's distrust of all people had resulted in lectures about not talking to people I didn't know.

"What do your parents do, Wilona?"

I'm not going to get out of this without saying something. "My grandmother is a seamstress." I looked away from his penetrating gaze.

"No parents, then?" he said.

I shifted uncomfortably and shook my head without looking up.

He took a step closer to me and lifted my chin so I was looking right into his dark eyes. They were cold and unkind. "How old are you?"

My eyes darted around. *Is there a way out of this? Is he going to hurt me?* I saw the other guard to my right. He had his hand on the hilt of his sword. He wouldn't be of any help. I bit the inside of my cheek to keep from crying out. "I'm seventeen."

He let go of my chin and turned to his friend. They exchanged some sort of silent conversation. Then he looked back at me with a forced smile on his face. The expression was about as convincing as a hungry wolf.

"Best be on your way then. It'll be getting dark soon."

I nodded and slowly took a few steps onto the road. I let out a breath I didn't know I had been holding but my hands were shaking. I glanced over my shoulder.

The men mounted their horses and the beast smiled at me. "Be careful out there, Wilona. There are a lot of dangerous people in the woods these days." They turned around and rode away from me and my village.

As I watched them leave, I felt a weight lift off of my chest. It was my first interaction with anyone who worked for the king, and it was not something I wanted to repeat. As soon as the horses were out of sight, I raced home.

Nearing my house, I slowed to a walk, working hard to catch my breath. I couldn't tell my grandmother about this. It would only upset her. *Besides, they left and went the other way.* They probably just wanted to scare me. *I'm sure they enjoy scaring people. Why else would they join the King's Guard?*

I opened the front door a crack and listened for any signs of my grandmother. Silence. I stepped inside and froze. Grandmother was sitting in the kitchen.

"Wilona." She shook her head.

I squeezed my eyes closed. *Guess she wasn't still in town.*

"Where were you?" she asked.

I moved the basket behind my back. "I went for a walk."

She frowned. "With a basket?"

I was almost eighteen. There were people my age who already had homes of their own. *When will she start letting me make decisions for myself?* I sighed. "Okay, you caught me. I went to the woods to pick berries."

She stood and walked over to me. "You know I don't like it when you go to the woods. It's just not safe for you."

"I can handle myself."

She glanced at the dagger. "You don't even know how to use that thing. Besides, it wouldn't do you any good if you ran into the King's Guards."

I rubbed my nose and looked away from her, wondering if I should just tell her about the guards. *It will only make her upset if I tell her.*

"What happened?"

I avoided eye contact. "Nothing happened." I lifted the empty basket. "Just no berries today." I walked past her to put the basket in the kitchen.

"Wilona, be honest with me. I know when you're keeping something from me."

I sighed. I was a terrible liar. The words tumbled out, too quickly. "I ran into two King's Guards, but I'm fine. They talked to me but then they left."

Her face fell and she sunk into a chair. "Wilona, it might be time we had a little talk."

Something in her tone of voice was different. My stomach knotted. She patted her hand on the chair next to hers. I sighed and plopped down on it. She leaned back in her chair and pinched her nose between her finger and thumb. I waited.

The ringing of bells cut through the silence. I jumped to my feet. It wasn't a feast day or time for service. The bell tolled again. It was ringing in a series of three rings with a pause in between. I'd never heard that pattern.

My grandmother looked at me, face ashen. She stood. "We have to get you out of here right now." She dragged me to the back door of the house.

I pulled away from her and grabbed her hands. "What are you doing?"

"There's no time, Wilona. They've found you." She threw open the back door. The men I had run into in the woods were smiling back at me. The hair on my arms stood on end.

"Looks like we found the right house," the beast said.

My grandmother pushed me away from the door and stood in front of the men. "Run. Don't look back. Run!"

I ran toward the front door, heart threatening to break free of my chest. My grandmother let out a scream amidst the thundering sound of their boots behind me. A hand clasped around my wrist, pulling me back. I screamed and another hand covered my mouth. *They've come back for me.* A dangling corpse filled my vision, lifeless body hanging from the gallows.

The beast whispered in my ear. "There's nobody here to help you. You'll be dead before those White Ravens even know we found you."

Why does he want me dead? He knows I wasn't hunting. What Ravens? He had let me go in the woods. Why show up at my house? Whatever the reason, he planned to harm me. *Fight back.* I pulled my dagger out of its sheath and he knocked it away. I tried to wiggle out of his grasp as he raised a knife above his head. Swallowing hard, I closed my eyes tight. *I can't die like this!*

There was a blur of movement. I found myself out of his grasp and he was on the ground, gripping his throat. There was blood flowing under his hands and a look of terror in his eyes. He dropped to his knees and fell back on the ground, unblinking.

The other guard grabbed me by my hair. He produced a small knife out of his waistband and held it to my throat. He turned me so that we were facing the newcomer, the person who had saved me.

The figure pulled back a hood, revealing a strikingly beautiful woman. She had green eyes and light blond hair that fell in messy ringlets. Her nose was small and pointed, mouth formed into a tight angry line, eyes narrowed. She reached inside her cloak, removing a sword, and gripped it with both hands. She bent her knees, getting into an attack position. My eyes widened. I had never seen a woman fight before.

"If you want her," she said, "you have to go through me!"

The man holding me shifted. He laughed as he tossed me aside, knocking me to the ground. I crawled away to put more distance between myself and the impending battle. My heart was still pounding and my hands were trembling. I looked toward the back door and saw my grandmother on the ground. I couldn't get to her without putting myself in the middle of a fight. *Please be okay.* The guards came here because of me and my grandmother had protected me from them. I didn't see any movement from her. What would I do if she was dead? I needed to get to her but that wasn't possible while the other guard was still alive. I returned my gaze to the unlikely pair as they faced off.

He unsheathed his sword and pointed it at the blonde woman. "What are you going to do with that thing?"

"You shouldn't underestimate me," she said.

"You're just a woman." He spat on the ground.

Her eyes never left his. She didn't seem rattled by his taunting and took a step forward, making the first move. She swung her sword with practiced movements, catching him off guard. He looked surprised, but managed to dodge it, taking a couple of steps back.

"This might be more fun than I thought." He lunged at her, causing her to spin away and her steel made contact with his, blocking his blow.

She returned his aggression with a quick thrust to his abdomen, piercing the skin. He backed up, howling in pain. Then he narrowed his eyes and charged her, swinging wildly. She smiled. In his haste, he left his body unguarded. He raised his sword above his head, preparing to strike. She ducked down and in one clean motion, sliced across his waist. Blood spewed everywhere.

He finished his swing but it didn't even touch her. Then he fell to his knees, eyes wide. He wrapped an arm around his waist and stared, open mouthed at the wound. All the color drained from his ruddy face. He struggled to speak, but couldn't get any words to come out. With a look of sheer panic, he fell to the ground and stopped moving. I sat there, feeling numb, staring at the dead man's lifeless, open eyes.

"Wilona," the woman said gently, "we need to go."

I looked up, her words breaking me from my trance. *Grandmother.* "Grandmother!" I shouted, looking around frantically. I raced to the back door.

She was laying on the ground on her side, one arm outstretched. I turned her over so I could see her face. Her eyes had the same lifeless look as the man I just watched die. *No!* A lump rose in my throat and my eyes stung with the beginnings of tears. *This is my fault.* These men had come here to kill me.

How did I let this happen? I'd done nothing, I was useless to protect myself or anybody else. I should have done something, anything. *It's my fault she's dead.*

"Wilona, we need to go." The woman said more forcefully.

I glared at this stranger who had just saved my life. "What's going on? How do you know my name?"

She lifted her wrist to show me a leather bracelet. A circular snake eating its tail, an Ouroboros, was burned into it. "My name is Saffron, I'm here to keep you safe. I'll explain everything later but right now, we have to go."

I stared at the Ouroboros on her bracelet and reached for my pendant. *It looks just like mine.* I'd dreamed of this day, the day somebody would fill in the gaps. Shouldn't I be happy? I swallowed down the metallic taste that filled my mouth. *Not like this. Not without my grandmother.* I shook my head. "I can't just leave my grandmother here!" My vision was blurry from the tears.

She grabbed my arm and pulled me up. "Wilona, I'll explain everything soon, I promise. But right now, you need to come with me. Your grandmother would understand."

I heard horses approaching. Her eyes widened and the color drained from her face. "Now." It was a command.

I nodded and followed her out the front door.

"Mount the horse!" She told me pointing to one of two waiting horses. "Stay with me. We have to go fast. Now."

I allowed myself one backwards glance at my home. I had a feeling this would be the last time I would ever see it.

CHAPTER 2

I chased Saffron down the road through the village, away from the woods. As we passed the last few farms in the outskirts, I realized I was about to travel further away from home than I had ever been before.

Darkness swallowed us as the last remnants of civilization vanished. We were left with only the stars and the full moon. I looked up at it, thankful for the extra light.

"We've got to move faster!" Saffron shouted as she picked up her pace. She didn't wait for my response, increasing her speed immediately.

Despite the fact that I had taken lessons at my grandmother's insistence, I was still fairly inexperienced at horseback riding. Panting, I struggled to hang on to my horse. My legs gripped the sides in a desperate attempt to keep my balance.

We were on a well traveled dirt road. I had no idea where we were headed. Anger rose inside me as I realized my grandmother had been keeping things from me all these years. Guilt quickly replaced the anger. My grandmother was dead. I'd never get to talk to her again. She'd never correct my embroidery or help me make a pie. My heart sunk and my breath came out shallow and rapid. *She can't be gone.* Tears stung my eyes and my throat felt like it was swelling shut. *This has to be a dream. This can't be happening.* The gap had widened between my horse and Saffron's. Blinking the tears away, I pushed my horse harder to keep up.

The faster pace helped clear my head. I focused on the cold wind on my face and the way the moonlight cast glowing pools on the road around us. A howl in the distance reminded me that we weren't the only ones awake at this time of night. I shivered and glanced behind me. All I saw was the dust from the dry roads rising in clouds as my horse's hoofs hit the dirt.

After several hours of riding, Saffron slowed her horse down and mine followed her lead. She dropped back to ride next to me. "We need to rest the horses and get them some water." She led us to a stream and we dismounted.

I didn't want to rest, I wanted to go home. My grandmother's lifeless body appeared in my mind. I winced and pushed the vision away. Grandmother *was* home and now she was gone. *I don't have a home anymore.*

I rubbed my eyes and dropped my hands to my side, letting numbness flow through me. It would be better to feel nothing than feel everything. Defeated, I sunk to the ground and pulled my knees to my chest.

"We'll be at a safe house in a couple of hours. I don't want to risk stopping to make camp." Saffron said. She brushed her hair off of her face and I caught sight of the leather bracelet.

I'd forgotten about that. Something inside me ignited, a flicker of hope. "Your bracelet. It has the same symbol as my pendant."

She turned her bracelet so the symbol was on the inside of her wrist, hidden from me. "It's how we find each other. Those of us who have been protecting you."

"People are protecting me? That doesn't make any sense. I don't understand why the King's Guard tried to kill me. Please, I need to know what's going on." My hands were shaking and I clenched them into fists.

Saffron sighed. "It's a long story and I don't want to get into all of it here. I promise I'll tell you everything soon."

"Can't you just give me something?" I lifted the pendant out in front of me. "All I have left in the world is this stupid pendant."

"Keep that hidden for now. It'll all make sense before long."

Saffron pulled the pendant from my fingers and tucked it under my bodice.

"I'm really sorry about your grandmother. She was an amazing woman," Saffron handed me the reigns to my horse. "She was willing to give up her own life to keep you safe and I intend to honor her sacrifice."

I opened my mouth to say something then closed it, unsure of how to respond. The sadness I was struggling to bury was bubbling to the surface again. I bit down on my lip. *No more tears. Not now.*

"Time to go." Saffron interlaced her fingers for me to use as a step.

As she mounted her horse, I checked to make sure the pendant was under my bodice. That remaining piece of my family felt heavy around my neck. It was all I had left. I was alone. When my parents had died, I'd become an orphan but I had never really felt like one until today.

I'd been too young to cry for my parents when they died. I didn't even have any memories of them. My grandmother had made me feel like I belonged, we were a family, just the two of us. She kept me from feeling sorry for myself. Without her, the full weight of the loss of my parents was suffocating. My chest felt heavy and breathing felt like it took too much effort. As our horses picked up the pace on the road, slow tears streamed down my cheeks. I let them fall, mourning the loss of my family for the first time.

We entered a large town as the sun was rising above the horizon. The whole world was cast in a warm glow. I visited the village frequently with grandmother, but had never traveled beyond the farmlands that bordered it. This town was at least five times larger than the village I was used to.

The streets were packed with carts, carriages, and other riders, forcing us to ride single file. I saw children running around in front of the shops and people hurrying by carrying purchases. The constant noise and distractions made it difficult to focus on the road ahead of me. I wanted to stop and look at everything.

We reached a wide open square. It looked like a nice place for people to gather but it was eerily empty. The hoof steps of our horses echoed through the uninhabited space. I shivered. Where were all the people?

My blood went cold. On the other side of the square was the longest gallows I had ever seen. From them, there were eight bodies dangling in the air. Two of them were small enough to be children. My mouth dropped open in shock. I pulled up on the reins, making my horse stop. My eyes widened, I couldn't look away.

Saffron brought me back to reality. "Let's go."

My trembling hands tightened their grip on the reins. I shook my head and closed my eyes, trying to clear the image from my mind. Taking a deep breath, I followed Saffron. "Why are those people there? What did they do?" I asked.

"The King's Guard doesn't need reason. They just enjoy killing. Most of the people in the larger towns live in a constant state of fear." She said.

My jaw clenched. *This shouldn't be happening.* "Why doesn't anybody do anything?"

Saffron glanced at me, the ghost of a smile on her mouth, then turned away.

I had grown up hearing stories about how dangerous the king was, how powerful his necromancy was. People lived in fear of being killed only to be brought back as members of his undead army. In Illaria, there was a fate worse than death.

The King's Guard had been a rare sight in my tiny village. They usually just passed through on their way to the coast or the larger towns to the west. The one hanging I had seen was of a criminal who had been convicted of murder. At least that was what my grandmother told me he was hung for. Now, I wasn't sure if that was true. It didn't matter. I was seeing the truth now, the things she had sheltered me from and they made me more angry than afraid. Wasn't there anybody who had the power to stop this?

We picked up the pace to get through the square more quickly. I held on to the heat that was seeping through me.

Feeling angry was better than feeling sad.

We were approaching the edge of town and I thought we would keep going, but Saffron turned down an alleyway and dismounted. A man was standing there waiting for us.

I dismounted my mare and Saffron put her hand up for me to stay where I was. I stood there, stroking the nose of my horse. Saffron and the man spoke in hushed tones. She handed him a small coin bag and they shook hands.

"He's going to take the horses from here," she said.

I followed her on foot through the twists and turns of the alleys. The town was even larger than I originally thought. We reached a small, plain looking building with a green door and a bronze knocker. The knocker had a circle engraved on it with small triangle that intersected the top line. It had the same shape as the Ouroboros. I traced my finger over it and leaned in to look at it more closely. *This isn't a coincidence.*

Saffron looked at me. One corner of her mouth was raised in a smile. "Most of us use this simplified Ouroboros so it just looks like a design. The symbol you wear is illegal."

Instinctively, I reached down to make sure my pendant was tucked under my bodice. My head ached. *More unanswered questions.*

I threw my hands up in the air. "I suppose I have to wait on the explanation for that, too?"

"In time, you'll understand everything." She lifted the knocker and pounded it against the door three times. Then she paused and did it again. Just like the bells in my village. After the fourth succession of knocks, the door swung open.

"Follow me," she said as she went through the open door.

The building had no windows and was lit with only a few scattered candles. It took my eyes a few moments to adjust to the dim light. Every wall was covered in a tapestry. As I walked, my feet sunk into plush rugs. We were standing inside of a grand foyer. I would have never guessed that the unassuming building was holding such luxury.

The door shut behind me and I turned at the sound. A thin woman in a silk gown was staring at me. The fabric looked a little worn, like it was an older dress, but the construction was exquisite. I had only seen gowns like this once, when my grandmother was asked to repair the dress of a noblewoman who stopped for a night in our village.

"Welcome to my home." She dropped into an exaggerated curtsy. Her voice was feminine but had a rough edge to it. Like she had gravel in her throat. She wore her dark hair piled on top of her head in elaborate curls. Her brown eyes watched every movement I made.

I wasn't sure how to respond to such a greeting. I gave a half bow.

She smiled at me. "We'll work on that." With a flourish of silk, she walked past us. "Come, come ladies. We have much to do."

Saffron was still wearing her half smile. She swept an open hand in the direction that the woman had just walked. "After you."

I hesitated for a moment and then followed her. We walked through a sitting room complete with ornately carved wooden chairs, and a piano. Then she took us up a narrow stone staircase to a second floor. The woman waited in the hallway for me.

"I have a bath filled for you, my lady," she said. "There is also a change of clothes for you." She opened the door to a small room containing a tub, bed, and a small dressing table.

"Thank you," I said.

She nodded at me. "We'll talk more when you are recovered from your journey."

I entered the room and the door shut behind me. Looking into the water, I wondered if there was any way to wash away the events of the last day. I peeled off my dress and a cloud of dust filled the air. The crumbled dress on the floor reminded me of my grandmother's body on the ground. I kicked the dress away and covered my face in my hands. Turning my back on it, I ran my hands through my tangled hair. This had been the worst day of my entire life.

Shaking my head, I looked down at the pendant hanging

around my neck. I traced my fingers over the symbol as if I'd find an answer etched in it. The serpent was as familiar to me as my own skin. I'd studied it so often as a child. It always seemed so futile to me. Eating its own tail. I felt like I understood what it was feeling today. The further I had come in this day, the more unanswered questions I had. As if I were creating my own problems, just like the snake.

I stepped into the warm water and sunk all the way under. It was quiet under the water, peaceful. As my lungs started to cry out for air, the lifeless bodies from the gallows penetrated my thoughts. I pushed myself up to the surface, splashing water everywhere, gasping for breath.

Hoping to clear the visions of death from my mind, I looked around for distractions. The room was well appointed, with a large bed and thick carpets. There were no windows. The door was the only way in or out. Goosebumps formed on my arms. I was alone but I didn't feel safe. I wondered if I'd ever feel safe again.

After this bath, I was going to find out what was really going on. My stomach filled with butterflies. Quickly, I scrubbed off as much of the dirt as I could. It was time to start getting some answers.

The gown that was left out for me was nicer than anything I had ever owned. I put it on carefully, not wanting to damage the stitching or snag any of the little beads that were sewn on. It was heavy and uncomfortable. I glanced longingly at the simple dress I left on the ground, then shuddered as I recalled the vision of my grandmother. She had made me that dress, but I wasn't sure I could wear it again.

When I reached the sitting room I found the woman waiting for me. Saffron wasn't there.

"Have a seat," she said with a slight curtsy.

I wrinkled my brow, studying her. When she didn't move or say anything else I resigned myself to having a seat in one of the ornate chairs. The cushions were decorated in fraying embroidery. At one point, these chairs would have been exceptional works of art. The frayed cushions deterred from the ornate wood, making them look less impressive up close.

I had spent a lot of time embroidering designs for my grandmother's seamstress business. I wasn't as good as the craftsman you could find in larger cities, but my work was always praised by the people in our village. I thought back to a time I embroidered the Ouroboros on a scrap piece of fabric. I thought my grandmother would be impressed. Instead, she threw the scrap in the fire and told me never to let anybody see the symbol. Now I knew what I created was illegal. I wondered about Saffron's bracelet. Were there others out there wearing the Ouroboros?

The woman sat on a chair across from me and smiled at me.

I smiled back and adjusted my position in the chair. I arranged my hands on my lap, and then moved them to the armrests and back again. I cleared my throat as quietly as I could in the thick silence.

She scooted to the front of her chair and set her clasped hands on her lap. Her posture was perfect. "I know you've been through a lot the last few days." Her smile was warm, genuine.

I nodded. My eyes darted to the stairs hoping to see Saffron. She had been the only constant thing in my life since my near death experience.

"She'll be down in a moment," she said, her eyes darting toward the stairs. She looked back at me. "I'm afraid I have been very rude. I never introduced myself. I'm Lady Genevieve. This is my home." She made a sweeping gesture with her arm.

"I'm Wilona. Thank you for having me in your home," I said. "And thank you for the bath and the clothes."

She smiled. "It's the least I can do."

I wasn't sure what to say. It took every ounce of my focus to keep from looking to the stairs again. This woman had allowed me into her home and shown me nothing but kindness. I didn't want to be rude to her. She fidgeted in her chair.

"Maybe you'd like something to eat while we wait?" Genevieve said.

17

I wasn't feeling hungry, but I thought back to the last time I ate. Bread.

"If it's not too much trouble."

She stood and gave me another of her curtsies before leaving the room.

I sank back into the chair and worked my fingers through my wet hair, trying to untangle the dark curls. My eyelids were growing heavy. I stood up and started to wander around the room, worried that sitting too long would result in me falling asleep.

Directly across from me was a massive tapestry. It showed a battle between two large armies. Up close, the details were stunning. I could make out the facial expressions on some of the key figures and saw the blood from the wounded soldiers. At first, I was too interested in examining the quality of the work to notice the narrative. Then the symbol blinded me. One of the armies wore the symbol I did around my neck as its crest. The other army had the symbol of the king. I gasped and walked backward to the chair I had been occupying only moments before.

I sat down, face flushed, hands cold. I had to look down to keep from staring at the bloody battle in front of me. I studied my hands and concentrated on slowing my breathing. Once I felt like I had regained control of myself, I pulled the necklace out from under my bodice. I looked at the symbol on my necklace and then back at the symbols covering the tapestry. The Ouroboros engraved on the charm seemed to glow. It was the same symbol. I dropped it as if it had burned me. *Why am I wearing a royal crest around my neck?*

Anything related to the previous king was considered treason. That's why this symbol was illegal. *I could be hung for wearing this.*

"Wilona?"

I jumped at the sound of my name. *Saffron is back.*

18

CHAPTER 3

I was pacing the room when Saffron entered. She had removed her armor and wore fresh clothes. She looked around the room. "Where's Genevieve?"

I shrugged. "She said she was getting food."

"She'll be back soon, then." Saffron walked to a plush armchair and sat down. For a split second, a tired look crossed her face, then she recovered and looked at me with sharp, focused eyes. "We have a lot to talk about and you have a lot of questions."

Jaw set, I held up my pendant. "Why am I wearing the old king's crest?"

She stared at me, unblinking.

"That's what it is, right?" I pointed behind me. "It's all over that tapestry."

Saffron followed my gaze and studied the tapestry for a moment. "That's the Battle of the Dead."

"Battle of the Dead?"

She raised an eyebrow. "Your grandmother didn't teach you about this?"

I shook my head. "She didn't like to talk about the old king. She told me it was too dangerous. I got bits and pieces from the villagers sometimes."

In less than a day, my whole world had been turned upside-down. The pendant, my grandmother's death, the bodies hanging in the square, this battle I had never heard of, all of it was connected. I was starting to realize how much had been kept from me. I clasped my hands behind my back and studied the tapestry again.

"Your grandmother had every right to be cautious. Tell me what you do know," Saffron said.

"I heard the old king was defeated in a terrible battle. Lots of people died."

Genevieve walked in and set down a tray of food then sat down in an empty chair. "Don't stop on my account, please continue."

I looked up at the ceiling, trying to piece together the information I had overheard the last several years. "The king is a necromancer and can bring back the dead. He can also control monsters and uses dark magic. People are afraid of him."

"That's all true," Saffron said. "The king is a very powerful sorcerer."

My brow creased as I recounted what I listed of the king's powers. "Monsters? That part is true?"

She nodded.

I ran my hands through my hair and turned away from her. *This just keeps getting worse and worse.*

"What does this have to do with me?"

She sighed. "Everything. I'll start from the beginning."

I dropped into a chair across from her. My insides churned as I waited for the answers to come. Part of me wanted to know everything and part of me was afraid to find out the truth.

"King Osbert used to be a duke. He was one of the king's dearest friends, but he was obsessed with power. He spent many years learning dark magic with one goal in mind: take over the kingdom and claim the throne for himself. He was trained in sorcery, as many noble children are. Few have natural talent. He did. His ambition drove him to begin training in dark sorcery, reading books that should be destroyed and learning from others who shared his love of darkness. He was relentless in his search for dark power ,leading him to find the Stone of Mortare."

"What's the Stone of Mortare?" I asked.

She spoke quietly. "It's what controls the Reapers."

I flinched. I had heard stories about the king's undead assassins but always hoped they were elaborate tales to frighten children. "They're real?"

"I've seen them," Saffron said.

"And they're controlled by a stone?" My mind started to wander. "Why hasn't anybody taken it from him to end this?"

"It's very well hidden, protected by magic. Still, in the beginning, some tried. They're all members of his undead army now." Saffron's gaze was unfocused as if recalling a memory from long ago. She sat silently for a moment.

I leaned forward in my chair. "So what happened next?"

She shook her head to snap out of it and looked at me. She cleared her throat and continued. "He used the Reapers to create a massive army of the undead. Anyone who resisted joining him against King Augustus was recruited to his undead army. Some people joined because they were afraid of him. Some joined because they were forced to. His army was too big. King Augustus didn't stand a chance. They fought valiantly, but it was for naught. So many people died during those months of turmoil."

"How did I not know more about this?" I couldn't believe that something that had happened during my lifetime had not been talked about more often.

"King Osbert made it against the law to discuss the old king. He enforced it brutally. So people were afraid to talk at all." Saffron grabbed an apple from the tray and started to eat.

I sat there for a moment, staring at the tapestry and listening to Saffron chew.

"Why risk it then?" I said.

"Risk what?"

I pulled the necklace off of my neck and held it out in front of me.

"Oh yes." She sighed and set down her apple.

I dropped the necklace in my lap and tried to piece together some way this was all connected. Who was I to be part of this in any way? Since when do peasant girls get involved with royal politics? My heart stopped as the pieces started to connect in my head.

"Please, Saffron," I pleaded, "just tell me the truth."

I already knew what she was going to say before the words left her mouth, but it didn't seem possible. I needed to hear it from her.

Saffron gave Genevieve one last look and then turned to me. "Here's the truth. You are a princess. King Augustus was your father."

My jaw went slack. I tucked my hair behind my ears. It was the same conclusion I had come to, but it still didn't feel real. *I'm not special, I'm not different from anybody else. I don't feel like a princess.* The pendant in my lap felt heavy. I stared down at it, unable to touch it at that moment. *My parents had been the king and queen.* Now I knew why my grandmother had never talked about them. It was hard to miss people that you knew nothing about. Every new fact I learned made them more real, making the pain of their loss slice though me like the opening of a long healed wound.

Genevieve joined the conversation. "As soon as your father discovered that the duke had control of the Reapers, you were placed into hiding. Your parents always planned to come for you once it was safe. Nobody expected them to die." She looked down and wiped a tear from her cheek.

Saffron took over. "It's true, Wilona. But we have been watching you since that day. There is a group of us who have been keeping you safe. We wanted you to have a happy life. We were going to tell you when you turned eighteen. Once the King's Guard found you, we had to speed up our plans."

Picking up my pendant, I traced over the symbol with my index finger. My fist closed around the necklace. I wasn't sure if I hated it or loved it right now. I slumped into the chair, suddenly feeling exhausted.

After a few deep breaths, I collected my strength and stood up. "What now?"

A wide smile crossed Genevieve's face. "Spoken like a true

princess. Despite all you have been through, you're ready to act."

I tried to smile at her but I felt numb. My mind was still processing everything I heard. Having dead parents was one thing. Having dead royal parents was totally different.

"Wait a minute," I began, "how was my grandmother alive?" Saffron gave me a sympathetic look.

I could see it written across her face. My shoulders sunk. "She wasn't my grandmother." *I loved her with all my heart. How is it possible that she wasn't my grandmother?* I never felt so alone.

"She was your governess from birth, Wilona. She loved you. She cared for you alongside your mother until you were two. Then she volunteered to protect you until the crisis passed. When your parents died, she raised you as her own blood."

My vision blurred as tears started to trickle down my face. I did love her. I wasn't even her real granddaughter and she died for me. It was too much. Too much death, too much hate. I wiped the tears from my face.

"I don't want to be royal." I looked at Saffron, then Genevieve. "Can't we just tell that to the king? Tell him I don't care what he does. Just leave me alone. Let me live in peace. I don't want a palace," I pulled up a section of the skirt I was wearing, "or fancy dresses. I just want to live in my little cottage with my grandmother." The tears were flowing freely now. There wasn't even any point in wiping them away. I sat there in front of these two women I barely knew and sobbed.

I hid my face in my hands. My shoulders shook and I struggled to catch my breath. Everything that I had been through cascaded around me.

A warm hand rested on my back. I looked up from my hands to see Genevieve kneeling next to me, her forehead wrinkled in concern.

I used the back of my hands to wipe the tears from my face. After a few deep breaths, I forced myself to stop shaking. Finally, the tears subsided and I started to breathe normally again. I didn't want to look at the other women in the room. "I'm sorry."

"Shhh, dear," Genevieve said, rubbing my back gently. "It's okay. You're safe here."

The sound of a throat clearing made me turn.

Saffron looked sympathetic. "I know it's a lot, Wilona. And Genevieve is right, you're safe here, but you'll have to move on quickly. I'm sorry, but there's too much to do."

I jumped to my feet and balled my hands into fists. "What do you mean *you know*. I just lost everything I had. And then I found out none of it was actually mine in the first place." My cheeks burned with frustration. "All I have left is a necklace with a symbol that can get me killed and my name..." I started laughing.

Both women looked at me as if I was going crazy.

"My name!" I said through the laughter. "My name probably isn't even my real name." I reached the point where I either had to find the humor in the situation, or I would have to keep crying. I wasn't sure if there were any more tears left.

Saffron stared at me, face impassive.

I stopped laughing, took a deep breath and looked to Saffron. "Am I right?"

She nodded. "You're right. Your name is not Wilona. That was a name your grandmother, um, Margaret, gave you to hide your identity. It was the name of her sister who was killed by an undead soldier."

She rested a hand on my shoulder. "Your birth name is Elisabetta. Your parents called you Etta."

"Etta," I said quietly. "Etta," I said it a bit louder, trying it on. I stood up and walked over to the tapestry again, searching the men wearing my family's coat of arms. I pointed to a larger figure with a thick black beard and gold armor.

"Is this my father?"

She nodded.

I studied his face for several long minutes. He had dark hair and blue eyes like me. I could see what looked like black curls hanging out behind his helmet. *So that's where my curls come from.*

The back of my throat was burning. I didn't want to cry again. I turned from the tapestry. "The king has taken everything from me."

Saffron gestured to the chair for me to sit.

I sat in the chair that faced away from the tapestry so I didn't have to look at it.

"You won't have to rule," Saffron began. "But you're a princess. As long as the king lives, you're a threat to him. You won't be safe until he's dead. To make that happen, we'll need your help."

The mention of death brought me back to the somber tone of our conversation. My whole body started to tingle and ice flowed through my veins. This wasn't fear. It was something else, an emotion I had a hard time identifying. Hatred. I had never experienced pure, blind hate before. It was overwhelming, making focus difficult. I felt like I was alone in the room. Glancing behind me, my eyes found the king in the tapestry. My upper lip curled and I narrowed my eyes at the embroidered figure. I wanted to tear it out of the tapestry. I wanted him to feel pain, no it had to be worse than that. *Something has to be done about this king.*

CHAPTER 4

"How can I help?" I asked. "If the King's guards see me, they'll kill me and anybody I'm with."

"I work for a group called the White Ravens. We have many friends. Like Lady Genevieve, here, they want to see the end of the evil king's reign. We even had people living in your village keeping you safe and watching over you."

"For how long?" I asked.

"Since you were placed into hiding." She smiled at me. "You aren't as alone as you think you are."

I smiled at her. Saffron had given me no reason to doubt her friendship. I'd spent my life largely cut off from the rest of the world. My grandmother was the only person I had ever had a true connection with. No friends or other family. And right here in front of me was a woman offering her friendship along with the promise that there were others who were waiting to welcome me. People who had been acting as protectors even when I thought it was just my grandmother and myself. I clutched my hand to my chest and a flutter of hope rose within me. Maybe things were going to work out. Was it too much to hope for?

Saffron held up her wrist, showing the symbol to me. "We have been working on a plan to overthrow the king since he defeated your father's armies. We're getting closer every day. You've always been part of the plan but we hoped to bring you in when you were a little older. Now we just have to pick things up a bit."

I stared at her bracelet and thought of the symbol on the door. Was it possible that something good would be able to come from so much bad? Maybe the Ouroboros wasn't such an ominous symbol, after all. If there were people willing to show that they didn't support the king, maybe there was some hope. Maybe the snake eating its tail wasn't about being alone and making your own problems.

Perhaps it was about something greater. Something that didn't have an ending, something that defied death itself. These people had watched out for me after my parents died. In a way, it was almost like my parents were still looking out for me.

Lifting my chin toward the ceiling, I mouthed a silent *thank you*. I was grateful that despite everything, I had people willing to help me. That also meant that they expected things from me and I intended to repay the favor.

"What is this plan?" I asked. I had no idea how I could possibly help to overthrow a sorcerer king. My skills were pretty much limited to sewing and finding useful plants in the woods.

"We'll go over everything, eventually," Saffron said. "For now, I need you to focus on just one part. The reason we are here."

"And that is?"

Saffron lifted her chin in Genevieve's direction. "Lady Genevieve is going to help you learn how to act like a royal. You're a princess, you need to learn how to act like one."

"Like princess lessons?" My voice was higher than usual.

Genevieve smiled at me. "Something like that, my dear. We need the people to believe that you are your father's daughter. They won't care that you were raised like a peasant. They will expect certain things from you. You have a role to play. It's an important one. You need to know everything a princess of seventeen should know, and we only have three days to get you there."

I sighed. This was not what I was expecting.

"Now, your highness," Genevieve said.

Your highness. I tried to say the words out loud but they stuck in my throat.

Genevieve patted my shoulder. "You need to eat something and get some rest. The next three days will be the longest you have ever had."

I reached for the tray of food and found something to eat. I had no idea what was in store for me.

*****

The next morning, I woke before the sun was up. A servant instructed me to dress and meet Lady Genevieve in the dining room.

I rubbed the sleep from my eyes and stifled a yawn as I entered the room.

Lady Genevieve sat in a deep purple chair in front of a polished wooden table. She stood when I entered and lowered herself into a curtsy. "Your highness."

"You don't have to do that," I said, waving her away with my hand.

"Yes, I do. And you should expect it of everybody who addresses you outside of your innermost circle," she said as she rose from the curtsy.

I sighed. "This is going to take some getting used to."

She smiled at me. Then the smile disappeared and her voice turned stern. "You're not going to like me much these next three days. But I have to make a lady out of a farm hand. It's not going to be pretty."

"I wasn't a farmhand," I said.

She held up a hand. "It doesn't matter. Anybody below nobility might as well be a farm hand."

I wrinkled my forehead. I wasn't sure I would be able to think about people like that. All I knew of life was the people below the nobility.

She walked over to me and pushed my shoulders back. She tutted. "Such bad posture." She circled me, making adjustments to how my hips, arms and head were placed.

I stood there afraid to move. The position she placed me in felt so unnatural.

"Now walk to the table." She walked backwards so she could watch me walk.

I took a few tentative steps, then picked up my pace a little.

"No, no, no!" she shouted at me. She walked over to me and began the whole process again.

We spent the next hour working on getting me to correctly walk to the table so we could have breakfast. Breakfast took two hours as she explained how to properly use every piece of silverware on the table and the proper way for me to eat my food. If every meal was going to be this much work, I wasn't sure I even wanted to eat. Maybe I could just eat in my room by myself. *She'll probably starve me if I don't do it her way.* I sighed and told myself it would get easier. *It has to.*

We spent the afternoon learning how to make small talk, the correct way to word compliments, how to use a fan, and dance. Lunch was preceded by another lesson on how to walk and how to eat. I was getting frustrated. She was right, I didn't like her very much.

I glared into my soup bowl. Learning how to be a princess was harder than it should be. *Why do all of these little details matter? How will this help defeat the king?*

"Do you really think it can be done?" I asked, "defeat the king, I mean."

"Perhaps. I suppose we have to hope it can be done," she said.

"Why are you helping me?"

She pushed her soup bowl aside and folded her hands on the table. "I had a family once, like you. Mother, father, brother. A husband and two beautiful daughters. They were all taken from me."

I looked away from her. "I'm so sorry. What happened to them?"

"My mother was taken hostage by the duke before the Battle of the Dead. My father was a member of your father's advisory council and they tried to control him by holding my mother hostage. My parents would never bow to a man like the duke. My father pretended to be helping him while leaking information to your father. When the duke found out, he killed them both. He killed my brother in the Battle of the Dead. To make an example of my family, he came after me. I was at the market," she wiped back a tear, "and came home to find my house in flames. My husband and children trapped inside."

My brow creased. "How could somebody be so cruel?"

She wiped away another tear. "I don't know, but he has to be stopped. If there is anything I can do to prevent somebody else from losing their family, I will do whatever it takes."

I pushed away my bowl. The thought of food made my stomach churn. I knew what it was like to lose family, but it had to be so much worse for Lady Genevieve. I didn't know my parents and my grandmother wasn't exactly young. How much worse was it for her to lose her children? Innocents who did nothing wrong? I shook my head. "Why hasn't anybody stopped him already?"

"People are afraid. They've lost hope. That's what you'll bring to them when you show them you survived. When you stand up straight and walk with confidence. You'll give them back that hope, and maybe they'll start fighting back."

Finally, it was time for dinner. Lady Genevieve helped me dress. Apparently, a princess has to wear uncomfortable clothing and four layers of dresses in order to eat an evening meal. When I walked into the dining room, she applauded me.

"I wasn't sure you could," she said. "But you learned how! You looked like a princess walking in here. You can only walk like this from now on. No going back to the slouchy farm girl walk."

I smiled despite the insult. It was the first time all day that I felt I had accomplished something.

Saffron joined us for dinner. Lady Genevieve had me teach her all of the proper uses of the silverware and how to eat each course. I was rewarded with a beaming smile from Lady Genevieve.

"You're a fast learner," Saffron said.

"Good thing, too," Lady Genevieve said. "I was worried when you asked me to do this. I didn't think it was possible. We have a lot to cover the next two days, but she should be able to pass as a royal who was raised by peasants by the time you two leave."

After dinner, the history lessons began. Saffron and I went to the sitting room and she began to teach me the history of the kingdom. Since the king didn't allow for any discussion of the old king, there wasn't much history being passed down to younger generations.

"A princess would be well versed in the history of her people," Saffron said. "You need to know your country's history and your family's history."

I nodded. I was looking forward to learning more about my family.

She rested her chin on her hand. "Let's see. Where should we begin?"

"My family?" I suggested.

"Of course." She smiled. "Now, your father was the seventh king in your family line. The Aqualine kings have a long and happy history. He ruled for twelve years before the Battle of the Dead."

"What about my mother?" I asked. I had heard snippets of stories and comments about the king, my father's, life growing up. I'd never heard anything about the queen.

"Your mother was from Gallia. A small, peaceful country. The stories say your mother and father married for love instead of political alliance."

"So that's why I was taught Gallic," I said. Growing up, I'd had lessons daily. My grandmother insisted that learning Gallic was important because we lived so close to the port. Gallia was a boat ride across the sea, making them our nearest neighboring kingdom.

"Your mother would be proud to know that you learned her language," Saffron said.

I tried to picture what my mother might have looked like. Based on the tapestry, I looked a lot like my father.

31

"The day you were born," Saffron continued, "I remember the celebrations and the parties. The king and queen had been married nearly ten years before you were born. People were worried that there would be no heir to the throne. The Grand Duke would inherit the throne if there was no heir and nobody wanted Osbert on the throne. I suppose he must have decided to take it the day you were born."

My birth had been the catalyst for the war that cost me my family.

The next two days were exhausting. I spent them learning how to braid my hair, dress myself, and curtsy. I learned how to hold my hands while speaking and how to greet new people. It was a whirlwind of information that would probably have come naturally to me had I been raised in a palace.

On the third day, I was nearing my breaking point. "Why am I doing all of this? Wouldn't it be better for me to be just like the people? Won't they understand that I was raised as a peasant?"

Genevieve sighed and plopped into the chair, in a very unladylike fashion. "We have been over this, dear. The people will expect you to look and act at least a little bit like a princess. Besides, there may be reasons that you don't fully know yet." She snapped her mouth shut and her eyes widened.

I lifted an eyebrow. Genevieve had given me some extra information. I knew they were hiding things from me, but they were very good at keeping secrets. Genevieve's exhaustion was clouding her judgment. I sat down next to her and leaned into her. "Genevieve, you have to tell me. Give me something to help me focus so I don't mess this up."

She looked at me and then looked toward the door. We were alone in the sitting room. Her voice was low. "I'm not supposed to tell you yet."

I knew she was close to cracking. Over the last three days, I had learned that Genevieve could not keep things inside. She said exactly what was on her mind at all times. I would guess that keeping this secret was driving her crazy.

I pleaded with her. "Please. I promise I will pretend that I don't know."

She sighed again.

I could feel her resolve breaking.

"Okay," she agreed. "But only because it isn't really a secret. It is more that we didn't want you to worry." She took a deep breath. "We are working on gaining allies in other countries. We need them badly if we are to succeed. We need them to believe that you really are the princess, and it will be hard to convince nobles and royalty you are a royal if you act like a peasant. They don't spend time with peasants. They will expect you to have certain qualities, even if they know of your upbringing. We will need you to seal our alliances with them."

I thought for a moment then stood up and then turned to face her. "So that's what you need me for?" I let out a sigh of relief. "Thank goodness! I was worried I would be expected to fight or something. I can shake hands and talk to people." I smiled. "I think I'm getting pretty good, too."

Genevieve stood. "Don't get too full of yourself, you're not there yet and I still have a whole afternoon with you."

I lifted the fan we had been working with. "Back to work, then?"

She nodded.

CHAPTER 5

When we left Lady Genevieve's home, I hugged her goodbye. She was hard on me during my lessons but I knew it was for a good reason. I hardly recognized myself. I was now wearing a traveling gown fit for a lady of the court and my hair was woven into an intricate braid atop my head. Out of habit, I tried to push my hair behind my ears, even though there wasn't any hair hanging in my face.

I didn't realize how well funded the Ravens were until Saffron led me to the carriage she had secured for our journey. We had a driver who would take us to our next stop in Yorkton, a day's journey from here.

Inside the carriage I sat with my back straight, gloved hands clasped in my lap. My face was set in an expression of disinterest. I didn't want the driver to realize it was my first carriage ride.

The driver loaded my new trunk on top of the carriage with a thud. Any one of the dresses in the trunk was worth more than my grandmother made in a whole year. Saffron directed the driver to secure my luggage with extra care. She was a convincing maid.

My shoulders and lower back were starting to ache from holding the unnaturally straight posture. Once Saffron seated across from me, the driver shut the door. The carriage rocked as he climbed to his seat. I let out a long breath and slumped against the cushion behind me. The carriage lurched forward and the tension started to drain from my body.

Saffron smirked at me.

"At least I didn't unlace the corset," I said.

"I can see why you didn't want to be a princess," she said. "I honestly didn't know all that was involved. That dress looks painful."

"Want to trade?" I asked her.

She smoothed the grey cotton skirt she was wearing. "No, thank you. I'm happy with my clothes."

We sat in silence for a few minutes. I looked out the window and watched the countryside roll by. It was a different way of seeing the world compared to horseback. *It was too quiet.* I tugged on the trim around my sleeves.

"Saffron?" I asked.

"Yes?" She lifted her chin.

"Is your family in the Ravens?"

"No, my family is dead." She looked out the window.

"I - I'm sorry." I didn't know what to say to her and turned my gaze to my hands in my lap. Maybe she did know what I was going through. Was the whole kingdom full of orphans as a result of the king's brutality?

She broke the silence. "My father was the Captain of the King's Guard and died defending your father in the Battle of the Dead."

My shoulders dropped. "I'm sorry."

She gave a half smile. "It's okay. I was thirteen when it happened. My father and I were close, but I knew what his job was." Saffron turned the bracelet on her wrist around in circles.

"And your mother?" I asked.

"She died in childbirth when I was young. I don't remember it. My aunt took me in for a while after my dad died. When the King's Guard came for her, she hid me under the floorboards." Her nostrils flared. "I heard her screams as they killed her."

I covered my mouth with my hand then lowered it to my neck. "Like Lady Genevieve's family." The king didn't just kill his enemies, he went after their families, too.

"You were all alone." I shook my head. "I'm so sorry."

"I was alone for a while but the Ravens found me." The

darkness that had been on her face faded. "They offered me a place, a skill, a community, and a cause. I never looked back."

I wasn't that different from Lady Genevieve and Saffron. All of us had lost everything that was important to us because of the king. Then there were the people hanging in the city square. And the people forced to fight for a king they didn't believe in, even after death. All of these families ripped apart. My fingernails bit into my palm and my heart rate quickened. *This has to stop.*

"The king needs to die."

Saffron smiled at me. "He will. He's going to pay for everything he's done."

We stopped for lunch at a small tavern a few hours into our journey. The driver stayed with the carriage. The smell of cooked meat and roasted vegetables flooded my nostrils as Saffron and I entered the small building. We found a table in the corner and sat down. A barmaid greeted us and took our order.

As she walked away, the dark room lit up as somebody opened the door. Two black armor-clad King's Guards walked into the tavern. I stopped breathing.

Saffron reached her hand under the table and gave my hand a squeeze. She mouthed *stay calm*, then took a long drink from her cup.

One of the guards walked up to the bar and started talking with the barmaid. I watched him out of the corner of my eye. I didn't want him to know I was staring. All of my movements felt stiff as I forced myself to drink from my cup.

The barmaid was being friendly to the guard. She didn't really have a choice. He reached out and touched her hair. She tried to mask her wince.

A shout from the kitchen gave her an excuse to break away. She handed him two glasses of ale and went through the door to the kitchen. I started breathing again as he walked to a table near the door.

A moment later, the barmaid come back with two plates of food for our table. She set them down in front of us and took our empty glasses back with her. When she returned to the bar, the guard followed her to pick up where he left off.

She gestured toward our table, probably telling him she needed to bring our drinks. He glanced over at us.

My heart was beating so hard it was threatening to leave my chest. I looked back at my food.

Saffron looked completely calm as she ate the chicken on her plate.

Boot steps approached our table then stopped.

I looked up. He was a mountain of a man. His head almost touched the ceiling, and he was as wide as a bull.

My fingers were numb and I couldn't breathe.

He bent down, his face nearly level with mine. "And who might you two lovely ladies be?" His breath was terrible.

I wrinkled my nose and turned my head away.

"You look familiar..." His rough finger pulled my chin toward him.

"Sir, you should not address my lady so informally." Saffron's voice was clear and bold.

He looked at her as if he was noticing her for the first time. Then he stood back up and started laughing. He smiled at us, showing decaying teeth.

I covered my nose and turned away. *No wonder the barmaid was so unnerved by him.*

"This is no lady," he said. "Morgan, come over here! I think I've got something."

I shifted in my chair. Even though I didn't know how to properly use it, I was really missing my old dagger. I looked to Saffron for instruction. She was still sitting as calm as can be. I tried to tell myself that if she wasn't worried, we were going to be okay. But as the second guard joined our table, I started to shake.

"Morgan, do you think this girl looks familiar?" He pointed at me.

Morgan bent down to look at me. His nose nearly touched my face in his inspection.

Pressing back against my chair, I turned my face away.

"She does kind of look like that drawing we got a few days ago." Morgan stood up.

"That's what I thought, too," the first man said. "Wasn't that reward only paid if we bring her in dead?"

I swallowed hard. *Dead?* Sweat started to bead on my forehead. *How can I get out of this?* Instinctively, I grabbed at my wrist for the dagger that wasn't there. Panic surged through me and my breathing quickened.

"I think you're right." Morgan drew his sword. "But maybe we should have a little fun with them first. It's been awhile since I've seen such a pretty girl."

The first man shook his head. "We don't have time for distractions. Let's just kill them." He pulled out his sword.

My eyes darted around the room, but Saffron and I were the only ones in sight. Her face was relaxed, calm. The memory of her rapid movements and steel slicing through the guards that attacked my home flashed through my mind. She was my only hope at getting out of this alive.

He pointed his sword at my throat. "Stand up, you two. Outside. We'll go through the back. I want to kill you slowly."

My whole body trembled as I walked. My legs felt weak and I stumbled as they pushed us through the door. I felt so helpless, so out of control. I wanted to do something but didn't know what to do. *How do you fight back against two armed guards?*

As soon as we were outside, Morgan tossed his sword aside and put his hand around my throat. I tried to cry out but I couldn't speak. I pushed and kicked and thrashed. Every movement cut off more air to my body. Tears streamed down my face. I tried again to cry out but no sound passed through my throat.

Out of the corner of my eye, I saw Saffron charge at the other man. The glint of sunlight on metal reflected off of her twin daggers. In one fluid movement, she slit his throat. His eyes widened as he grabbed at the gaping wound. A gurgling sound emitted from his mouth. He fell flat on his face, dead.

Morgan tossed me aside and lunged for his sword. I hit the

ground hard, gasping for breath. Saffron dropped her daggers and picked up the dead man's sword. She bared her teeth at my captor. Without hesitation, he rounded on her, slicing her across her upper arm.

Blood bloomed across her white blouse. "Saffron!" I cried out. She ignored me and struck back, just missing him as he dodged her blade. He attacked her, causing her to jump and spin away from him. Her agility was the only way she was avoiding his blows. He struck quickly, never really taking the time to pause between strikes. On his next blow, Saffron's sword was knocked loose, dropping near her assailant's feet. He struck her again, this time on the leg, tearing her skirt. She backed away, outside of his reach, weaponless.

He sneered at her. "After I kill you, I'm going to kill your friend, slowly."

Heat rose up through my body. *Oh no you're not.* My eyes darted to where Saffron had dropped her daggers. I pushed myself to standing and looked at the battle in front of me. I bolted around them and tumbled to the ground, reaching for the daggers. "Saffron!" I held the blades of a daggers, offering the hilts to her.

Saffron's breath came in heavy pants. She reached out her hand and swiped the blades from me. In one graceful movement, she threw the first dagger at the man, striking him in his ribs. He groaned in pain and reached down to pull the handle of the dagger from his chest. Saffron crossed the space between them in a split second and sliced the across his throat with the second dagger, delivering the killing blow. With a push of her hand, the man toppled backward, dead.

She walked over to where I was standing and sat down on the ground next to me, breathing heavy. She rested her head on her knees.

I was still rubbing my bruised throat. "You're amazing." My voice came out in a hoarse whisper.

She inhaled deeply through her nose and exhaled from her mouth. "I am what I have to be. No different than you."

I knelt down next to her and the blood caught my eye. I had

forgotten about her wound during the fight. "You're hurt. We need to get you taken care of."

She looked at her arm, then back to me. "It's fine. We'll be to Yorkton soon. I can get it taken care of there."

I reached over and tore the sleeve off of her blouse.

She pulled her arm back from me.

"Stay still," I said, pulling her arm back. "You need a bandage." I wrapped the sleeve around the open skin and tied it off. "There. That'll help until we get to somebody who can clean it."

"Where'd you learn that?" she asked me.

I shrugged. "I might not have learned everything I was supposed to learn, but I picked up a few things living as a peasant."

She smiled and held her hand up in the air. "Help me up."

She grunted as I helped her up, then she brushed off her skirt. We walked back to the carriage in silence.

When the driver saw us, his eyes widened and he dropped the flask he had been drinking from. He raced over to us. "What happened?"

Saffron waved her hand at him. "Don't worry about it."

He looked toward the tavern as if he expected somebody else to join us. His hands were trembling. "How can I not worry about this?"

"Because we'll double your fee," she said. "Let's just get to our destination quickly."

We were rocking and bumping our way down the road within seconds of the door closing behind us.

Every swallow was painful. I gently ran my fingers over my neck. My hand was covered in Saffron's blood. *It should have been mine.* That's who they were after. *How did I let this happen?* I was useless to defend myself. I had only known Saffron a few days and in that time she had had to save my life twice. What if Saffron wasn't there? What if there had been four guards? At the rate I was going, I wouldn't live to see my next birthday. *I'm being hunted.*

"Saffron, what drawing were they talking about?"

She shifted in her seat, wincing when she moved her shoulder. "The king has been searching for you since you were smuggled away. He's never known for sure if you were alive, but he didn't want to take any chances. Each year, on your birthday, he commissions artists to make a drawing of what they think you'll look like at that age. He distributes the drawings to his guards."

"And they just kill anybody they think might be me?" I asked.

She shook her head. "There were a few restrictions. The king didn't want his guards to

have the power to kill any girl they wanted. He didn't want people to know you might be alive. They had to check with the town priest to confirm that the girl's age was close to yours. See if they had record of the birth. If the girl was an orphan or didn't have proof of being born in that town, then they could kill her."

My mouth was wide open. *How many girls had been killed for me?* "They don't have to ask permission anymore, I guess."

Saffron looked grim. "It seems that is the case. He must have gotten word about the dead guards at your grandmother's house." The color drained from her face.

Maybe her wound was worse than we thought. "What is it? Is your shoulder hurting?"

"He might have your grandmother."

"My grandmother is dead. You said so yourself." My pulse quickened.

"He's a necromancer. That means he can bring back the dead. If his men got to her before ours, he could bring her back and ask her anything. She'd have to tell him."

My hair was falling out of the elaborate braid. I pushed it off of my face. "Will he know where to find me?"

She shook her head. "We didn't tell her those details for this exact reason. I just hoped it would never be needed."

"Where are we going?" I asked.

"To see a friend. We'll have to make the stop short, though. I don't think we can keep you anywhere for too long that doesn't have guards. It's too much of a risk. I'd guess the king has sent his Reapers after you by now and I'm no match for them."

I swallowed hard. *The Reapers are after me.* "There has to be something I can do to fight back. Something I can do to protect myself."

"Even a trained warrior isn't much use against the Reapers. They only have one weakness: fire. Even that doesn't stop them, it just slows them down. Could scare them off for a while, but only a sorcerer could make enough fire quickly enough to have any effect. The sooner we get you to the Ravens, the better."

"There are sorcerers working with the Ravens?"

She nodded. "One of the most powerful in the whole kingdom. He's the leader of the Ravens." She glanced out the window. "The sooner we can get you there, the better."

"Why not go straight there, then?" I asked.

"To be a princess, you must understand diplomacy. There isn't anybody at the Raven camp who can teach you like Sir Henry can."

I looked back out the window, trying not to see Reapers in every shadow or flicker of movement. "You're sure there's no way I can give up this whole princesses thing and just be a normal girl?"

"You've never been a normal girl, Wilona. You were born for this." Saffron rested her head against the seat and closed her eyes. Our conversation was over. I opened my mouth to say something, I wanted to know more, then closed it, not sure of how to argue against something I was still trying to wrap my head around.

Settling back in my seat, I pulled the pendant out from under my bodice. As we bumped along the rocky road, I considered what my life could have been like. What if the king had just assumed I was dead and had never come for me? What if my parents had been just like everybody else? What was it that made made me so special? How could one little piece of metal have so much control over my life?

CHAPTER 6

Every so often, I risked a glance at Saffron. Her chest rose and fell in slow, deep breaths. I wasn't sure if she was really asleep or if she was just resting. Neither would surprise me. After what I had been through today, I wasn't sure if I'd ever be able to sleep again.

The vibrations of the carriage changed. They weren't as rough as they had been. I glanced out the window. We were traveling down a well maintained road. It was smooth and well groomed. The streets were empty.

My stomach churned. *Something isn't right here.* Time seemed to slow down as we passed through the town. There was no sign of life anywhere. All of the shops were closed. None of the doors or windows were open. The only sound was the rattle of our carriage. "Where is everybody?"

I reached across and tapped Saffron on her elbow. Her eyes snapped open, instantly alert. I pointed to the window. She looked out, jaw set. "Something isn't right."

The carriage jolted and stopped.

I held my breath as visions of heavily armed King's guards overwhelmed my mind. *Please don't be the Reapers.* "Saffron?"

"Stay here," she whispered. She pulled open the door and shut it behind her.

I tucked the pendant back under my bodice and closed my hands into tight fists. Voices from outside carried through the carriage but I couldn't make out the words.

My whole body shook as I waited for Saffron's return. The

43

voices turned to shouts and my blood went cold. *I have to do something.* I looked around the carriage for a weapon. *There has to be something I can use.* I found a bottle of wine next to one of the seats and picked it up. *Better than nothing.* I opened the door a crack and peeked outside. The unmistakable sound of steel on steel rang through the air. Gripping the bottle by the neck, I quietly stepped out.

A body was sprawled face down on the ground in front of me. I clasped a hand over my mouth to keep from crying out. He wore the black leather of the King's Guard. A puddle of blood was staining the road under his abdomen. I swallowed back the sick feeling in my stomach and crept to the front of the carriage.

Saffron was engaged in combat with another King's Guard. She was red-faced and grunting with effort. The guard was a heavyset man and his movements were slow. Neither of them could see me. Saffron kept her injured arm at a distance from the man as she swung her sword. He dodged her blow and sliced at her neck. She jumped back just in time to avoid his blade.

I had seen her take on more challenging opponents than this man, but her injury was preventing her from keeping up. I held the bottle out in front of me. *I wish I knew how to fight so I could help her.* Saffron caught my eye and looked away quickly. I ducked down behind the carriage so I would be out of the line of sight of the guard. He turned his head behind him but didn't look down. I let out a breath. *That was close.* Saffron found my eyes again and gave me a single, small nod. I swallowed hard, trying to figure out what she wanted me to do.

I looked at the bottle again. The only thing it was good for would be to hit somebody with it. I wouldn't do much damage on his body with the armor he wore. *His head.* A blow to the head would do damage to even the largest man.

I lifted the bottle above my head and gently rested it on top of my head, waiting for Saffron to look my way again. Once she did, I lifted the bottle and brought it down on my head, showing her what I intended to do. The faintest smile crossed her face.

Saffron ducked down and put her leg out, causing the fat man to stumble and fall to the ground. "Now!"

I jumped out from my hiding place and slammed the wine bottle over the man's head. He went limp. The purple liquid ran down his face. I dropped the broken bottle and stumbled back from him. My breathing came out as quickly as if I had been running and my heart was throbbing in my ears.

Saffron narrowed her eyes at the man. In two large steps she reached him. She raised her blade above him, preparing to finish him off, then pulled the blade back. Kneeling down, she pressed her fingers against his neck.

She stood and locked her gaze on me. "He's dead. Blow to the head hit him just right."

The words rang through my ears and I stumbled backward a few steps, eyes locked on the unmoving body. *I killed a man.*

My breathing came out in short bursts, too fast. No matter how much air entered my lungs, I couldn't catch my breath. It was as if my breathing was trying to match the speed of my heartbeat. The world started to spin and I reached out trying to find something to hold on to.

Saffron grabbed my arm and turned me away from the body. She went in and out of focus as I recalled what had just happened. Saffron locked her green eyes on mine. "Try to slow your breathing. You are fine. You did the right thing."

I looked at her, trying to follow her instructions. My breathing started to slow down. "I shouldn't have done that. I didn't mean to kill anybody." I covered my face with my hands. Saying the words out loud made it more real.

Saffron pulled my hands off of my face and lowered her face so she was level with mine. "Do you think he would have let us go?"

My shoulders dropped, defeated. "No." I glanced at the body again. He had been trying to kill us. If we hadn't killed him, he would not have thought twice about finishing us off.

"Is it over, lady?" The driver popped his head up from the other side of the carriage.

"It's over. You can come out," Saffron said.

He was slack-jawed, eyes fixed on Saffron. "Who are you?"

"It's best you don't know the details," she said.

He nodded, closing his mouth.

My cheeks flushed. She wasn't going to tell him that one of the bodies was there because of me. For days, I'd been thinking that the king needed to die. Until today, the idea seemed almost innocent. Somebody out there would make him go away. I wouldn't have to deal with the realities of what it meant to kill a person. I looked at my hands, sticky with spilled wine. No blood from the dead man was visible on me, though I knew it was there. I'd see it for the rest of my life. His blood, his life, gone because of me.

Saffron's voice jolted me from my thoughts. "We need to get to our destination. Quickly."

"As you wish, lady." The driver's hands were shaking as he held open the door for us. He shut it and we took off down the road almost instantly.

I forced myself to take a few deep breaths. My cheeks were wet from tears I didn't know I had been crying. I wiped my face.

Out of the corner of my eye, I noticed that blood was flowing down Saffron's arm. The fighting had aggravated the wound. I handed her a handkerchief that had been tucked in my sleeve and she pressed it against her injury.

"How did they know we'd be here?" I asked.

She shook her head. "I don't know. The whole town was empty. Makes me think maybe Reapers came through and took everybody away. The guards might have been there to check for anybody the Reapers missed. Things like that happened before, when the duke was building his army."

"What about the children?" I asked.

Saffron let out a sigh. "He takes them, too. Though I'm not sure what he does with them."

A small fire was growing in my stomach. *How could he do such things?* I wanted to scream or punch something. My mind went back to the man I had killed.

The body count in my wake was rising daily. The guards at my grandmother's, the guards at the tavern, and now two more. If he was helping the king, he was just as guilty, but I couldn't help but feel like I was starting to make some choices about what kind of princess I wanted to be.

"Everything I'm doing is going to help get rid of the king, right?" I asked.

"Yes," Saffron said.

"When he's gone, all of this death, it'll stop, right?"

She pressed her lips together. "Your first is always the hardest. It will get easier."

My eyes widened. "You expect that I'll have to kill more people?"

"I hope you won't have to, but if you do, it won't be as bad as today." She took a breath. "We're about to start a war to remove the king from his throne. Things will get worse before they get better."

I wrapped my arms around myself and leaned back against the seat. These last few days had been the worst in my life. Trying to imagine days filled with more fear, more death, or more heartache was almost impossible.

"How am I supposed to do this?" I whispered.

Saffron's eyes softened and she smiled at me. "Don't worry, you have lots of people on your side. We'll keep you safe."

I relaxed into the seat as best I could and pulled out the pendant again. Just minutes ago, it had felt like a curse. Now it was beginning to feel like a calling. Was I strong enough to answer?

CHAPTER 7

The sun was dipping low into the horizon when we finally turned off the main road. The carriage rolled past an animal enclosure and a large stable. We came to a halt in front of a modest home. Saffron locked her eyes on me. "This is your first test, princess. Act the part."

I swallowed hard. I wasn't sure who lived here, but I was already acutely aware of the fact I was expected to sway people to join the Ravens. I reached up and felt my hair, trying to pin it back in place. Then I smoothed out my dress. There were splashes of wine along the skirt and my hands were still covered in wine. I cringed. This was not how a princess was supposed to look.

Saffron reached across the carriage and pulled my necklace free from under my bodice.

I clasped it protectively and felt exposed with it out in the open. "You sure this is okay?" My chest tightened as I remembered the soldiers in the bar.

She sighed. "You've got to get used to it, Etta."

I flinched at the sound of the new, unfamiliar name. During my training with Lady Genevieve I had still been called by Wilona. Nobody told me I was going to have to switch it up, though I suppose it made sense.

Etta. I tried the name out in my head. It felt uncomfortable, like wearing somebody else's clothes. Looking down at the expensive dress, I laughed to myself. *I am wearing somebody else's clothes.*

"Etta," I whispered it, barely audible, then shook my head. No matter what I did, it didn't feel like it fit me. Taking a deep breath, I closed my eyes and tried to imagine what my parents looked like. *I am their legacy. They gave me this name. Why does it feel so wrong?* For some reason, I didn't feel like I had earned the name of a princess. I still felt like an impostor.

The driver opened the door for us and helped each of us out. He had my trunk waiting for me already. Saffron gestured with her hands for me to walk in front of her. I took a deep breath and lifted my chin. Lady Genevieve's lessons filled my mind.

As I stepped toward the front door of the home, it swung open to reveal a man in farmer's clothes. He greeted me with a warm smile.

I smiled back at him, feeling surprisingly at ease in his gaze. His white hair and hunched posture made him look older than 60. He had a thin face and red cheeks. Despite the fact he wore farmer's clothes, they were well cared for and clean. Most of the farmers I met were covered in dirt.

"I'll take that, young man," he said to the driver as he reached for my truck. He lifted it with ease and set it inside the house. When he stepped back out he was holding a purse of coins. "What was the total for the trip?"

"I told him we'd double it," Saffron hurried to add. "He was an excellent driver."

The old man nodded and counted out seven gold coins. Probably more money than the man normally made in a whole year. "How's seven gold?'

The driver's face lit up. "Thank you sir, very kind." He nodded his head as he spoke into a small bow.

"Thank you for taking such good care of my niece and her friend." He gestured to Saffron, then to me. He dropped the coins in the driver's outstretched hand before closing his full purse.

"Any time you need a ride, sir, please summon me. My name

is William."

"We'll keep you in mind for future work, William."

William bowed again and then turned to leave. As the carriage rode out of sight, Saffron greeted the old man with a hug.

I relaxed as I watched the friendly scene unfold. *How would a princess react in a situation like this?* Lady Genevieve would tell me to command attention, not get lost in the crowd. I cleared my throat and lifted an eyebrow.

"Oh!" Saffron turned to me. "I'm so sorry, your highness. Please allow me to introduce to you my dear friend, Sir Henry." She gestured to Sir Henry and then to me, "Sir Henry, this is her royal highness, Elizabetta Aqualine."

Sir Henry stepped past Saffron to stand in front of me. I maintained a bored expression and stiff posture. He bowed low. "Your highness, it is an honor to have you in my home."

I held out my hand to him. "Thank you, Sir Henry, for having me."

He kissed the top of my hand and I pulled it back. I gave a polite smile, not wanting to seem too eager or too friendly, though I had already failed at that when I first arrived.

"Please, come in." He touched my elbow and guided me into his house. "We have much to discuss."

The home was sparsely furnished, but clean. There was a sitting room, a small kitchen, and a table for meals. In the sitting area, there were four wooden chairs facing the fireplace. We each took a chair in front of the empty fireplace. It was too warm for a fire right now but the newly burned logs and ash told me that it was used at night to keep the home warm.

Sir Henry handed us each a polished wooden goblet full to the brim with a dark, sweet smelling wine. I waited for Saffron to drink first, not sure of the etiquette or expectation in this situation. She took a long draw. I took a small sip and wrinkled my nose. It was my first taste of alcohol and I was not impressed. *Why do people drink this stuff?*

Sir Henry watched me as I sat there with the goblet in my hands. He took a drink from his. Then another before he opened his mouth to speak. "You almost have me fooled, girl," he said with a sparkle in his watery blue eyes.

I flushed and glanced sideways at Saffron. She covered an obvious smirk with her goblet. She wasn't going to bail me out of this one.

My eyes grew wide. *Fooled?* Maybe Saffron had made some sort of mistake. Maybe I wasn't the princess she was looking for. Maybe I was just a normal girl. For a moment, I considered the possibility of returning to a normal, less exciting life. One where I was not being hunted. The reality of what my life had become tumbled down on me. The King's Guard were looking for me. I could never go back to being a normal girl.

He must be testing me. I straightened in my chair and blinked. "I'm sorry, Sir. I don't understand."

He laughed. "I know your story. I know Saffron told you to princess it up for me."

My cheeks felt warm and my flush deepened.

"It's okay, I'm a friend." He sat down in the chair next to Saffron and turned it so it faced mine. "You have an important job ahead of you, and that's why you are here."

I relaxed a bit and glared at Saffron.

"Sorry, I couldn't help it." She smiled at me. "Plus I wanted to see what you could do away from Lady Genevieve. If it makes you feel any better, I'm impressed. When they told me I had to have you ready in just a few short days, I didn't think it could be done."

That makes two of us. "Wait, who told you?" Saffron had been with me since I left my grandmother's house. When did she meet up with somebody?

"I met a contact while you were with Lady Genevieve," she said. "The Ravens have eyes everywhere."

"Lady Genevieve is the best," Sir Henry chimed in. "She can turn anybody into a princess with enough time."

"How much is enough time?" I asked. The idea that anybody could be made into a princess made me nervous.

"Oh, I don't know." He tapped his finger on his chin as he thought. "A few months, maybe more, depending on the pupil."

"She had three days," Saffron said.

His eyes widened. "Maybe there is something to be said about blood, then." He squinted at me and looked me up and down. "I would have guessed you'd been with her a month."

I sat up a little straighter and smiled. At least my time with Lady Genevieve was worth the effort.

Saffron turned from me to Sir Henry. "We only have two days before we have to head out again."

His eyes narrowed. "I was told I'd have a week. You marrying her off already?"

My head snapped to him. "Marriage? Nobody has said anything about marriage. I'm not ready to be married." I had seen girls younger than me married in my little village, but my grandmother always told me I'd have to wait. Since I'd never had much interest in marrying one of the few single men in my village, I had never worried about it. Now I realized she was making me wait until I found out who I really was.

Saffron lifted her hand. "This has nothing to do with marriage. The king knows she's alive. He's probably got the Reapers looking for her."

A dark shadow crossed Sir Henry's face. "This does make things more of a challenge. Did he change the law?"

Saffron nodded. "I don't think the guards have to check with a priest any more." She paused a moment. "We rode through Redding. It was empty. Shops closed, people all gone. Just like last time. I think he's building his army."

Sir Henry sat quietly, fingers steepled under his chin. "Then we'd better get going right away. You two can't linger here." He stood. "First, I'll show you to your room, then we meet back in here to begin."

Nervous butterflies filled my stomach. *Reapers. Undead army.* Saffron had said this was just the beginning. That things would get worse before they got better. *How much worse can things get?* People were going missing, people were dying for no reason. That seemed pretty bad to me.

I stopped in the middle of the room. When the others

realized I wasn't following them, they turned to look at me. "There's really no way the king will believe I'm not a threat? Why would he waste so much energy on a teenage girl?"

"He sees you as a threat for many reasons. Mostly because if you wanted to, you could rule," Sir Henry said.

"I don't want to rule. I'm not a leader."

"You don't have to," Saffron said. She turned to Sir Henry. "She's had a very long day. She needs a few minutes."

She walked back to where I stood and placed her hand on the middle of my back. "Come on, let's get you cleaned up."

Saffron and I were to share a small room with two little beds. On a table was a wash basin and a wash cloth. I washed the travel off of my face then started scrubbing the wine from my hands. No matter how much I washed, they didn't feel clean.

A hand placed on top of mine stopped my progress. I dropped the cloth in the basin. My hands were red and raw from scrubbing.

"They're clean," Saffron said, "you're safe." She walked away, leaving me staring at my reflection in the bowl.

The girl staring back at me didn't look different. Same blue eyes, same narrow nose, same pink lips. But somehow, this girl wasn't the same girl anymore.

Closing my eyes, I gripped the side of the table and took a few breaths before I turned around. Saffron was changing from her maid outfit into a simple house dress. I looked at the dress with envy. I wasn't yet used to the corset and layers of fabric I was wearing.

Saffron caught my glance and gave me a sympathetic smile. "I've got an extra house dress in my bag. You can wear it while we are here."

I didn't waste any time changing from the heavy dress into the lighter clothes. I went back to the sitting room feeling a hundred pounds lighter.

The fire was crackling softly in the now dark room, giving it a warm glow. I joined Sir Henry, once again having lessons alone. He gestured to the chair at his right so I sat next to him.

This time, I fell into the chair, all pretense of being a princess forgotten.

He gave me a sideways glance. "After you leave here, you'll have to be Princess Etta all the time."

It was a strange thing to hear. I felt like I was putting on a disguise and playing a role of somebody who wasn't me. Yet, it was me. It might even be a truer form of myself because it was who I was supposed to be. I had spent a lot of time the last few days trying to imagine what my life could have been. What if I had been raised in a palace instead of a cottage? What if I had spent all my days wearing gowns that weighed almost as much as me? If I was Etta, was I still Wilona?

Almost as if he could read my mind, Sir Henry cut in. "You know, it's not all bad. Being a royal." He turned to face me with his kind eyes.

"It's a lot to take in," I confessed. "I keep wondering what it would have been like if my parents hadn't died."

His eyes locked on mine. "None of that matters. Everything you have been through will make you stronger, not weaker. You'll make a great queen."

"I already told you that I don't want to rule."

He didn't break his gaze. He looked as if he was trying to tell me something without words. What did I know about this man? I thought back to the conversation when we arrived.

I gasped. "They're planning to marry me off."

"I'm not a Raven so I can't speak to their plans." He held his hands up in front of him, "I'm just here to teach you diplomacy and geography."

I narrowed my eyes at him. It's been a long few days. I tried to shake the paranoia from my mind. *Isn't that what princesses do? Get married to forge alliances?* If I'm not ruling here, they'll eventually have to find me a place to go.

"Are they going to marry me to the leader of the Ravens?" I asked.

He shook his head. "I might not be able to tell you much, but I know that won't happen." He looked behind him. The room was empty. Saffron had left the house when I began my lesson. Possibly to meet with another Raven contact.

"Princess, we need to get going on the lessons. We don't have much time."

I sighed. Frustrated that he wasn't going to tell me more, I relented. "All right. Tell me why a princess needs to know these things."

"A princess should know how to talk to people from all over the world. There are different customs, greetings, and expectations from different people. You don't want to insult somebody because you didn't know the correct way to greet them. And you should know where these people come from, what their homeland is like, and what their government is like. Do they have excess wheat that can be traded? Do they have a shortage of water? Do they have an army of sorcerers that are waiting to attack us? Knowing about the cultures and places of the world is very important for any leader."

I lifted my eyebrow at the word "leader."

He smiled. "Don't worry, we'll start you small." He stood up and walked to the little table that held the wine jug. Under the table, standing on its side, was a tattered brown book. Books were expensive and rare. Each page was handwritten and the fragile pages were sewn together. Most books were made by monks who lived on the islands in the sea. He carried the book as if it were a newborn baby and then set it gently in my lap.

"This is an atlas," he said. "It has maps of all of the known world." He flipped open the first page, and I saw a drawing of a shape with lines going across it and small words written inside the shape. "This is Illaria. See here?" He pointed at a star on the map. "This is the capitol, where the king's palace is." He dragged his finger across the page. "This is where we are, outside of Redding. And this is where you lived, near Campari."

We spent the next several hours going over all of the maps in his book. We broke only for a small meal that Saffron brought us. As he went through each map, he told me about the government and the customs of the country we looked at. He told me stories of wars and alliances. He told me about the past marriages of past kings and who we thought would be the best to make an alliance with us now.

The fire was down to glowing embers by the time we finished. I rubbed my eyes and stumbled into the bed, falling asleep in the dress I was wearing.

The next morning began with a quiz over everything I had learned the night before. Anything I got wrong was reviewed. Then we practiced greetings for several hours. Saffron came to my rescue midday with another meal. We took a small break and I walked around in the field outside of the house. The wind cut through the thin house dress, refreshing me. I wasn't sure I could fit any more inside my head. Reluctantly, I walked back to the house, knowing I had more in store for me this afternoon.

I arrived inside to find a large map spread across the entire dining table. Saffron and Sir Henry were standing next to it, making marks with charcoal sticks. I approached with apprehension. The other maps we had looked at were small, and we hadn't written anything on them.

Saffron looked up at me. "Ready for more?"

I sighed. "This is a lot to learn in such a short time."

Sir Henry stopped moving the charcoal and looked at me. "I know. We would have liked to give you the whole year to prepare, but it just wasn't possible." His mouth turned down into a momentary frown, then he pulled it into an impassive line.

I had a flash of a warning knot in my stomach, but pushed it away. I was probably imagining things. "What's this?"

"This is a world map," Henry said proudly. "Here's Illaria and here is Sardinia." He moved his finger across the sea to an island. "Here is Gallia. These are our two best hopes of alliances. You'll be traveling to each of them."

I looked at Sir Henry in disbelief. "I'm not ready!" I blurted out. "How can I convince these people to help us? I don't even have any idea what we would be asking for."

He held his chin in between his thumb and forefinger and looked at me thoughtfully. "What do you think you have been doing the last few days? This is what Lady Genevieve and I have been preparing you for."

"I don't feel like a princess, or anybody important. There has to be some senior official in the group, what are they called?" I gestured with my hand as I tried to recall the name of the group responsible for my rescue.

"The White Ravens," Saffron said. "And we're going to be leaving to go to them tomorrow morning."

Sir Henry clasped my hands in his. "I know this is a lot to take in, but it's important and we need you. The Ravens will help you to see the big picture when you arrive. They will finish getting you ready to meet with the Kings of Sardinia and Gallia. I know you can do this." He gave me that warm smile I had grown accustomed to in the short time he had acted as my teacher.

Saffron placed her hand on my shoulder. "It has to be you."

I think she meant the words as a comfort but they only served to cause my stomach to churn. I didn't feel like I was the right person for this job. I was worried that when I met the kings, they would see a peasant girl playing dress up. I took a deep breath and let it out. I wasn't sure how I felt about all of this, but I knew the Ravens were my best chance at survival and my best chance at destroying the king.

CHAPTER 8

I woke before dawn the next morning to prepare for travel. Though I had spent much of the last week moving from one place to another, I still wasn't used to the long days with limited rest. We were making the last leg of our journey on horseback. I dressed in riding clothes. They were nicer than what I owned while living in the village, but not as elaborate as the dresses I had been wearing at Lady Genevieve's.

Sir Henry was still asleep as we prepared to leave that morning. Saffron didn't want to wake him. We had said simple goodbyes the night before, knowing it would be an early departure. Saffron handed me a cup of hot tea to sip on while she readied the horses. I sat in one of the wooden chairs in front of the ash filled fireplace.

"Etta?" I jumped at Sir Henry's voice.

I turned to see him approach me in his dressing robe. His white hair was messy from sleep but his watery blue eyes were alert. He glanced around. "Is Saffron outside?"

I nodded. "She's preparing the horses. Did we wake you?"

He shook his head as he sat in the chair next to me. "No, I've been awake for a while. I don't sleep much anymore."

I wasn't sure if he was referring to his age or something more sinister as the cause of his insomnia. I sat in quiet thought, wondering if he was going to continue speaking. We had said our goodbyes already and I was not sure of what to add. He had taught me a lot over these two short days, but we didn't really have any conversations that were not related to maps, geography, or diplomacy.

He sighed and rearranged himself in his chair so he was turned toward me. "Etta, you're a smart girl. That's clear by how quickly you learned from me. You've probably already thought about this, but I wanted to mention it anyway. Please, Etta, don't trust anybody." He fixed a pleading gaze on me.

I was taken aback by his words. I was curious about the White Ravens and their plan for me, but I felt like I didn't have a choice. If I couldn't trust them, who was I supposed to trust? The king was trying to kill me, and I didn't know how to survive on my own. The White Ravens were my only option. I had to hope their intentions for me were noble. I certainly believed in their cause of removing the king. I was about to open my mouth to say as much, but Sir Henry began to speak again.

"There is a lot you don't yet know. There is only so much I was allowed to tell you or they wouldn't have brought you to me. You need to do whatever it takes to make sure you are getting the whole truth from people before you believe them. You have a long journey ahead of you. This won't be over quickly. Use your mind and trust your intuition."

Sir Henry reminded me of my grandmother. She always told me not to trust anybody. I used to think she was just paranoid in her old age. Now I knew she was protecting me. I couldn't help but feel like Sir Henry's worry was coming from the same place. Even though he was telling me not to trust people, I found myself believing him, trusting him.

I leaned against the chair to steady myself. "Who wouldn't let you tell me?"

He glanced around the room. "They know I won't get involved unless the true heir is on the throne." He pointed to me. "You are the true heir. When you step up to take your rightful place, I'll happily serve at your side. You remember that."

"I don't want to rule. You know that." My voice sounded like it belonged to somebody else.

"I know you aren't ready yet, but you will be. I believe that."

He seemed like he wanted to say more, but at that moment the front door opened. He patted my knee and stood.

Saffron walked into the home and greeted Sir Henry with a nod. "Good morning, Sir Henry. I'm glad you are awake so we can thank you for your hospitality." She smiled at him and gave him a friendly hug.

"I'm happy I can occasionally be of use. Since I've been in hiding out here, I obviously don't get many visitors. You two were a welcome distraction from farm life." He smiled at me, and inclined his head in a bow. "Safe travels, your highness."

I gave him my best formal curtsy and followed Saffron to our horses. I glanced back at him as he waved to us from the front door. My mind was racing. What did he mean? It makes sense not to trust people, I don't know if I'll ever really trust anybody again after what I've been through.

True heir. What did he mean by that? Of course I didn't want to rule. Look how my parents turned out, they're both dead. Why would I want that? What made him think that I would change my mind?

The pendant around my neck felt heavy. I tucked it under my bodice. *I'm not meant to be a queen.*

*****

I was riding a dark brown mare this time. Saffron had packed my dresses into saddle bags on the side of each of our horses. She didn't pack a tent or any provisions. I took it as a hopeful sign we had less than a day of riding ahead of us this time.

We rode at an easy pace, not wanting to go too fast in the low light. My horse was next to Saffron's on the empty road, matching her horse step for step.

"Wilona," she said.

I looked at her. "Yes?"

"I want you to know something about Sir Henry. He's been living completely isolated for the last fifteen years. He has a tendency to get a little paranoid. He thinks people are after him."

"Are they?" I blurted out.

"They were, at first. He served with your father, and he was very high ranking. But I don't know if anybody really remembers him, anymore." She trailed off, a note of sadness in her voice.

"Is he active in the Ravens?" I asked.

"He acts as a safe house for us so he gets news when people stop by. Other than that, he doesn't want to be involved. He keeps saying he'll come out of hiding eventually."

When the true heir returns. Suddenly, I felt like I had the wind knocked from my lungs. If I was the only survivor of my family, then I was the only one who could rule by birthright. Who did they find to place in that role if the family line ended with me?

"Saffron? Who will be ruling the kingdom?"

She pulled up on her reigns, momentarily stopping her horse. "The Ravens have a wise and just ruler who will step into the role of the king. He wanted to be the one to tell you himself, so I was asked not to talk to you about the details. You'll meet him in a few hours when we arrive at camp." She urged her horse forward and I followed.

Why did I have to wait? Who was this secret would-be king?

"Saffron? Do I have a cousin or something?" I couldn't believe I hadn't asked this question sooner. I had been so focused on staying alive, I didn't stop to wonder if anyone else in my family had survived.

She smiled. "Better than that, but I don't want to ruin the surprise."

Frustrated, I pushed my hair out of my eyes and tried to figure out what she meant by *better*. Who was this person? More importantly, what did they want with me? My head started to ache and I longed to be back in a time when my life made sense. *I'm really starting to hate surprises.*

We rode in silence for the next several minutes. I watched the sky turn from pink, to orange, to red as the sun rose. The road was cut through the tall, yellow grass and I could see it ahead for miles. No trees, no towns, no coverage. We were totally exposed. In the distance, I thought I could see the hazy outline of mountains.

My eyes darted all around the landscape. Every rustle of grass, every bird cry made me flinch. I kept picturing the king sweeping down on us with his Reapers. I shuddered.

"How much further do we have to go?" The sooner we reached our destination, the better.

"We're headed to the mountains," she said.

As we rode, the distant mountains grew nearer, I could see the thick trees covering them. Some of the tension in my shoulders released as we approached. Being back in the woods was like a dream. I turned my eyes back to the road and saw a cloud of dirt approaching. The tension came back. The cloud moved closer to reveal a carriage headed right for us.

"Pull your hood over your head," Saffron said.

I covered my head with my lightweight cloak and dipped my chin down to avoid showing my face. After the encounter in the carriage, I wasn't sure I could handle another run in with guards. My mind raced as I imagined what I would do if we were stopped. Could I attack somebody again? Was I ready to do that? I gripped the reins tighter and slowed so Saffron could ride in front of me as we prepared to pass the carriage. My heart was beating so fast I thought it would burst from my chest.

The carriage approached in a cloud of dust, nearly obscuring us from view. It was in a hurry and moving quickly. Saffron picked up our pace and I followed suit. The faster we passed this carriage, the better. I risked a glance at the shiny black carriage as I rode by. My stomach knotted as I saw the fiery phoenix and skull of the king's crest. The pounding of my heart filled my ears. I quickly looked ahead again, praying I hadn't drawn attention to myself.

Thankfully, the carriage bolted by us without slowing down. The speed and the dust were enough to make us nearly invisible to the driver. I picked up my pace for a minute to bring my mare next to Saffron. As the rumble of the carriage faded, she slowed a little so she could talk to me.

"We need to move faster."

I tightened my grip on the reins. "I'm ready."

I struggled to keep up with her new pace but pushed myself to keep going. As we raced across the countryside, my mind kept going back to our encounters with the King's Guard over the last two days. My stomach felt like it was full of rocks. I leaned forward on my horse, willing her to go faster. *We are going to make it.* I pushed the guards out of my mind and tried to focus on the mountainside in front of me. The hills were getting nearer. We were so close.

The sun was directly above me, signaling the midpoint of the day. I pulled my hood back down to wipe the sweat from my brow. The bright light was so intense I had put the hood back on to help shade my eyes.

"We're close," Saffron shouted. "Stay right behind me. The trail is narrow."

I held back so I could ride behind Saffron. As we neared the mountain, shrubs made way for trees. Saffron cut right through, and we started to go up. As we rode into the shaded forest, tension left my body. I let out a breath. The trees were close together, barely wide enough for a single horse to pass through. It darkened as we neared the heart of the forest. I dropped the hood from my cloak so I could see better.

The scent of fresh bread mixed with the smell of the trees. *I must be hungry.* Just when I was starting to question how much further, the trees thinned and we entered a clearing bustling with people. There were structures and tents all around the clearing. Children ran by playing with wooden swords. People were cooking and a woman was weaving on a huge loom. It was like a hidden village right in the middle of the woods.

Saffron gracefully dismounted and handed the reins to a boy who was passing by. He nodded at her and took her horse without exchanging any words. I stared at the activity around me for a moment, mouth open.

"Welcome to the home of the White Ravens," Saffron said. She held my horse's reins and I dismounted, staring with wide eyes.

The boy who had taken Saffron's horse was back. She handed the reins of my horse to him. "Thank you, Charlie," she said.

Saffron put her hand on my shoulder. "Come, Wilona. There's somebody I want you to meet."

I followed her through the clearing. The people we passed stopped what they were doing as we walked by and watched us. I could hear whispers in my wake.

We left the cleaning and walked through the trees again into another, smaller clearing. There were a couple of benches near the trees but otherwise the clearing was empty of any other structures. Next to one of the benches two figures were deep in conversation.

The first was only slightly taller than Saffron, with dark curly hair and a trimmed black beard. He looked to be in his thirties. He was gesturing with his hands as he explained something to the other figure, a younger man with fair hair that hung to his shoulders. He was taller than the other man and seemed focused on the conversation. The dark haired man froze, his hands in the air as he noticed us. His brown eyes grew wide and he smiled. He dropped his hands and walked quickly over to us.

Saffron took a few steps toward him and they met in a tight embrace, followed by a kiss. I looked away from them and glanced at the other man. He was looking away as well. I caught his eye. He frowned at me and then walked out of the clearing. I watched him walk away, wondering what I had done to upset him.

Risking a peek at the happy couple, I saw they were pulling apart. Saffron was beaming. I had never seen her so happy. She grabbed the man's hand and walked over to me. He was wearing a friendly smile across his face as he locked eyes with me.

"Etta, I want you to meet Max, leader of the White Ravens." She let go of his hand and stepped toward me. "Max, this is Etta."

Hi Jenna!
The author of these books is a good friend of mine. So of course I bought __many__ copies and these are for you ♥

— Jess

Max smiled at me. "There is no doubt you are your father's daughter."

I glanced at Saffron then back at Max. "Um, thank you."

Saffron let out a small laugh. "Wilona, Max is your brother."

CHAPTER 9

I looked from Max to Saffron, eyes wide. How could this be? I was already overwhelmed with everything that had happened to me in the last week. I didn't know how I was supposed to react to finding out I had a brother.

Sitting down on a bench, I rested my face in my hands and took a few deep breaths. When I looked back up, they were both staring at me. Saffron's eyebrows furrowed. Max was unreadable. I ran my fingers through my hair. "I'm sorry, but it sounded like you said Max is my *brother.*"

Saffron walked to the bench and sat down next to me. "I know it's a lot to take in, and I'm sorry I didn't tell you sooner. We thought it would be best to wait until you arrived."

I stomped my foot on the ground like an angry child. "How is this best? You should have told me." *How could she keep something like this from me?* I trusted her.

"The focus was to get you here safely." She clasped her hands in her lap. "I'm sorry, but I was under orders to wait until we got you here. We didn't know how well we could trust you."

I raised my voice. "Trust me? As in, worried I'd run to the king?" I stood up and glared at Max. "You're my brother. You should have come for me a long time ago. Do you realize what I've been through?"

His smile faded. "You don't know what you're talking about. Trust me, keeping you away kept you alive. Everything has always been about keeping you safe."

My fingernails were cutting into my palms. I relaxed them and took a deep breath. I looked around. The Ravens were living in tents in the middle of the woods. I had grown up in a warm home with a loving grandmother. Maybe I was being too hard on him. "I"m sorry. I should be happy, I am happy. It's just been a very strange week for me."

Max smiled at me, flashing a set of straight, white teeth. "I understand. Everybody here has been through a lot. Things will make sense soon."

I nodded once. "Thank you, Max. How long have you been with the Ravens? Were you hidden away, too?"

"I was, but for reasons different than your own," he said.

I stared at him, silently willing him to continue.

"Our parents weren't married when I was born. So they hid me away to keep our mother's reputation pure. They were in the process of changing the rules of ascension when the duke started the uprising."

"Did they get it changed?" I asked.

He crossed his arms over his chest. "No. Some people think I don't have the right to rule because our parents weren't married when I was born. If it hadn't been for our sick grandfather, they would have been. In reality, they should have waited to consummate their love, but they didn't."

Saffron set her hand on my knee. "You'll find that most people know how much your parents loved each other and have put their support behind Max."

He rolled up his sleeves and I noticed a tattoo on his wrist. "What's that?"

It was a stylized dragon that traveled from his wrist up his forearm. He looked down at it and pulled his sleeve higher. "It represents my membership in the Order of the Dragon."

The tattoo extended up past his elbow, wrapping around his bicep. The dragon's mouth was open, breathing fire, and the tail twisted around his arm. I had never seen such an intricate tattoo. "What's the Order of the Dragon?"

"It's an organization for sorcerers who align with fire. I'll tell you more about it later. Right now, we need to head back for dinner."

Saffron had mentioned that the leader of the Ravens was a sorcerer. I wanted to ask more questions. Sorcerers rarely passed through my little village. The only magic I had seen were little tricks to impress local children.

As I followed him out of the clearing and into the woods, I tried to find features that we had in common. We both had dark, curly hair and fair skin. He was much taller than me and he had brown eyes in contrast to my blue ones. He was an imposing figure in his black robes with his dragon tattoo. I wrapped my arms around my body as I followed him. It had been a long day. *Please, no more surprises tonight.*

We returned to the large clearing which was now occupied with tables. The people that had been busy at work around the camp were seated at the tables or walking around with plates of food. The space was filled with pleasant chatter.

Max glanced over his shoulder. "I want to introduce you to the camp. This way." He continued walking until he was near a large table covered with food. People were lined up to fill their plates. They stopped what they were doing when Max approached and turned to watch him, faces eager.

A hush fell over the space as heads turned toward Max. Then I realized with horror that they were also staring at me. My cheeks felt hot and I bit my lower lip.

"Sorry to interrupt your dinner, everybody. This news is too good to keep to myself." Max spoke with a strong, clear voice. He held the crowd's attention without effort. "I want to introduce you all to my sister, Princess Elisabetta Aqualine. She has returned to us to help us take back our kingdom."

Cheers erupted from all around me and my eyes darted around. There were more people here than I had originally thought. The sound of the cheers seemed to stretch forever in the clearing. A flicker of hope rose inside me and a smile filled my face. The people seemed happy to see me, warm even. *Maybe this won't be so bad.*

Max put an arm around my shoulder.

I flinched at his touch. There was something cold about it.

The people around me were staring. They were waiting for me to do something. I flashed my best princess smile and gave a tiny wave.

They rose to their feet, clapping and cheering for me. I still had a hard time believing I was really a princess, and hearing this introduction from somebody else was surreal. The clapping seemed to go on forever. As I stood there trying my best to do what they expected of me, I was surprised to feel a small swell of pride.

Max raised his arms and gestured for them to quiet. I was amazed how quickly they responded to his action. "Thank you for your kind welcome. I'm sure my sister is looking forward to getting to know you all in the coming weeks. Please, enjoy your dinner."

Max leaned in to me and whispered in my ear. "It's time for you to act like a princess."

I jumped a bit at the comment and locked eyes with him. He looked serious and his head was still lowered near mine.

"Everybody here expects Princess Elisabetta. It's time for you to become her. You can go by Etta if you want." He stood again, finished with the conversation. Then he walked over to the large table and picked up a plate.

I stood glued to the spot, not sure what I should do. Thankfully, Saffron was nearby. She placed her hand on my back and guided me to the table. She handed me a plate. I went through the motions of walking down the line and letting people plop food on my plate.

Max was already seated and waved me over. "Etta," he said as he patted the bench next to him. I sat down. Saffron sat across from him. He winked at her but didn't break the conversation already in full swing.

I stared down at my plate, too tired to eat. My mind wandered to where I would be sleeping that night and when I could get to that place.

" - Ask the princess, see what she thinks," a man at the end of the table said. I looked up, horrified I was being brought into a conversation I had been ignoring.

"That's ridiculous," Max started. He turned to me. "No offense, sister." Then he turned back to the man who had spoken up. "She has been raised as a peasant her whole life. She just found out who she is a week ago. We don't need to bring her into this."

"I beg to differ, highness," the man said. "She is royal, ordained by the gods. That gives her insight that other people don't have."

I held my breath. *The gods must have forgotten to gift me with that talent.* I didn't want to answer any questions, and I had no idea what they were talking about in the first place.

"Fine," Max relented. "Ask her, then."

The man nodded and then looked at me. "Lady, if you please, I'd like your thoughts on the matter at hand."

I took a breath and looked at Max. He nodded at me.

"I'm so sorry, sir. I'm afraid I wasn't really listening to the conversation. I was daydreaming about sleep."

He smiled at me, then started to laugh. Max joined in. Then Saffron. The whole table was laughing.

My face went scarlet.

Max placed a hand on my shoulder as he caught his breath. "I don't think you need to worry about politics."

I bristled at his comment. *What had I been preparing for during my lessons if not politics?* I was about to say as much when Max spoke again.

"Saffron? Can you take Etta to her room? I think she needs to get some rest."

"As you wish, my lord," Saffron said.

Her formal response caught me off guard after the embrace and kiss they shared earlier. I made a note to myself not to bring it up with anybody. If Saffron was hiding her relationship with Max, I didn't want to get her in trouble.

Saffron showed me to a canvas tent with a bed roll. I bid her goodnight and closed the flap. Next to the bed roll was a trunk. I opened it to find all of my dresses and clothes neatly folded inside. I quickly changed into night clothes and gratefully crawled under the blanket.

I thought about everything I had been through. The world seemed bigger now. A week ago, I was a peasant girl, on track to become a seamstress. Now I was involved with rebels who wanted to overthrow the king and place a brother I never knew I had on the throne. Sir Henry's words echoed through my mind. *Don't trust anybody.*

CHAPTER 10

The next morning when I peeked out of the flap of my tent, I saw the man I had seen yesterday with Max, sitting on a stump. His arms were crossed and he looked bored.

Yesterday I saw him only briefly but I was pretty sure it was the same person. He had shoulder length honey blonde hair and stood head and shoulders taller than me. I was surprised he looked to be near my age.

"About time you woke up." He stood and dropped his arms to his side. "We've got things to do and I'm stuck with you all day."

I tilted my head to get a better look at him. Though he was tall, he wasn't very broad. Couldn't be much of a fighter.

He raised an eyebrow at me and I noticed just how green his eyes were.

"Well?" he said.

I'd gotten used to people being overly nice to me. I didn't know how to handle somebody who so clearly didn't want to be around me. My heart sunk a little. *So much for making friends.* I blinked a few times. *What does he want me to say?*

He rolled his eyes. "You ready to go?"

I looked down at my dressing gown. "No. I'm not dressed." I pulled the tent flap over my body.

He laughed. "Well, *princess*, you better get ready. Max gave us a list of things to do and we're already behind."

I dropped the tent flap back in place and stomped into the tent. *Who was this man to speak to me like this?* I dug through the trunk and found the least formal dress I owned. Riding clothes.

"All right," I called as I pushed my way through the tent flaps. "Let's go do this important stuff that Max wants us to do."

Without any other comment, he turned from me and started to walk away. I shook my head and followed him. Max's comment from last night came back to me. I was supposed to be acting like a princess.

"You know," I shouted up to him, "you aren't making me feel very welcome."

He stopped and spun around. "I'm so sorry, *your majesty*. I'm sorry you don't feel special."

"I'm sorry I'm taking you away from whatever important dish washing duties you might have, but -"

"Dish washing! Ha! You don't know what you are talking about." He stepped up to me and leaned down so our noses were almost touching. "I'm a sorcerer. And I'm taking my test in two weeks. I should be spending this time studying or practicing or working with Max. Instead, the whole camp has been obsessed with your arrival and I've missed out on days of training. That would be bad enough as it is, but now I have to baby-sit you all day!"

My face was hot. *I didn't ask for any of this.* "Hey!" I said. "I didn't ask for your help. You can go do your magic tricks and I can take care of myself."

He raised his eyebrows. "Magic tricks?" He shook his head. "You have obviously never seen a true sorcerer in action before. As for taking care of yourself." He shook his head.

"I'll be fine on my own!" I lifted my chin and started to walk away from him. *How am I suppose to spend the day with this person? He is insufferable. I shouldn't have to put up with this.* Maybe I could find Saffron. I was sure she'd understand. Maybe she would be just as irritated by him as I was.

"How'd that work out for you before?" he asked. "The taking care of yourself thing. I heard about the guards at the tavern. And the road. What if it's Reapers next?"

I stopped walking. My shoulders sunk. He was right. *I don't know how to take care of myself.*

"Fine. Let's get this over with and then you can go pull rabbits out of hats."

He pushed past me, back on the original path we had started down without saying a word. I rolled my eyes at his back and followed.

He is the most irritating person I have ever met in my life. "Where's Saffron? Or my brother? Can't they show me around?"

"They're busy," he said.

"So they needed to keep you distracted?" I asked.

He glared at me. "No. For some reason, they felt like you were important enough to be in the care of a sorcerer."

"Are you actually a sorcerer if you haven't passed your test?" This time I was genuinely curious, and I used a softer tone. This man and Max were the first sorcerers I had ever met.

He sighed. "No, not officially. I've been training with your brother for ten years."

A pang of jealousy shot through me. He had spent the last ten years with the brother I just found out about. "How did you become his apprentice?"

He gave me a sidelong glance. "That's a long story." He turned away from me for a moment then stopped walking. "Look, I'm supposed to give you a tour and show you around. I'm going to do it because I always do what Max asks me to do. And because I agree with him, you need protection."

"Fine." It was pretty clear he didn't want to waste time getting to know me. Looking around I realized we were standing in the space where we had eaten dinner last night.

He lifted an open hand and gestured to the middle of the space in front of us. "This is the common area. You probably already figured that out. We eat meals here and have meetings here or do anything that involves the whole camp."

The common area seemed to be the heart of the camp. People came from all directions to walk through it and there were worktables set out on the outside of the clearing. I saw a man working on a cart, hammering away at a wheel. Two children were sitting next to a woman weaving on a large loom.

They were braiding strips of fabric at her feet. I heard a loud clanging sound and looked for the source of the noise.

"That's the blacksmith. He has a little work area set up right behind those trees." He pointed toward the sound.

"Hey, Ashton!" called a stocky man who looked to be only a little older than my guide. "Want to introduce us?" He stopped in front of me and gave a bow. After the way I had been treated this morning, I was taken aback.

"Your name's Ashton?" I asked, suddenly feeling foolish for not asking sooner.

"Never introduced himself, huh?" the newcomer said to me. "He's got no manners. Orphaned, raised by -"

"That's enough, Micah," Ashton said through gritted teeth.

Micah pressed his mouth into a tight line. He took a step backward, as if he was afraid of Ashton.

I was impressed by Ashton's ability to quiet him so quickly. Micah was solid muscle and looked like a fighter. Ashton was tall and lanky, he didn't look like he'd ever lifted a sword. I nodded my head in greeting at Micah. "Nice to meet you."

He smiled at me. "It's nice to finally meet you. We weren't sure if we'd get to meet you of if you were going to be traveling outside the kingdom right away."

My heart sunk. I didn't like the reminder of my upcoming diplomatic missions. "It was nice talking with you, Micah. However, Ashton and I have some things to do. Maybe I'll see you again later?"

Micah shifted his footing uncomfortably. "Um, yes, princess. Later." He gave an awkward bow and walked away.

"I should have let him keep talking to you," Ashton smirked. "But we finally found something we have in common. I was just as happy to get away as you were. There's just something about Micah that makes me uncomfortable. Besides, I hate small talk."

No kidding. I still wasn't ready to let go of the earlier argument. I bit my lip to keep my smile from spreading.

"Come on." He was serious again. "Let's see the rest of the camp."

"So, Ashton," I said.

He glanced at me. "Yes, my name is Ashton."

"I'm -"

"-Etta, I know." He didn't look at me as he walked.

I flinched. The new name didn't sound right coming from him. "I'd rather you call me Wilona."

He stopped and narrowed his eyes then softened them. He smirked. "Okay, Wilona."

We spent the next several hours visiting the different areas of the camp. The stables, the aviary, the gardens. There was even a chicken coop. The camp was larger and more organized than I would have guessed based on the location in the middle of the woods.

"Where did all of these people come from?" I asked.

"You mean, how did they come to join the Ravens?"

I nodded. "There's so many people here. Old, young, men, women. So many different trades and skills."

"The king has created a lot of enemies. Well, his guardsmen have, at least. Most people who seek us out have lost something. Homes, loved ones, children. Or they've seen the horror that the king puts his own people through. The original Ravens were made up of soldiers who fought for your father. They grew from there."

I sat down on a fallen log and rested my chin in my hands. "Tell me more." I felt like a child asking for another bedtime story.

He sat down on the other end of the log. "Well, there's a lot to tell. I'm not sure where to start."

"How about how you got here?" I suggested.

"That's kind of personal, don't you think?" His previously self-assured attitude was gone.

I struck a nerve. "I'm guessing you know more about me than I know about myself." I shrugged. "Seems fair that I should know something about you."

He sighed. "You aren't going to drop this, are you?"

I flashed my best sweet smile. "Nope."

He relented. "Okay, but the short version. Here goes. I was

living in a boy's home with the Sisters of the Blossoms. When the Battle of the Dead happened, the home was in the path of the fighting. I don't remember much, but from what I was told, few of the children survived. Those of us who did were taken in by a knight of the Aqualine army. He was one of the founders of the Ravens. So, basically, I grew up here, in these woods."

My heart softened toward Ashton as I heard this story. It wasn't very different than my own. I knew what it was like to be an orphan.

We sat in awkward silence for a few moments. Ashton cleared his throat. I looked over to see him stand up quickly.

"We better be moving on," he said, keeping his voice flat and unemotional.

As much as I wanted to keep asking questions, or even try to comfort him, I knew it was time to get going. Any small connection I felt was in my head. Ashton had no intention of getting to know me. I stood and brushed the tree bark from the back of my skirt.

"Lead on," I said, doing my best to sound bored.

Our tour concluded with a walk to the battle headquarters of the Ravens. We walked past a large tent that was my brother's quarters. Most of the major meetings regarding strategy were held there. Then I was led to the weapons training center. A series of fenced in spaces set in clearings among the trees acted as outdoor training grounds for different weapons. One space for sword, a range for archery, an enclosure set up with obstacles for close quarters training. Ashton led me past the training spaces into the woods. We stopped in the small clearing where I had first met him and Max.

"This is where we come to practice sorcery," he said, "figured you might want to know where it is since Max spends a lot of time here." He headed back through the trees, and I followed him away from the sorcery area, doubting I'd have a reason to know where it was.

Ashton let me wander around the area on my own while he

talked with a man who was sharpening swords. I wandered to the archery area and ran my fingers over the arrows filling a barrel. Hanging on a tree nearby were several different sized bows. I touched the smooth wood and wondered what it would be like to shoot one.

I thought back to the tavern where I had felt so helpless. I didn't want to ever feel that way again. *I need to learn to fight.*

"Etta!"

I froze. My new name felt unfamiliar in my ears. *Guess I'll have to get used to it.* I spun around.

My brother stood in front of me. He was smiling but the smile didn't reach his eyes.

"Have you shot one before?" He nodded toward the bows.

I shook my head. "No. I don't really know anything about weapons."

"Saffron told me you expressed an interest in learning how to fight."

I tucked my hair behind my ears. "Yes, that's right." I glanced at the bows hanging on the tree. "It's just that those men in the tavern made me feel so helpless."

He held up a hand. "I get it. I happen to think it's a great idea."

I smiled. "Really?"

He nodded at me. "Think about what you'd like to study. We'll get you started on weapons training tomorrow. I already have plans for you this afternoon."

"What plans?" I asked. *Please don't stick me with Ashton again.*

"You're with me after lunch," he said as he started to walk away. "We'll see if you have any skills in magic."

CHAPTER 11

I stood in the center of the clearing across from Max. Both of my hands were resting in his. I looked up at his relaxed expression. His eyes were closed. We had been standing like this for several long minutes. I risked a glance to my left where Ashton sat watching us. His eyes caught my glance and he flashed an amused expression at me. I looked away quickly, feeling my cheeks redden. Somehow, Max was trying to determine if I had any magic. Butterflies filled my stomach as I waited. Did he expect me to have magic? Would he be disappointed if I didn't have any magic? What happened if I did?

I took a deep breath in just as Max let go of my hands. They dropped to my sides and I stood there afraid to move.

He opened his eyes and took a step back, then frowned at me. "There's magic in there somewhere. But it's not what I'm used to, and I don't know if we will be able to release it. You should have been trained when you were younger. It might be too late."

I have magic? Relief washed through me, followed by confusion. How had I gone my whole life with magic inside me? Wouldn't I have known? I thought back to my life in the little cottage. Nothing interesting ever happened to me. Then again, I didn't know anything about magic. Maybe nothing was supposed to happen, especially if I was somehow different. "What do you mean - it's not what you're used to?"

He pulled a metal ring out of a crate on the side of the

clearing. Tossing it to me he said, "It means that I have never felt magic like yours."

I caught the ring and looked down at it. It was just a simple metal ring. Nothing special or unique about it. I stared through the ring, not able to concentrate on it. Instead, I was lost in thought. Where had this magic come from?

As if he knew what I was thinking, he continued. "Magic runs deep in our family. Most of the members of our family had at least a little bit of magic. It's a shame you weren't hidden with a noble family. Noble children used to take lessons to see if they could channel it. They'd teach them little things, see if anything stuck. Any child that demonstrated true power would be given more in-depth training as they got older. If they wanted to, they could continue to the sorcerer level."

"So this is something that our parents could do?"

Max shook his head. "I'm not sure what they could do because they were never trained as sorcerers. It's possible they had they ability but chose not to follow that path."

I absentmindedly flipped the ring over in my hands. *What I wouldn't give to have one conversation with my parents.* If they had studied magic, would they still be alive? "So this is what makes the king so strong. Why he was able to defeat our father."

Max nodded. "That is why learning how to control magic is the most important skill we have. Every person who joins the Ravens is tested to see if they have magic that they can learn to channel."

"Does that mean we have a lot of sorcerers?"

"So far," Max said, "Ashton is the only one who has shown a natural aptitude. It seems that while magic might be common, being able to control it is rare."

I looked down at the ring and gasped. It was no longer in my hands. It was floating above me. I jumped, causing the ring to clatter to the ground.

Max smiled at me. "You just passed the test."

I looked from Max's broad smile to Ashton. He was staring at me with his mouth hanging open. The look of surprise sent a jolt of pride through me. *Guess you're not so special, after all.*

The rest of the afternoon was spent trying to get me to move the ring from one side of the clearing to the other without touching it. It had been hours and Max was losing his patience with me. The only way I could get the ring to move was if I was holding it. Then I could get it to glide across the space and land softly on the ground. It wouldn't budge if I wasn't touching it to begin with.

"Unless we can get you to move that without touching it, we have only taught you a parlor trick. It has no real merit," Max spat out.

I dropped my outstretched arms to my sides, hurt by his insult. "I'm trying."

Max pressed his palms into his eyes. "Ashton, you work with her until dinner. Etta, try harder. It might be easier if I'm not here watching."

I frowned as he walked from the clearing and strode into his quarters.

Ashton let out an exaggerated sigh as he retrieved the ring from its position across from me and dropped it at my feet. "Let's try it closer to you and then if you get it, we can move it back a little bit at a time."

"You don't have to stay," I said. "I can keep practicing on my own. I know you don't want to be here."

"I told you," Ashton said, "I do what Max asks. Now, try moving the ring."

The last thing I wanted was to let him see me fail. I pressed my lips together and rolled up the sleeves of my dress. Maybe I just needed to concentrate harder. Closing my eyes, I took a deep breath. The sound of the wind in the tress and the birds chirping filled my ears. The scent of pine soothed me. It was almost like being back in my woods. *You can do this. It's just you and the ring. Nothing else.* I pictured myself alone in the trees near my home then opened my eyes.

Focusing on the metal ring, I imagined it moving where I wanted it to go as Max had instructed. The ring shook and my heart quickened. It started to rise. A loud popping noise broke through the trees and all of the birds stopped singing. I jumped back in surprise. When I looked down at the ring, it was gone. I stared across the cleaning to where I wanted the ring to move and didn't see it there. I slumped down onto the ground, resting my head in my hands.

"It's fine," Ashton said. "Not everybody is cut out to be a sorcerer."

I didn't look up. I didn't want to see the gloating smile I knew Ashton was wearing.

"Etta!" Max's voice was loud and angry.

I lifted my head to search for him.

He emerged from his tent holding several pieces of metal in his opened hands. "What did you do that for?" He walked toward me and dropped the metal pieces at my feet. It was the ring, only now it was shattered.

I brushed my fingers over the pieces of metal in complete shock.

Max's features softened. "You didn't do this on purpose, did you?"

"No. I don't know how this happened."

Max sighed. "Well, at least we know there's strong enough magic in there for you to be able to do some damage." He reached down and helped me up.

"Ashton, you'll work with her again tomorrow. We need to find out what she can do."

My stomach knotted as I realized I'd be spending the day with Ashton. He glared at me as if I were purposefully ruining his life.

I had about an hour of free time before dinner, so I walked back through all of the places Ashton had shown me earlier, trying to get a better feel for the camp. My arms felt heavy and tired, as if I had been working in the garden harvesting crops all morning. I didn't realize magic would be so physically exhausting.

My feet seemed to have a mind of their own, leading me through the trees while my mind replayed the event with the ring over and over in my head. What had I done to the ring? How did it end up in Max's quarters, shattered? It was my first chance to impress my brother and instead, I had made myself look foolish.

The sound of birds drew me toward the aviary. Inside, owls and ravens greeted me with friendly cries. If you could ignore the smell, the aviary was a nice place to visit. Finding some seeds, I started to feed the birds. A tiny, white owl flew down from a corner perch and landed briefly on my arm. She let me touch her soft feathers before flying away. The birds seemed so happy. *At least they were easy to please.*

The door opened behind me and I turned to see Saffron enter, holding a tiny scroll in her hand. She smiled when she saw me. "I heard your brother kept you busy today."

I dropped the last of the seeds from my hands into a bowl in front of a large gray dove. The bird pecked away at the seeds. My shoulders dropped and I realized how tired I was from spending the morning trying to make something happen with the magic I didn't know I had. One morning with my brother and I'd already managed to disappoint him. My life continued to get more complicated every day. "Yes, it has been a long, strange day."

I watched her place the paper into a tube on the leg of a white dove. She stroked the bird before picking it up and walking out of the doors with it in her hands.

I followed and watched her release the bird into the sky.

"Where's the bird going?" I asked as I watched it reduce to a small speck of white against blue.

"Message for our secondary camp in the mountains," she said.

I raised my eyebrows. "We have another camp?"

Saffron nodded. "We have two more camps. They are much smaller than this one. There is one in the mountains of Marimont and then one near the King's castle. The camp by the king only has four men at a time. We used to have one more small camp. Outside your village so we could watch you and keep you safe. We broke it down after we moved you."

I had no idea how big of an operation the Ravens really were until that moment. Hope welled up inside me. If they were this large, and organized, maybe there was actually a way to bring down the king.

"How was your tour this morning?" Saffron asked.

"It would have been better with a different guide," I said.

She chuckled. "Ashton's not so bad. He's been through a lot," she paused, "actually reminds me of you in a lot of ways."

I huffed. "I hope I'm never as conceited as he is."

Saffron put her arm around my shoulder. "Try not to take it personally. Besides," she shrugged, "it might be good practice for all of the lords and ladies and royals you'll be meeting in a few weeks."

I winced at the thought of mingling with all of the highborn people I was going to have to meet. I was starting to like the Raven's camp. I made a mental note to not get too attached to anything. I didn't want to start to think of this place as home only to have it ripped away from me.

"Now," Saffron began, "tell me about sorcery training."

"It was bad." I covered my face with my hands. "Max didn't tell you?"

She shook her head. "I haven't seen him at all today."

I stopped walking and she stopped with me. I knew I shouldn't say anything, but I asked anyway.

"Saffron, what's with you and Max? I mean, I saw the kiss but you act so formally around him."

She sighed. "It's a long story, really. What it comes down to is that we were in love once. A very long time ago. Before the Ravens, even. We were children, but it was love." Her eyes looked far away, her gaze glassy.

"What happened?" I asked.

"Nothing, really," she said, breaking the faraway look. "It's just not possible for us to be together. So we had to go our separate ways. We hadn't seen each other in months and we fell into old habits."

I furrowed my brow. "Why can't you be together?"

She locked her eyes on mine. "Because he is going to be king. He'll have to marry for political reasons rather than love."

My breath caught in my chest. I knew royalty couldn't marry

for love but seeing Max have to toss aside his childhood love made it more real. *Wait.* "Weren't my parents in love?"

Saffron's mouth twisted. "From what I've heard, yes, they were. But your mother was a princess, so she could marry a king."

A princess. My mother was a princess before she married my father. I knew that was how it worked, but I didn't think about it before. *I'm a princess.* I felt the color drain from my face.

"What's wrong?" Saffron asked.

"The diplomatic missions I'm being sent on." I couldn't finish the thought.

Saffron pulled her mouth into a tight line. She nodded. "Yes, Etta. You'll have to do the same as Max."

Before Max is even king, they're going to marry me off. I knew it was coming, but I thought I'd have more time. I thought I would get to help the Ravens put Max on the throne first. *I'm not ready to get married. I'm still trying to figure out who I am and what being a princess means.*

I grabbed Saffron by her shoulders. "Why now? Can't it wait?"

She gently lowered my arms. "We need to forge an alliance with a country that has an army. Marriage is the best way to do that. You have the most important job. Without an army, we can't defeat the king."

The space around me seemed to turn slightly sideways and I steadied myself with a few deep breaths. I was overreacting. This wasn't news. Everybody knew that princesses marry high ranking nobles, princes or kings, even. *What does it really matter if it happens now or later? It's not like I'm giving up a great love of my own. Maybe it's better this way. I won't have to fight and I won't have time to fall in love with anybody. Maybe I'll even love my husband.*

As much as I tried to find the good, I couldn't fight the nagging feeling in the pit of my stomach. It was as if I was forgetting about something important. Some reason why I couldn't marry. I just couldn't put my finger on it.

CHAPTER 12

"Again!" Ashton shouted from his place lounging in a low hanging tree branch.

I pushed my sweat stuck hair from my forehead off of my face and focused on the four little boxes set on stumps in front of me. Each box contained one of the four elements: water, fire, air, and earth. I concentrated hard. Trying to get a reaction from any of the four boxes. My body ached from the constant state of tension. I sighed and spun away from the stumps, massaging my temples.

"It's no use," I cried out.

He jumped down from the branch with the grace of a cat. He landed quietly on the ground.

"You're overthinking it," he said for the hundredth time. "That's why we have children do this. Kids don't overthink things the way adults do."

I clenched my jaw. *Easy for you to say. You aren't the one out here staring at little boxes while somebody watches you.*

"That's not helping." I glared at him. It had been nearly two days of staring at boxes in the worst heat I had ever experienced.

"Watch," Ashton instructed. Once again, he took my place in the center of the boxes and stood in front of them. He rolled his shoulders and stood up straight, eyes locked on the center box, fire. He closed his eyes and took a deep breath. Then opened them and reached toward the box. Flames shot out of the box, letting off a fierce heat.

He dropped his hands, causing the fire to shrink back into its place inside the little box. He looked at me. "See?"

I put my hands on my hips. "Yes. I see. You keep showing me, but that isn't helping. You already know your element. You stare right at the box you need and focus all of your energy on it. I have to look at all of them, through all of them. To feel the right one. It's impossible." I threw my hands in the air, dropping them at my sides. "Plus, I can barely focus in this heat!" I pushed my hair back out of my eyes again.

Ashton looked around the clearing.

"Hoping somebody else can take over for you?" I asked in frustration.

"You'd like that, I'm sure," he said. He looked around again.

"What are you doing?" I shouted. The heat and the lack of progress had made me cranky.

"Calm down," he said quietly.

I forced myself to relax my tense shoulders. "I'm sorry," I said. "It's just - I feel so useless."

He smiled at me.

We weren't exactly friends, but over the last two days I had seen a different side to him. He was mostly a patient teacher. He took my training seriously, despite the fact that I knew it was costing him time he could be practicing himself.

"There's a theory I heard once," he said.

I raised an eyebrow.

"That adults can have an easier time finding their element if they, well, if they have a few drinks. Helps them let their guard down and be more impulsive. More like a child."

I smiled. "You're totally making that up."

He put his hands out in front of him in mock surrender. "No, I swear. I heard it from another sorcerer."

I pressed my lips together and thought for a moment. I knew it was probably a bad idea but I wanted to open one of those boxes so badly. "Do you think it would really work?"

He shrugged. "It's probably not going to hurt at the rate we're going. There's only one downside." He crossed his arms.

"We'd kinda have to sneak into town."

"Why?"

"There's no alcohol in the Raven camp. Max says it dulls our senses. So if anybody wants a drink, they have to go to the village."

I swallowed hard. Nobody had told me I had to stay in camp, but I knew the King's Guard was hunting me. *This is a bad idea.*

"It's about a mile away," Ashton said.

I looked at the little boxes that had been the source of all of my stress the last two days. If I could learn how to channel magic, I wouldn't have to worry about being safe. I could learn how to protect myself. *I'm tired of being so defenseless.* I nodded at Ashton. "I'm in."

He smiled. "Didn't think you'd have it in you, I have to admit." He looked up at the sun. "It's almost dinner. We'll go once the sun sets."

My stomach filled with butterflies. I felt guilty about sneaking out without telling anybody. I was sure I'd be in huge trouble if I was caught. Then again, Max was planning my whole life out for me without talking to me about it. The least I could do for myself was to have a few adventures before I was married off. Plus, this was for a good cause. Max said that a sorcerer was the most powerful thing you could be. He thought it was important. Maybe he'd understand. *Maybe nobody will find out.*

*****

Ashton was putting the element boxes into a satchel when I arrived at the Sorcery training clearing. The last rays of the sun shone through the trees. It would be dark soon.

"Are you bringing the element boxes?" I asked.

"We'll have to have you try them outside of town. The walk back to camp might be enough to sober you up." He pulled the satchel over his shoulder.

"I've never had a drink before," I said.

He raised an eyebrow at me. "Never? Not even on feast days?"

"Well, a sip at Sir Henry's but nothing more. My grandmother always said it wasn't appropriate."

"Never had a taste with your friends?"

I shook my head. "I didn't really spend time with other kids in the village. And I never really wanted to try it. I saw enough grown men acting like idiots because of it."

We started to make our way through the woods, Ashton leading the way.

"I thought I had the worse childhood." He smiled at me. "Being raised in the Ravens. But it sounds like you were kept pretty closed off. At least I played with other kids."

I pushed some of the stray curls away from my face. "I guess I never thought about it too much. To me, it was normal. I didn't know any different."

"That's true. I started sneaking out to this village when I was about ten. That's when I realized how different things were in this camp from how they are in other places. Then I got to go on a few supply runs when I was older."

I was surprised by how much he was sharing about his life and wanted to know more. "How old are you?" I asked.

"I'll be twenty next week. That's why I'm taking my sorcery test then. You can't take it until you turn eighteen but they only have the trials once every three years. So I missed out last time."

"Why eighteen?" I asked.

"The guild doesn't want you to practice magic without a master until you're eighteen. Once you pass the trials, you can legally perform magic on your own."

"What if you don't have a master?" I asked, thinking of my own situation. If I was able to channel magic, how would I learn?

"You can't do magic without a master," he said. "If you need training, I suppose Max will have to apply to be your master or find you somebody. If we teach you without registering you with the guild, we'll be breaking the law. Max won't do that. He's the leader of the Order of the Dragon, and he'd lose his title if he broke guild law."

There was so much I didn't understand. How had this whole other world existed around me for so long? "So you'll be done training with Max after you pass?" Maybe Max would take a new apprentice.

"I could be. Or I can keep going. There's advanced trials you can test for, higher levels. Depends on how high you want to move into the sorcerer's guild."

"It sounds complicated," I said.

"I can explain it all to you one of these days," he said.

I smiled. This was a different version of Ashton. I think I like this Ashton. Maybe he was like me. The woods always helped calm me back home.

"Max thinks I'll be able to test for the Order of the Dragon in a year or two. It's the highest ranking group for sorcerers who align with fire. I could be the youngest member ever."

There was so much I didn't know. "Is there an order for every element?"

"I'm not sure. I don't know much about the other elements." He climbed over a fallen tree and then turned to face me. He offered a hand to help me climb over it.

His touch sent a wave of heat through me. My pulse quickened. *Calm down. It's just Ashton.* I tried to focus on the fallen tree and not on my hand in his. He had changed over the last few days. He wasn't the same angry person I first met.

"I'm sorry," I said as I jumped off of the tree. I dropped his hand.

"For what?" he asked.

"I've taken so much time away from you. Time that you should have used to study."

He smiled. "I'm not so mad about that anymore. Besides," he shrugged, "Max says the true test of mastery is being able to teach."

I grinned. "What do you think Max would think of your teaching methods?"

"If we get you to unlock your element, Max won't care how

it happened," he said.

We alternated between bouts of silence and friendly conversation for the rest of the walk through the woods. As we neared the village, Ashton took us to a main road. Distant lights came into view. I shuddered as I thought about what happened to me last time I went into a tavern. I pulled my cloak up over my head. *This really wasn't a good idea.* It was too late to turn around. If this helped me unlock my element, it was worth it.

Ashton was walking next to me now. He seemed to know that I was nervous. He reached his hand out and grasped mine. I almost pulled away, but didn't. The same warmth spread from his hand up my arm. My cheeks felt hot. I was grateful for the darkness so he didn't see my flush.

We entered town hand in hand and Ashton took us to a small tavern. It was only lit with a few lanterns that filled the interior with long shadows. There were several patrons at the bar, laughing and talking while drinking their ale.

We found a table in a dark corner and soon had two large tankards of ale sitting in front of us. I stared into the amber liquid and wrinkled my nose.

Ashton lifted his glass. "Cheers."

I lifted mine and tapped it to his. He took a long drink. Steeling myself, I took a sip of my own. I set it down and curled my lip. *How do people enjoy drinking this?*

Ashton laughed at me. "It gets better. You get used to it."

I lifted the glass again and took a long drink. "Please tell me one is all I need."

"I think one will be more than enough." He laughed again.

I made myself keep drinking the liquid. Ashton looked completely entertained by me.

The tankard was nearly empty. "I feel funny. My head is," I searched for the word, thinking was getting more difficult, "foggy."

"We're on the right track, then." Ashton set down his empty glass and picked mine up. "I think you've had enough." He drained my glass then threw a few coins on the table. "Let's go."

I stood, then collapsed back into my chair. I started laughing and covered my mouth to muffle the sound. I couldn't help it. The customers at the bar top were staring at me. I gave them a little wave.

"Okay, darling," Ashton said louder than he needed to. "I think it's time to go home now."

"I fell down," I said, trying my hardest not to giggle.

"Yes, yes you did." He put his arm around my waist and helped me up.

"Thank you," I said. "You are so sweet. I can't believe I spent the last few days not liking you."

"I know," he said.

Somehow, we made it out of the bar to a wooded area right outside of town. Ashton practically carried me as I stumbled and giggled alongside him. The lights from the town twinkled through the trees but it was too dark to see anything in front of me. Lifting my hand in front of my face, I squinted to try to make out my fingers.

"I think it's too dark," I said.

"Don't worry," Ashton said.

In front of me, fire appeared, illuminating Ashton's face. I gasped as I realized he was holding the fire in his hands. He cupped his hands around the fire, smoothing it until it formed a ball. Lifting his hands, the fireball floated above us, lighting the space we were standing in.

"That's amazing!" I reached toward it and felt it radiating heat. It looked and felt just like a normal fire, but it was floating above me in a perfect sphere.

He smiled. "Well, let's see if it's something I'll be able to teach you one day." He set up the boxes on the ground in a circle around me. "You know, it's likely you'll align with fire, since Max does. Elements run in families. Maybe you should focus on that box first."

"That would have been helpful information before," I said.

"We're not supposed to tell people anything when they do the test," Ashton said. "They say that your element will speak to you."

"Did yours?" I asked.

"Clearly," Ashton said, "but that's the story for a different day."

"You know what to do," Ashton said from outside the circle of boxes. "Do any of them speak to you?"

Before doing anything else, I walked right up the fire box and stared at. Nothing happened. "It's not working."

"Keep going," Ashton said. "Don't try so hard."

Don't try so hard. With a sigh, I turned in a slow circle, pausing every so often to offset the spinning in my head. *What was in that stuff?*

Maybe I needed to touch the boxes. Walking up to each box, I touched it with my fingers. Air. *Nothing.* Earth. *Nothing.* Fire. *Nothing.* Water. *Water.* A chill ran up my spine. I sat down in front of the box and picked it up. I examined it from every angle then held it in my cupped hands. It was colder than I thought it would be. And the material was smooth. As if it were made of ice.

"Wilona, the box." Ashton stared at me, mouth open.

I gasped. It wasn't as if the box were made of ice, it *was* made of ice.

I held the box up to Ashton. "Is this normal?" I asked.

He shook his head. "You align with water. I should have known." He swallowed hard, his face in a tight line.

I wasn't feeling dizzy or giggly anymore. The ice on the box snapped me right back. I stood, staring at the box in awe. "Ashton, this is so amazing."

He wasn't smiling.

I pressed my eyebrows together. "What's wrong?"

"Nothing." He relaxed his face, trying to hide his disappointment or disapproval.

"It's not nothing," I said. "Tell me what's - "

" - Shhh" Ashton froze, shoulders tense. He turned from me in the direction of the village.

I stood still, heart pounding. I let the box tumble from my hands. *Somebody is here.* I heard the muffled voices and the crunching of feet over the forest ground. Whoever it was, they were not afraid of making noise.

Ashton stood in front of me, facing the direction of the noise, arms up in a defensive position.

Four King's Guards broke through the trees. They smiled when they saw us and drew their swords. A tall, olive skinned guard spoke, "Looks like we'll be claiming ourselves a reward, fellas. Those guys in the tavern were right. She looks just like the drawing."

"You might as well just let us kill you now. We'll do it quickly if you surrender," said another.

"Aw, don't tell them that," said a third. "I like it when they try to fight back. Makes for good entertainment."

My heart was beating so hard, I was sure everybody could hear it. My eyes swept across the woods, scanning for a way out. Maybe we should just run. It was dark; we might be able to lose them.

I looked to Ashton, hoping to catch his eye so I could signal to him. His gaze was locked on the men in front of us. His jaw was set, shoulders tense. He stood with his legs apart, knees bent. He looked like he was ready to jump. *He's going to attack them.* My stomach tightened as fear mixed with excitement. I'd never seen a sorcerer fight before. Was he powerful enough to stop them all?

A twig snapped, drawing my attention back at the threat in front of us. The men took a few steps forward, twisted grins across their faces. I shrank back, terrified. *Maybe I should just run.*

"I will give you one chance to turn around and leave us." Ashton's voice was clear and calm.

The men looked at each other and laughed. Then they continued to advance on us.

I shifted my gaze back and forth between Ashton and the men approaching us. Ashton never flinched. He raised his hands above his head and dropped them quickly toward the ground. He turned his hands, palms up toward the sky and a line of fire sprung up between us and our attackers. They paused, looking toward the tallest man. He nodded at them and they charged us, yelling, with swords raised.

Ashton lifted his hands and the line of fire grew into a wall, burning the men as they charged us. The battle cries turned to screams of pain as they were burned alive in seconds. Ashton brought his hands together and the flame burned so bright I had to turn away. When I looked back, there was nothing left of them but ash.

CHAPTER 13

I thought we managed to sneak into camp undetected but when I pulled back the flap to my tent, I was greeted by Max. He wore a scowl on his face. I swallowed hard and closed the flap behind me, hoping to shield Ashton from my brother's gaze.

"Ashton," Max called out, "I know you're out there."

For a moment, I thought maybe Ashton had left, but then he came through the tent. His gaze was downcast and he looked pale.

Max sniffed the air. "You used your magic." He glared at Ashton. "A lot of it. Sit." He pointed to Ashton and myself, then to the bed. "Explain."

I sat on one end of the bed, Ashton the other. I looked down at my hands, knowing that I had done something very stupid. I'd spent yesterday disappointing Max, and now I was breaking rules and nearly getting myself killed. I lifted my eyes and looked around the room through my lashes, chin lowered near my chest.

Max occupied a spindly chair in the corner. He stared at us with a gaze that could probably look right through me. I wondered if he could read minds. After seeing what Ashton could do, I was beginning to understand the true power of sorcery. I shuddered. If Ashton was just an apprentice, there was no limit to what Max could do.

Ashton sat up straight and rested his hands on his knees. "I'm sorry, Max. I had to use my magic to protect her." He inclined his head toward me.

I dropped my head. *This is all my fault.*

"You never should have taken her out of the camp in the first place," Max said. "What were you thinking?" His voice was getting louder with each statement.

"It's my fault!" I jumped up and faced Max. "I wanted to find an easier way to find my element, and I heard a story about drinking."

Max looked to Ashton. He didn't look like he believed that it was my idea.

"You risked her life for the element boxes? Ashton, you know what my plans are for her." He shook his head. "You could have compromised the whole camp. You put everything we've worked at risk."

My chest burned. *Plans for me?* "I thought you said that learning sorcery was the most important thing?"

Max's eyes blazed. "For a warrior, yes. But you're a princess. Your job is to marry a prince. I need you to make an alliance and help me to grow my army. I can't do that if you're dead."

I tightened my hands into fists. "What about self-defense? How do I protect myself?"

Max gave me a saccharine smile. "You'll have guards with you at all times. You don't need to learn self-defense. I only let you try this to keep you busy and to keep Saffron happy."

I clenched my teeth. *How could he do this to me?* "What if I don't want to marry some prince you pick out for me?"

"You don't have a choice." He stood and looked down at me. "I am your king. You are my sister and you are just a princess. Your duty is to marry whomever I deem will be of the most help to our cause. After your antics tonight, I'm going to see if we can move up the date and get you out of here sooner." He stormed out of the tent.

I sunk on to the bed and struggled to breathe. I felt like the wind had been knocked from me. *I have no control over my own life. Is this what being a princess is? Was it worth it?* If I left the Ravens, the king would find me and kill me. If I stayed here, I was going to be married off. *I never wanted this. I never wanted any of this*. I buckled into choking sobs.

Ashton wrapped his arms around me. I buried myself in his chest, grateful for the comfort and embarrassed that he was seeing me cry. He stroked my hair and whispered calming words to me.

I finally caught my breath and pulled away from Ashton. "I'm so sorry."

"Don't be. It's my fault. Max is right, it was a stupid risk. I shouldn't have brought you there." He rested a hand on mine.

"We didn't even tell him about my element. Maybe that would fix it? Maybe then he'd..." But even as I said it, I knew it made no difference. I turned to face Ashton, grasping both of his hands in mine. "Don't tell him. Please. Promise me, you'll keep it a secret. I don't want him to know that I found my element."

Ashton furrowed his brow. "I don't know why you'd want to keep that a secret."

"I don't want him to know," I pleaded. "I can't handle upsetting him any more than I already have. Besides, you heard him. He doesn't even want me to train, anyway. So there isn't any point."

"I don't know, Wilona. I've never kept anything from Max. I've been his apprentice a long time."

Tears blurred my vision. I wasn't sure why I wanted to keep this from Max, but something was telling me it was the right thing to do. "Please," I whispered.

He sighed. "Very well, Wilona. We'll keep it our secret, for now. But we'll have to tell him soon."

I nodded. It was a start. Ashton's gaze met mine and butterflies swam in my stomach. That warm feeling was back and it traveled through my whole body. I was overwhelmingly aware of his hands in mine. I pulled back, and jumped up off the bed.

Ashton cleared his throat and stood. "I should go and you should get some rest."

I nodded. My throat felt tight, like I wouldn't be able to speak if I tried.

*****

Saffron woke me the next morning by throwing clothes at me. "Get up."

I sat up, startled. "What's wrong?" I asked.

"You really upset your brother." She shook her head. "I don't want to hear the excuses, just get up and get dressed." She left the tent.

I looked away from her. *Great. Now Saffron's mad at me, too.* Maybe being sent away to some random castle wouldn't be the worst thing in the world. At least there maybe I could find some people who weren't mad at me.

I pulled on the trousers and tunic she threw at me, grateful to be out of the heavy dresses. When I emerged from the tent, Saffron handed me a piece of bread and started walking. I hurried to keep up with her as I ate.

"We have five days to teach you how to stand up for yourself," she said as we walked.

"What do you mean?" I asked, my mouth full.

"Your brother left camp to see if he can secure your engagement. The original plan was for you to visit the courts and make an impression. Now he just wants to find somebody who can benefit our cause. He doesn't think highborn women need to know how to fight. I disagree. I cleared my schedule. I have five days to make you into a warrior."

My heart leapt. *Finally, I get to do something useful.* Learning how to fight was a way of regaining at least a little bit of control. If I could protect myself, I wouldn't be completely dependent on these strangers I was surrounded by. Sir Henry's warning still rang in my mind, reminding me I shouldn't depend on anybody. I caught Saffron in a hug.

"Thank you," I said. Finally, I felt like something good was happening.

"You're welcome." She gave me a one armed hug in return.

We started walking again. Her strides were so long, I almost had to run to keep up.

"Where's Ashton?" I bit my lower lip.

She glanced at me but didn't break her stride. "He's with your brother. Max wasn't happy with him, but he has his test soon and needs to be ready."

"Saffron? Are you sure I have to be married off right away?" My voice shook.

She slowed down her pace and her eyes softened. "You know the answer to that."

A small fire started to burn in the pit of my stomach. I had always done everything I was told. Always followed the rules, but there was a part of me that didn't want to anymore. "Why can't Max just marry somebody?" I slapped my hand over my mouth as soon as I asked the question.

I saw a flash of pain in Saffron's eyes. "He will, eventually, but he'll make a better match once he claims the throne. In order for him to claim it, we need more manpower." She stopped walking and rested her hand on my shoulder. "Royalty doesn't have the freedom of falling in love. At least, not usually. That's the only benefit to being a peasant. When you are royalty, your life belongs to your kingdom and to your people. If you had been raised in a castle, you'd already be married."

I swallowed. The little fire inside that wanted to rise up against this was losing fuel. "This is the only way for me to help?" I asked. "The only way we can bring down the king?"

She nodded. "Everybody is afraid of the king. They won't step up to fight him. But if they are connected by marriage and take our princess as part of their family, they'll do it."

I sighed. I trusted Saffron and if she said this had to be done, it must be the way. Her words made sense and I hated them, but I needed to find a way to eliminate the king.

We walked quietly for a minute before Saffron turned to me with a wild light in her eyes. "Time to get it all out." She tossed me a wooden sword. She came at me, sword raised and I did my best to block her. As she made contact, my sword shot across the practice ring and landed with a dull thud.

My hand was stinging and I shook it out. "I wasn't ready."

"Let's go again," she said.

We went again. I lost count of how many times I had to run after my thrown sword. My shoulders ached. I'd never been this bad at anything in my life. I picked up the sword and dropped it at her feet. "Saffron." I sighed. "Is there any other way I can defend myself besides using a sword? I don't think I will ever get the hang of this."

"You're probably right." She put the swords back in the open shed with the other training weapons and pulled two daggers off of her waist. "Let's switch to dagger." She handed me a slim silver dagger with a black leather hilt. It was lightweight and felt comfortable in my grasp. I studied it for a moment and touched the sharp edges and point.

"A dagger is a good weapon for you." Saffron pointed the other dagger at me as she spoke. "It's small and compact, so you can hide it under dresses. And it works well in close quarters in case you need to fend off an attacker."

She threw the dagger past my head and it stuck into the fence post with a thwack. "You can also use it for attackers that are a bit further away with some practice."

I passed the small weapon between my hands. I tried to imagine throwing it at one of the guards who attacked me. I frowned. "I don't think this will do much against armor."

"You're right," she said. "But you can aim for the face or the neck. Usually it's exposed."

The thought of stabbing somebody in the face sent chills through me. Breaking the bottle over that guard's head had been very effective, even if it had been accidental. What would I be able to do with a real weapon and some practice? Could I kill somebody intentionally?

Saffron touched my shoulder. "Don't worry. This is all precautionary. It would be a worst case scenario. You'll most likely have people with you to defend you."

She sounds just like Max. She was teaching me how to do this, but did she believe I could? I weighed the dagger. Then I lined up with the fence post and threw the blade. It bounced off of the post and landed with a dull thud on the ground.

"It takes practice." Saffron smiled. "Let's focus on the up

close tactics first. Places you can stab a man that will cause the most harm."

I spent the next several hours learning about anatomy. I learned where I should aim if I wanted to kill, and where I should aim if I wanted to just slow somebody down. She showed me the typical weak areas in armor and how to angle the blade when I struck. After that, she showed me where I could hide the blade on my body in different types of clothing.

"Can I try throwing it again?" I asked.

"I don't see why not." She looked to the sky. "The archery fields should be empty this time of day. We'll head there so you can use a proper target."

"Thanks for doing this for me. I know Max didn't want me to do this," I said.

"Your brother might be my oldest friend, but we don't agree on everything."

"It must be hard. Giving him up," I said.

She stopped and stared at me. "Let me tell you this right now, Etta. Anything worth doing is going to be hard. You are going to face some of the most difficult situations in your life in the coming months. But it will be worth it. It's what we have to do. I believe in the Ravens." She pressed her lips together. "I believe in your brother. Max will be an amazing king. The kind who can save our kingdom. For these things, we must all sacrifice."

I swore I saw the shimmer of tears in her eyes. I didn't know how to respond. Would Max be a good king? I hardly knew him. He didn't seem like the type to let people get close. Was that a good thing or a bad thing for a king? I tried to imagine him on a throne with a crown on his head. In my mind, he wore his black robes, surrounded by fire. His eyes flashed red and he wore a maniacal smile. Chills ran down my spine. For some reason, Max with a crown didn't seem to match up.

Saffron cleared her throat and started walking again. Pushing away the unsettling vision of Max, I followed at her heels, silently, afraid to cause her any more pain.

The archery field was indeed empty when we arrived. We

started five feet from a large hay-filled scarecrow that acted as our target. She showed me how to grip the dagger so I could throw it in one fluid movement. The first time I tried, it sunk right into the target's face. I grinned.

"Wow." Saffron laughed. "That's some beginner's luck. Let's back you up to see if you can do it again."

We backed up, little by little. Every time I threw, my blade met its target. After the disaster with sorcery and sword fighting, I was relieved to find something I could actually do.

She let me try her other dagger, a heavier blade, to see if I could still find the balance. Once again, I was able to hit my target.

"She's brilliant."

I heard clapping from behind me and turned to see the spectator. Not wanting to seem like I was overly proud, I bit the inside of my cheek to keep from smiling too widely.

Saffron waved the man over. "Master Edward! Nice to see you. Come on over."

Master Edward was an older man with thinning white hair. He had a fat, red face and a large belly that hung over his trousers.

"Your highness," he said, inclining his head toward me.

I offered a small nod in return. He was the first person I had met at the Ravens who had used my formal title. It didn't feel right. I didn't feel worthy.

"Saffron's got you throwing blades when you should be using a real weapon." He glanced between the blade in the target and the one in my hand.

"Well, she tried teaching me to use the sword," I said.

He waved his hand dismissively. "Swords. Brute force and flashy heroics. You need a real weapon. Something more elegant." He swept his hand through the air to the bows hanging on the tree behind us.

"Master Edward is our archery master," Saffron explained.

He crossed to the tree and removed a bow, then held it out to me. "Let's see what you can do."

He spent a few minutes showing me how to hold the bow,

how to line up the arrow and how to aim.

My fingers tingled as I held the bow and my face hurt from smiling. The weapon felt right in my hands. I nocked the arrow, and pulled the string back until the arrow rested against my cheek. I took a few deep, steadying breaths while I aimed, then released the arrow. It launched toward my target, hitting just inches from where I had been aiming. I smiled and looked to Master Edward.

He clapped his hands together. "I knew it when I saw you throw that dagger. I have only worked with one other natural archer in my lifetime. It's a pleasure to see it runs in the family."

My eyes widened.

"I was fortunate enough to train your father when he was about your age." He smiled at me. "I worked with him for about a year before I was called away. In reality, he only needed that one year because he was so gifted."

I straightened and looked down at the bow in my hand. It felt like my parents were looking down on me. Little by little, the pieces were starting to come together. For the first time in days, I felt a sense of pride in who I was rather than dread at what was expected of me. "Can I learn more?" I looked from Master Edward to Saffron.

Saffron shrugged. "That's up to Master Edward. Do you have time to add a new pupil?"

Master Edward's face lit up. "Of course. Wild boars couldn't keep me away."

"You'll have four days with her before Max gets back. I'm not sure what her schedule will be like when he returns," she said.

He nodded. "Four days should be enough for her to learn the basics with her natural gift."

I smiled as I ran my fingers over the smooth wood of the bow. I was finally learning to defend myself. Gone was the weak, scared girl I had been when Saffron found me. In just this short time, I had become something else. I lifted my chin. *Nobody is going to hurt me ever again.*

CHAPTER 14

I woke before dawn with butterflies in my stomach. Today I would begin my archery training. I had four days to learn how to be the best possible archer I could be. Feeling my way around the tent in the darkness, I found the trousers and shirt Saffron had given me. I dressed in the dark, too excited to go back to sleep. *Four days.* Soon I would be married. *But not today. Today is my day.* I had to make the best of every minute.

When I reached the archery field, I was surprised to find no targets set up. Instead, I found Master Edward at a wooden table set with various tools.

He inclined his head. "Good morning, your highness."

I winced. "That's really not necessary."

"Of course it is. It's the same title I used with your father, and I will use it with any true heir to the kingdom."

There wasn't going to be any arguing with him. "Should I grab a bow?"

He shook his head and handed me a small axe. "You don't have a bow yet, you need to make one." He slung a pack on his shoulder. "It's about an hour walk each way to the trees we need." He nodded. "You can carry the axe."

I followed him away from camp, axe in hand. We were going up hill and the terrain was getting rockier. I was panting slightly as we ascended. Master Edward wasn't even breaking a sweat.

"Do you come up here often?" I managed between breaths.

He turned his head over his shoulder to look at me. "At

least once a week. I like to always have a new bow in progress."

"Do you bring all your students up here?"

He shook his head. "You're the first one. Most of them wouldn't benefit from a custom bow."

That motivated me to pick up my pace. We were going to make a custom bow just for me. I'd never had anything that was made especially for me. Even though my grandmother worked as a seamstress, my clothes had always been modified dresses that she purchased or traded for. But it wasn't just about having a possession. It was what having my own bow represented. Master Edward believed in me. He thought I could truly learn to defend myself. That I was worthy of such a gift. It was nice to have somebody here see me as more than just a girl who was going to be married off.

I laughed to myself. How things have changed. It was still hard to believe that I was not the peasant girl from the village. Though I didn't feel quite like a princess, I knew I couldn't go back to what I had been before.

The incline continued and the pine trees thinned as we walked. I started to see different shrubs and vegetation from those at the camp. A little critter skittered away from us.

"That's a chipmunk." Master Edward pointed. "Bet you didn't have those in the farm country you were in."

"Nope. Rabbits and squirrels," I said.

"We have those, too, but they don't come around much where people can get to them. They're tricky here in these woods."

I looked through the trees to see if I could catch a glimpse of any more chipmunks or any of the elusive rabbits.

The pine trees had nearly disappeared, replaced by shorter trees with leaves rather than needles. They were only a couple of feet taller than me. They stood straight and proud, with thick, low-hanging branches and leaves so green they looked like they were glowing. I had never seen trees like this before. I brushed my fingers on the trunks of a few of them as we passed. They were smooth and cool to the touch.

We reached the summit of the hill we had been climbing and Master Edward sat on the ground. He patted the space next to him and I joined him. From his bag he removed a couple of apples and we ate while I caught my breath. He looked at peace as he surveyed the hill below us. His breathing was even and steady. The break was probably added for my benefit.

The woods were below us, sloping gently down the hill we had just spent an hour climbing. The village in the distance looked like it was made of miniature boxes.

I hugged my knees to my chest. "It's beautiful here."

"Aye. I used to take my granddaughter up here." He shifted uncomfortably.

"Your granddaughter?" She had to be close to my age.

He sighed and pointed to the village. "My daughter and her family lived in that village. She died of fever leaving three young children and her husband behind. Her husband served your grandfather and was away often. I gave up my post as Archery Master to help him care for my grandchildren. Went back to making bows again. The two oldest, both boys, followed in their father's footsteps and joined the king's army. The youngest, Anna..." he swallowed.

"It really doesn't matter." He shook his head. "They're all gone now. More senseless deaths added to the list of casualties at the hand of the king." He stood abruptly and offered a hand to me to pull me up.

"It's not good to dwell on the past. The important thing is to move forward. And this, my dear," he gestured to the trees all around us, "is going to move us to the future."

"Trees?" I raised an eyebrow.

"Not just any tree." His eyes twinkled. "These are Scarlet Elder trees. They make the best bows in the world. People will hike for months to find one to make their bow."

I pulled on one of the branches. It was nearly as thick as the trunk and was difficult to bend. How did this tree support these branches?

Master Edward did the same, pulling on a branch next to the

one I held. "Strong and steady branches. They shape more easily than other woods, yet hold their shape better. There are those who believe these trees were created by magic because they are so perfectly matched for making a bow. No other tree even comes close."

After what I'd seen Ashton do with his fire, I knew there was a lot I didn't know about magic. "Do you think they're magic trees?"

"Considering their properties, I think they are magical."

"So, I'll have a magic bow?"

"In your hands, I wouldn't be surprised," he said.

I lifted the axe. "So I need to cut down a branch?"

He nodded.

"How do I know which one to cut?"

"You'll know," he said. "Take your time. I'll wait."

I spent some time circling trees and tugging on branches. They all looked the same. How was I supposed to pick one? I considered asking Master Edward for some advice and glanced over my shoulder. He was gone from my sight. *I'm on my own.* The leaves on the trees rustled in the breeze. It was a pleasant sound, similar to rain. I could picture myself spending a lot of time here if I were to stay with the Ravens. *I don't get to stay.* Maybe I should just run away to the woods. I could see myself living in a place like this. I shook my head.

Don't be so selfish. The sad look on Master Edward's face filled my mind. *No more families ripped apart.* I was dreading the idea of marriage to a stranger but it was my chance to help put an end to all of the violence. There were worse things. The people in this kingdom lived in constant fear. All I have to do to help save them was to follow along with Max's plan. Maybe Master Edward would move with me and teach me archery wherever they sent me. He might like that. That happy thought drove me as I ran my fingertips over the smooth trunks.

I continued my circles around the trees, stopping to tug on branches. *Time to pick one and get back.* I reached for my axe but hesitated. A rush of cold filled me, as if I had just taken a drink of chilled water. The feeling pulled me away and I followed to a short tree a few yards across from me. It seemed to vibrate when I placed my hand on a low hanging branch. The branch felt like ice. It was buzzing with energy, then the feeling went away. I took a breath. *That was weird.* Shaking my head, I tried to regain my senses. Maybe the trees were magical. I ran my hand along the branch and found the place where it connected to the trunk. After several swings of my axe, the branch dropped to the ground. It was a long branch, about as thick as my leg. My heart was beating harder from the exertion of swinging the axe and I felt sweat on my brow. Wiping it away, I looked around, trying to figure out where I was so I could return to the summit.

Without warning, the sounds of the woods vanished. It was too quiet. My mouth went dry and I swallowed. Out of the corner of my eye something moved. Then I heard a rustling sound.

"Master Edward?" *Maybe it's just a chipmunk.* The hair on my arms stood on end.

I should have run back to the Archery Master, but a strange boldness took hold of me. With a grunt, I heaved the branch over my shoulder and walked toward the sound. It grew louder as I approached. A thick grove of shrubs in front of me moved. Holding my breath, I pushed the shrubs apart. There, on a rock was a huge black raven. It turned its gaze on me, an intense stare, as if it was trying to say something to me. The bird squawked and snapped its beak. I jumped, dropping the branch.

It hopped forward on the rock and lifted its leg revealing a small scroll. I looked around. There wasn't anybody else here. *I shouldn't be getting a message.* My heart pounded in my ears as I pulled the scroll from the bird. As soon as it was removed, the bird flew off in a thunderous flapping of its huge wings. I unrolled the small parchment and saw a message written in thin, tight cursive.

My darling princess, I hope this note finds you well. I have been searching for you for a long time, and it seems you have bested my guards. Perhaps I was too quick to dismiss you. I am holding a feast in your honor. Your grandmother hopes you will be able to attend.

- King Osbert, I

With a gasp, I clutched my chest. The forest seemed to turn on its side. The king. *He's found me. And he has my grandmother. It's not possible.* My blood went cold. Had she still been alive when I left her there? My head spun, trying to recall every second of that night. The details flooded in as a blur of overlapping events. As they came into focus I felt the color drain from my face. *She died. I saw it with my own eyes.* Had the king brought her back from the dead?

I'm not sure how I made it back to Master Edward. Or why I thought to bring the branch with me. As I approached the place where he sat, his grin faded.

The ground seemed uneven as I walked.

He stood and hurried to me. "What's wrong? Are you hurt?"

Numbly, I handed him the scroll.

As he read it, the color drained from his face. "Where did you find this?"

"A raven delivered it to me."

He shook his head. "This isn't possible. He shouldn't know you're here." He roughly repacked his bag. "We have to get you back to camp."

I worked on steadying my breath as we made our way down the hill. I was afraid to go back there. Afraid that he was waiting for me at the bottom. The walk back was going too quickly. My hands felt cold and clammy.

"It's going to be fine," Master Edward said from time to time.

I couldn't tell if he was trying to make me feel better or if he was talking to himself.

My mind whirred as I tried to comprehend the message. *He knows where I am.*

I felt like I was entering a dream when we arrived at camp.

Everybody was busy doing their normal tasks. Nothing had changed here even though inside, I felt like everything had changed. My eyes searched the people we passed as we made our way through the camp. My cheeks burned when I realized I had been looking for Ashton. *He's not here, and you shouldn't care anyway.* I used my forearm to brush the hair off of my face and tried to think of a plan. I wasn't sure what I should do. There was a small part of me that was hoping my grandmother was alive, and that little part of me was screaming out to go to her. The rational side of me was sending warning bells that shook my entire body. This had to be a trap.

When we approached Max's quarters, several long swords were propped against the side. I looked to Master Edward.

He shrugged. "Looks like she's got company." He pushed his way through the flap and I followed behind.

Inside the tent, Saffron stood at the head of a long table surrounded by six men in armor I had never seen before. They all turned to look at us as we entered. Murmurs went around the table and the men looked to Saffron. She nodded at them and everybody turned their attention to me.

I took a small step back from their stares. Master Edward gently nudged me forward. "I received a message." I held out the rolled parchment, struggling to keep my hand steady.

Saffron crossed the space to take it from me. She wrinkled her brow. "I was worried one of them would find their way to you."

I drew my eyebrows in and stared at her. "What do you mean?"

She sighed as she unrolled the paper. She turned to the men around the table. "It's the same as the others. I think we can safely say he knows she's alive but he's not sure where she is."

Saffron turned to me. "We have had reports of messages just like this showing up around the kingdom. Seven confirmed so far."

I bit the inside of my lip in an effort to keep my face blank. I hoped I didn't look as scared as I felt. The only comfort I could find was that he didn't know exactly where I was.

"Sir Gregory, go ahead," Saffron said.

"Are you sure?" A gray haired man asked Saffron.

She nodded. "She can handle it, and she has the right to know."

I swallowed hard and clenched my fists, preparing myself for bad news.

"I was at your village the day after you escaped. Went to give your grandmother a proper burial but she wasn't there. The villagers saw a battalion of King's guards pass through. They left with a cart. Most likely with your grandmother's body."

Fingernails bit into the skin of my palms. I wavered between sadness and anger. This king had taken so much from me. My parents, my grandmother, my chance at a happy life. Hot tears formed in the back of my eyes. I closed my eyes and took a deep breath. *Don't cry.*

"Thank you for telling me." I nodded at Sir Gregory then looked around the room at all of the people gathered. "Where were the other letters found?"

Saffron picked up a piece of paper off of the table and read a list of names. I recognized a couple of them from my geography lessons but didn't know them all.

"Why these places?" I asked.

"That's what we have been discussing." She set the list back down. "Two were sent to Raven camps. Two were sent to port towns. The other three to nobles in smaller fiefdoms loyal to the Ravens."

"He knows about the Ravens." I hugged my arms across my chest. "Has he always known?"

Saffron shrugged. "Perhaps. We just don't know. With the protective wards you have on you, we only have to worry about the guards."

"Wards?" I had no idea what she was talking about.

"Magical protection given by a powerful sorcerer. Cast on you before you were put into hiding. As long as the sorcerer who created the wards lives, the king himself can't hurt you. That's why he sends others out looking for you. If he could do it himself, you'd already be dead."

"That explains the drawings and the Reapers. He'll send them here, won't he?" I said.

Saffron nodded. "Yes. We've got a decoy in Redding. Enough of a false trail to keep them away for a day or two."

"Max?" I asked.

"He's already on his way back. Negotiations will resume once you are moved to safety."

"When?" I asked.

"As soon as Max returns, we'll get you out of here." She rested a hand on my shoulder. "Don't worry, we will keep you safe. Go with Master Edward. Finish your lessons. There's nothing you can do right now."

I nodded and turned to leave the tent. Hesitating for a moment, I wondered if I should ask the question I really wanted to know the answer to. *That's not a good idea.* Silently, I prayed for Ashton's safe return.

CHAPTER 15

I looked at the branch in my hands. Making a bow didn't seem as important as it had this morning. I pulled off the leaves one by one, tossing them on the ground.

"You found yourself a fine branch."

His words snapped me out of my trance. "Thank you." I stared at the branch. Maybe it was important to make it. After all, I still needed to defend myself. Now more than ever. "Do we still have time to make me a bow?"

The sparkle returned to his eyes and he laughed. "I think that would be a might fine distraction for you, your highness."

Next to the archery field stood a small wooden structure that looked like a roof on stilts. Under the roof was a work table and a series of tools. Master Edward showed me how to clear and smooth my branch to prepare it. Next, we carved a handle in the center and notches for the string. We set it in a vise that would hold it in place so it could develop the curve it needed.

"It'll be in there all night tonight." He tightened the stand. "Tomorrow, we'll add the string. Only wood in the world that can make a bow so quickly."

My shoulders sunk. "Now what?" I didn't want to have extra time to wait around.

He placed his forefinger and thumb astride his chin as he thought. He snapped his fingers. "How about I teach you how to make arrows? Just in case you ever have to make them on your own."

"That sounds great." I clapped my hands together. "Can we start right away?"

He patted his large stomach. "We'll start after lunch."

I wasn't feeling hungry so I grabbed a handful of berries to take to the birds. The aviary had become my favorite place in camp. The little white owl I met on my first day here was one of my favorite things about the camp.

Four doves and my favorite owl were inside the small structure today. I held out the berries in my open hands. The doves ignored me but the little owl swept down from her high perch and landed on a railing next to me. She nibbled the berries out of my hands. I laughed as her beak brushed my palm. She was a gentle bird. I reached out to stroke her soft feathers, and she let me touch her for a moment before flying back up to the top corner and burying her head under her wing.

It was a warm day and the interior of the aviary was a little too hot for my taste. Reluctantly, I headed outside. A few steps from the door I heard a loud snap. My heart started pounding. I flattened myself against the building and didn't move. *The king has found me.* I shook my head. The letter was getting to me. It's probably a rabbit. *A really big rabbit.*

Halfway through talking myself into peeking around the aviary, I heard voices. They were on the other side of the building and speaking in hurried, hushed tones. I tip-toed to the edge of the wall and peeked my head around. I couldn't see them, but I could now make out two male voices. I strained my ears to listen to the conversation.

"She got the message, then?" said an amused male voice.

I couldn't make out the muffled reply.

"So they still think he doesn't know where she is - good."

The second voice was louder this time. "They won't move her until tomorrow. Things are going exactly according to the plan."

My heart was pounding so hard, I was worried they would hear it. *There's a traitor in the Ravens.* The king *does* know where I am. The other letters must be decoys.

115

"Wait for the signal," the first man said.

I have to get out of here. There was a large tree a few feet away from me. If I could quietly get to the tree, I could hide there and make my way back to the common area one tree at a time.

I crept slowly toward the tree. *Snap.* I froze.

"What was that?" One of the men had heard me.

I heard the unmistakable sound of a sword being unsheathed. I ran.

My lungs burned with effort as I neared the common area. I could see people still sitting at the tables eating lunch. I tossed my head back to check behind me and ran right into somebody. I tumbled to the ground, panting.

I spun my head around wildly, making sure nobody was behind me then looked up to see Ashton smiling down at me.

His smile faded and he knelt down next to me. "What's wrong?"

I hugged my knees to my chest while I worked to slow my breathing. "Can't. Talk. Here."

He stood and pulled me up. "What do you mean?"

My breathing was returning to normal. "Not safe. We have to go somewhere safe."

His eyes softened. "Is it about the letters? Because Max has a plan for that. Everything will be fine."

I shook my head. "No. I mean yes." I let out an exasperated sigh. "Please. I just need to find Saffron."

Saffron was with Max in his quarters. For the second time that day, I entered without permission, which I instantly regretted when I walked in on the two of them mid kiss.

They pulled apart abruptly and Saffron's cheeks turned pink. I looked away and cleared my throat, trying to ignore what I just saw.

"What's going on? Ashton, didn't we talk about this?" Max's gaze was locked on Ashton.

He looked down. "I'm sorry, Max. Wilona said it was urgent."

Max let out a breath. "*Etta*, what can I do for you?"

I glanced around the tent then peeked out the flap.

Saffron's brow wrinkled. "What's wrong?"

"I overheard two men talking." I told them the story about the men behind the aviary. I watched Max for reaction as I spoke. His face went from an annoyed look to a scowl.

Max began pacing the room. "I have wondered if there was a traitor in the Ravens for a few months now. We just never found any proof, and everything that has gone wrong could have been coincidence. Now we know."

He stepped up to me. "We have to move up your departure."

I nodded and resisted looking at Ashton standing next to me. The back of his hand brushed against mine ever so slightly. The familiar warmth I now associated with his touch spread up my hand. I pulled my hands together and clasped them in front of me.

Saffron took a step forward. "We can't let them know we're on to them."

"I agree." Max looked at her before turning his gaze back to me. "We'll sneak out tonight after nightfall. They won't expect us to travel at night."

"I'll take her," Saffron said.

Max looked concerned for a moment, but nodded nevertheless.

"Etta, can you find something to do for a few hours that won't arouse suspicion?" Max asked me.

"You can go to the archery range," Saffron suggested.

"Archery?" Max frowned.

She put a hand up. "We'll talk later."

"Take Ashton with you," Max said. Then he turned his back on me to face the papers stacked on the table.

Ashton and I walked to the archery range in silence. We were the only ones there when we arrived.

I reached for Ashton's hand. He flinched, then let me lead him to the structure where my bow sat in the vise.

"I want to show you something." I ran my hand over the smooth wood of the bow. "It's mine," I said. "Though I suppose I won't get to finish it now."

Ashton touched the bow. "It's beautiful. I can tell it's going to be a great bow when it's done."

"Can you finish it for me?" My stomach tightened. "And hold on to it for me, until we…"

Ashton moved in closer. Our bodies were almost touching. He could probably hear my heart beating. He touched my cheek lightly and ran his fingers down the side of my face, leaving a trail of tingling skin. He leaned down and touched his lips to mine gently. For a second, I was too surprised to react but as his lips moved against mine, time seemed to stand still. It was as if we were the only people in the whole world. I pressed my mouth into his and wrapped my arms around his shoulders. I could feel the muscles under his tunic. I wanted him to pull me closer, to be completely wrapped up inside his strong arms. He slid his hand on the back of my head and the kiss grew deeper. Something was growing inside me that I hadn't felt before. I wanted more.

He pulled back slowly, cheeks flushed. "I'm sorry."

I pushed my hair out of my face. I knew we couldn't be together, but that didn't stop me from wanting to kiss him again. "Don't," I said. "Don't be sorry."

He cupped my cheeks in his hands and shook his head. "How did this happen?" He laughed.

I smiled at him and put my hands on top of his. I closed my eyes, burning this moment into my memory. "Come with me. Who could protect me better than you?"

"You know I can't." He dropped his hands. "Besides, even if I could convince Max, I have my exam next week."

"Then I can go with you." I practically jumped. "How perfect would that be? Nobody would suspect that I'd be traveling to the trials, and I'd be surrounded by sorcerers."

Ashton shook his head. "But not all of them are on our side. It's too dangerous."

"Nobody would know who I was, though. You could say I'm an apprentice, just like you."

He thought about it for a minute. "That might work, you know. Except for the fact that you're supposed to be going off to get married."

I shook my head. "There has to be a way to stop that. Why is Max so determined for me to get married right away?"

"I guess I can see why he wants to have you…" Ashton couldn't finish the sentence.

I knew it was a bad idea, but before I could stop myself, I reached for him and pulled him into another kiss. His arms wrapped around me and for the first time in weeks, I felt truly safe.

"Ah-hem."

I pushed myself away from Ashton and turned to face Master Edward. I covered my face with my hands to hide my flush. Of course. I was supposed to meet him here after lunch. *I'm in so much trouble.*

"I - uh - was just showing Ashton my bow."

He cleared his throat. "I can see that." He looked at Ashton. "I didn't realize you were back already."

"We made good time," Ashton said.

"It looks like you had extra motivation to get here." He waved a hand dismissively. "But it's none of my business, really. We live in dangerous times. None of us know how much time we get. It's important to make the best of it."

"You won't tell my brother?" I asked.

"What would I tell him? That you showed your bow to Ashton? I doubt he would be interested in that. Far too busy, your brother. Doesn't stop to notice the beauty in life."

I let out a breath and relaxed.

Ashton's shoulders dropped a bit. He smiled at me.

Master Edward's face grew serious. "Your brother is all about power. No heart. Not like you. I think you'll do what is right for the right reasons. I wish I could say the same of your brother." He pointed to the pendant clearly on display around my neck. "That symbol you wear says it all. Takes a true royal to bear such a strong crest. There's a reason your brother has a dragon on his arm and not a Ouroboros."

I reached up to grasp my pendant. "What do you mean? He told me his tattoo was for some sorcery order."

"Aye, that's right. Nobody has been eligible to take the mark of the Ouroboros since your great-grandfather. He was the last of the water sorcerers." He waved his hand dismissively. "It's not the time for a history lesson. You'll learn all of this soon enough."

I put my hand on my hips. "You know, it's getting old having everybody else know more about my family than I do."

"Patience, your highness. Right now, the focus is on keeping you alive."

I huffed, making me feel like a spoiled child, demanding something I wasn't allowed to have. "Do you know all of this?" I asked Ashton.

He shook his head. "This is all new to me. History wasn't a big priority in my lessons with Max. My guess is the only reason he even let me learn how to read was so I could decipher old spell books."

This wasn't getting me anywhere. I stood up straight and fixed my best serious expression on my face. "Master Edward," I spoke in a tone Lady Genevieve would be proud of, "I will drop this for now as long as you promise me, we can pick it back up at a later date."

The corners of his mouth turned up into a smile and he raised an eyebrow. "Agreed, your highness. Now, let's check on this bow of yours. I hear a rumor that you might not be here to finish it tomorrow?"

How would he know that? I stared at him. Master Edward seemed to have the pulse of the whole camp at his fingertips. I wondered if he'd be willing to travel with me when I went. The idea of leaving him behind, even if it was temporary, caused an emptiness inside.

He chucked. "Saffron found me. Sent me along to help keep your mind off of things." He turned some levers and used some tools to measure and pull on the wood of the bow.

He sighed. "I was hoping we could force it, but it's not ready yet. I'm afraid you'll have to use one of mine for now." He walked back outside of the structure to where he had propped a graceful bow against a tree. Picking it up and running his fingers over the wood, he handed it to me.

"This is beautiful." I traced my fingers along a flower pattern that had been carved into the wood. "Did you make it?"

He nodded. "For my granddaughter, but she never got the chance to use it. Now, it's yours." His eyes were watery. "It's made of Scarlet Elder wood. The properties of the tree will make it easier to hit your target. It's also lighter than bows made of other materials. You'll be able to get more shots out of it before you tire. My granddaughter was about your size. It should be a perfect fit."

My throat tightened and I blinked back tears. "Thank you." I hugged him.

He cleared his throat again. "No more hugging. No tears. It's time for you to learn how to shoot your new bow."

CHAPTER 16

I steadied myself with the new bow. It was longer than the practice bow and it took more strength to pull. I held my breath as I released the arrow. It hit the target but the force wasn't enough for it to stick. I cursed.

"You need to pull back further with this bow. You need more power." Master Edward stood behind me. "You need to get the power from your legs and midsection. Ground yourself. You're all arms right now."

I nodded and focused on tightening the muscles in my legs and stomach. The muscles contracted, responding to my effort. Nocking the arrow, I pulled back again, lining up my shot with the center of the target. Taking a deep breath, I focused on the muscles in my whole body working together. I pulled a little more and checked my aim. As I let out my breath, I released the arrow. It struck true with enough force to enter the target. I smiled.

"That's it. You've got it now." Master Edward started to walk away.

"Where are you going?" I asked.

"I'll be right over here. I've got something to work on. You have to keep shooting until you hit twenty in a row."

I raised an eyebrow. *Twenty?* I was tired just thinking about it. *This could take a while. Could I even pull the bowstring that many times?* I shook my hands out and took a deep breath. If my father could do it, I could too. I drew another arrow and aimed again.

Long shadows crossed the ground as the sun hung low in the sky. I put down the bow. My whole body was sore from the repetitive shooting of arrows. I shook my hands and rolled my shoulders.

Master Edward motioned for me to go to him. He was holding a quiver filled with arrows. While I had been practicing, he had burned the same flower pattern that was on my bow into the leather of the quiver.

"Thank you. For everything." I said.

"Just keep your bow with you on your journey and you'll be fine. I'd hate to be the King's Guard who meets up with you."

It was nice to have somebody who believed in me and didn't look at me as helpless. Smiling, I gave him a hug.

Ashton found me as we were walking back to the common area.

"Any news?" I asked.

"They hadn't come up with an exact plan yet when I left." He frowned.

We took a few silent steps before Master Edward paused. "I left something back at the archery field. You two go along." He waved us forward.

"You sure you don't want us to walk with you?" I asked.

He smiled at me. "I'll be okay." Master Edward looked to Ashton. "Keep her safe. You have no idea how important it is that she is safe."

Ashton nodded. "I'm beginning to figure it out."

My cheeks reddened as Ashton smiled at me.

It was almost dark when we arrived back at camp. The days had been getting noticeably shorter. People were wrapping up dinner and somebody was playing a fiddle at the edge of the clearing. I looked around for Saffron or Max. They were both missing.

Ashton squeezed my hand briefly and then let go. "You should eat something. It might be a while…" He froze, a dark shadow crossing his face.

"What is it?" Then I felt it. The temperature had dropped at least ten degrees and my fingers began to tingle.

Ashton pushed me away from the clearing, behind a large tree. "Stay here." It was a command.

I peeked from behind the tree as he stepped back into the clearing. The music stopped. Other people were starting to feel it, too. Something was happening. Something was here.

I smelled them before I saw them. It was the unmistakable scent of rotting flesh. The smell of death itself. My fingers started to tingle.

The Reapers walked without touching their feet to the ground. Their black cloaks floated around their bodies giving them an ethereal appearance. If it weren't for the floating and the smell, I would have thought they were men in long cloaks. The hoods covered their heads and there was a black hole where their faces should be. I covered my mouth to keep myself from crying out.

The space was filled with screams and panic as people fled. But the Reapers didn't even notice them. They were here for me. I turned away from the scene and pressed my back against the tree. My pounding heart was probably giving my hiding place away. I searched my memory for the stories I heard about the Reapers. Was there anything that could kill them? *They're already dead.*

I risked a glance around the tree and saw that they had fanned out around the clearing. *Ashton.* Ashton hadn't left with everybody else. He was right in the middle of them. They had him surrounded.

My throat tightened and I clenched my fists. *I have a bow.* It might not do any good, but maybe I could buy him some time to escape. I wasn't going to let him die for me. *Nobody was going to die for me.*

I nocked an arrow using the tree as cover. I took a deep breath and then stepped out. Pulling the string back, I aimed at the Reaper closest to me, then released.

It struck true and the creature let out an inhuman howl as it snapped its head in my direction. My veins felt like they had ice running through them as I loaded another arrow. I shot it a second time. It growled and all four of the creatures floated toward me. I knew the arrow wouldn't kill the monster, but they were leaving Ashton and that was all I could hope for. They were coming toward me, not concerned with speed as they approached their prey. I knew it was useless to run.

"Run, Ashton!" I cried out. I wanted him to get far away from here.

He ran, but toward the monsters, toward me. He ran past them and they didn't even flinch. He wasn't their target. Ashton stepped in front of me. My heart beat faster in my chest. *No. I won't let you sacrifice for me.* Too many people have done that already.

"What are you doing?" I screamed at him. "You need to go!"

"I'm not leaving you." He squared his stance and put his arms out. Flames grew from his outstretched hands.

The Reapers hesitated, stopping their progress for a moment, then continued.

Anger and fear rose up inside me. The ice running through me was burning. I looked down at my hands and saw small blue sparks in my palms. I focused on the sparks and they grew stronger, resembling icy blue flames. I stepped next to Ashton and raised my hands like his and forced the burning ice through my body into my hands. A rush of heat exploded from me and I was blinded by a blue light. Then everything went black.

*****

"Etta?"

Fingers brushed across my forehead. My head was pounding and my cheeks were hot. Slowly, I opened my eyes only to squeeze them shut again. The light was too strong. I tried again, blinking a few times to adjust to the light.

Saffron was looking down at me. "Thank the gods," she breathed. "I thought we lost you."

I sat up, too quickly, and stars danced in my vision.

"Easy, easy." Saffron put her arm around my back to

support me.

"Are you alright?" she asked gently. "You've been asleep for hours."

I nodded. "I - I think so."

She frowned at me. "What were you thinking? Trying to take on those Reapers with a bow?"

I looked around. Max was standing above me with his arms crossed. Ashton was behind him, avoiding eye contact.

I tried to remember the event. *Had I used magic?* It was a blur of fear and adrenaline.

"Thankfully you were with Ashton," Max finally spoke. "The Reapers only weakness is fire, but it only sent them away. They'll try again."

I swallowed and looked at Ashton. He was still avoiding meeting my eyes. Had I done something to upset him?

"Can you stand?" Max asked.

Saffron stood and pulled me up. I wobbled but maintained my balance. Max was frowning at me.

"Good," he nodded. "I've got to keep you safe for three weeks. Then you'll be leaving Illaria. Think you can manage to stay out of trouble until then?"

I stared at him, trying to figure out the best way to answer. *Leaving Illaria? In three weeks?* "Where am I going?"

"We'll talk about it later. Too many ears around here," Max said. Then he turned to Ashton. "Get her horse ready. You're taking her with you to the trials." With that he left, Ashton at his heels.

Saffron watched him until he was out of earshot then she pulled me in for a tight hug. "I was so worried about you."

I winced. The hug hurt but I didn't complain. Saffron made me feel safe. I didn't know what I would do without her. I straightened, worried that my travels were going to cost me my biggest ally. "Are you coming with me?"

She nodded. "I'm not leaving your side ever again."

My gaze traveled in the direction that Ashton and Max had gone. "Is Ashton upset with me?"

She frowned. "Max knows about your feelings for Ashton.

You can't hide something like that from him."

The color drained from my face. *How did he know?* I had just started to figure it out for myself.

"You have to end it, Etta. You need to stop it before it hurts too much. Don't end up like me, in love with somebody you can never have."

I bit the inside of my cheek. *Too late.*

*****

Ashton moved quickly as he secured my horse for travel. I felt useless standing there watching but they wouldn't let me help with anything. Still exhausted from the Reaper attack, I didn't press the issue. Distracted by the activity in front of me, I didn't notice Max approach and jumped when he grabbed hold of my elbow. He nodded toward a bench a few feet away and led me there. We sat together in silence for a moment.

"I know you've been through a lot." Max turned to look at me. "And I'm asking a lot of you, but I need you to trust me."

I waited for him to keep talking.

"We have a long road ahead of us and I might not show it, but I need you." He rested a hand on mine. "Without an alliance to a powerful kingdom, we will never get back our inheritance." He paused. "I know better than anybody how hard it is to put duty before your own heart. But it's the only way."

I swallowed. I didn't like where he was going with this.

"You have to end things with Ashton. Don't let it go any further. You'll both end up broken by it." His eyes softened for a moment before getting serious again. "I couldn't tell you this before. It has to be kept a secret." He lowered his voice. "Your marriage has been arranged. You are betrothed to the Prince of Sardinia. His father is unwell and it's likely you will be marrying a king by your wedding day."

My throat was tight and my eyes burned. My voice came out in a whisper. "When?"

"Three weeks from tomorrow."

Three weeks. How was I supposed to be ready to marry a prince in three weeks? What about Ashton? *Don't be stupid. You know you can't be with Ashton.*

I squared my shoulders. "I don't know if I can do this."

Max's jaw tensed. "You remember the night you went out with Ashton?"

I nodded.

"What did you think of that village? It was nice, right? Regular people living their lives."

My breath caught. He was using the past tense. "It was nice."

"It's gone now. The Reapers took out the whole village after they left here. It's the king sending you a message."

My heart dropped into the pit of my stomach. "What do you mean?"

"The king wants you to know that he'll do whatever it takes to get to you. The longer he stays on the throne, the more people will die."

"They killed all of those people? Just because I was there?" My hands were shaking and tears began to blur my vision.

He nodded. "He won't stop until you're dead."

My breath caught in my chest. *All of those people.* I pictured the people sitting in the tavern, having a drink with their friends. The village was about the size of the one I grew up in. All those people, children, all dead, because of me. I turned away from Max, unable to meet his gaze. *They died because of me.* I wrapped my arms around myself and struggled to breathe. All I wanted to do was to curl up in a little ball and cry.

Max turned my chin with his fingers so I was facing him again. "Don't you see why you have to do this? We can't fight him on our own. He's too powerful. And the longer we wait, the more people die. *Your* people. You are their princess. It's your job to sacrifice for them."

I wiped the tears from my cheeks and struggled to slow my breathing. My insides felt raw and twisted. Duty, sacrifice. I understood those things. Yet, my heart cried in protest.

"Look," Max's tone was gentle, "Sardinia is a nice place. The prince is a good person. You'll be happy there."

My throat was so tight I couldn't speak. I nodded, my heart breaking as I did. There had to be another way I could help. I needed to find a spark. Something unique to me that would convince them that I was more than just a bargaining chip to be married off. *Three weeks.* I had three weeks to figure it out.

CHAPTER 17

The trials were held every year in the Faron Mountains. We had a two day ride ahead of us to reach the base of the mountains. From there, we would be given the exact coordinates of the trials and would have to hike to the location. No horses and no weapons were allowed to go into the trial.

During our ride, nobody spoke. There was a feeling of gloom hanging over our party. I felt bad for Ashton. We were heading out to the event he had waited a decade for. Our journey should be filled with anticipation and excitement for the trials ahead. Instead, the attempts on my life had left us in a constant state of fear.

My run in with the Reapers had drained my energy and after only a few hours of riding, I was struggling to stay on my horse. Ashton pulled his horse up next to mine.

"You alright?" he asked.

It was the first time he had spoken to me since the attack. I wanted to be upset with him for ignoring me, but a rush of relief flooded through me. "I'm just a little tired is all."

"You look terrible." He frowned.

I raised my eyebrows. "You haven't spoken to me since the attack and that's what you say?"

His cheeks flushed. "That didn't come out right. I'm worried about you."

"Is that why you've been ignoring me?"

He sighed. "Max's orders."

"Oh," I said. "He talked to you, too."

He nodded. "I've never disobeyed him before."

I felt sick to my stomach. The thought of him avoiding me for the rest of my life was painful. "He told me I'm getting married in three weeks." I looked away from him. "He already found somebody."

"So soon?" Ashton said. "I knew they were discussing that but he had all of the meetings behind closed doors. I thought there would be more time."

Before I could ask Ashton anything else, my horse came to a halt. I hadn't been paying attention and looked ahead. Saffron had stopped, causing our horses to do the same. She put her hand out in a fist. Ashton went still and his eyes darted around us.

"This way. Fast," Saffron called over her shoulder and took a fork to the right. I caught the glimpse of dust coming down the road toward us as we headed in the opposite direction. Adrenaline shot through me and I no longer felt tired. Ashton rode next to me and we sped down the road.

Our turn took us through a wooded area lined with tall, leafy trees. As soon as we crossed into the tree line the temperature dropped. A chill went through me. *It's just from the shade.* We kept riding and I felt the ice running through my veins.

"Ashton, Saffron!" I shouted over the sound of our charging horses.

They whipped around to me. Ashton's eyes wide. He felt them, too.

"They're here. The Reapers. They found us," I said.

The faceless, hooded monsters flooded my vision. I remembered them floating toward me at the camp. Ashton holding them off with his fire, the strange blue sparks. *I had stopped them. I made them go away.*

My body felt like it was on fire. That cold heat running through me again. I knew the Reapers wouldn't stop coming for me. The best we could hope for was to send them away for a while. Maybe I could call on the same strange power I did back at the camp. *It's our only hope.* I dismounted, knowing the only thing we could do would be to face them.

"What are you doing?" Saffron yelled at me. "Get on your horse. We have to get out of here."

"I can do this," I said.

"She's right, Saffron," Ashton said. "She's the one who got rid of them last time." He dismounted his horse. "Hold the reins, Saffron. We'll take care of this."

Saffron glared at us. "We're going to be having a long talk about this later."

Ashton and I stood in the middle of the road, back to back. The air shifted and the smell hit me. Death. Decay. Then I saw them. All four of the Reapers, floating toward me. They were moving faster this time.

"Ashton," I called to him.

He moved to stand next to me. He raised his hands and I copied his movements. Ashton put up his wall of fire but they continued to approach, undeterred by his flames.

I felt the ice flowing through my veins. The power was still so new to me, but it was becoming more familiar. I reached inside, willing it to grow stronger. The cold burned as it traveled through me, creating the illusion of heat. Using all of my energy, I forced the burning ice into my extended hands, directing the power toward the approaching Reapers. Sparks of icy blue formed in my palms, sending a chill through me. My body wanted to give in, and my vision blurred. I fought away the exhaustion and called on more power. Finally, the sparks gave way to a surge of blue ice that looked like fire. My hands were burning from the cold, but the flames leaving my palms emitted no heat. The Reapers screamed as the blue fire reached them, their unholy cries echoing through the air. As they retreated, blackness claimed me.

I collapsed to the ground, panting. The world was spinning and I saw stars. I had to work hard to stay conscious.

Ashton dropped to my side and wrapped an arm around me. "Stay with me."

I offered a weak smile. "I did it." Then everything went black.

I woke in an unfamiliar bed with the headache I now associated with using the strange powers I possessed. I sat up slowly and looked around the room. Saffron and Ashton were sitting at a small table, deep in conversation.

"Hi," I said.

Ashton jumped to his feet and crossed the room in one large step. He pushed my hair away from my face and focused his green eyes on me. "Thank the gods." He pulled me in for an embrace then held me at arm's length. "It's amazing to see you do that, but scary waiting for you to wake."

Saffron sat down on the bed next to me. "Ashton told us that you passed out from fear in the first encounter."

I shifted. I was grateful that Ashton had kept his word to keep my magic a secret from my brother.

"I'm sorry," I whispered. "Everything happened so fast."

She nodded. "Ashton caught me up on everything. Why didn't you want to tell Max you found your element?"

I shrugged. "Seemed easier at the time. He was so eager to get rid of me."

She sighed. "He's doing his best, you know. There's a lot of pressure on him."

"I know." Something tugged inside me. "I just - I'm not ready for him to know." I searched my mind to find a reason I could use to keep her from telling him. "I don't want to add extra worry for him. Please, let me tell him when I'm ready."

Her mouth made a line and she was silent for a few moments. "Fine. But it needs to be before your wedding."

I nodded. That's a start. My eyes darted around the small, windowless room. "Where are we?"

"An inn. We had to get you off the road for a bit. Don't worry, nobody saw you." Saffron stood and walked back to the table. She picked up her sword and returned it to the sheath on her waist. "We can't stay any longer. We have to move again."

Ashton squeezed my hand. I squeezed back, enjoying the warmth of his touch. I turned to him. "How long was I out this time?"

"Four hours," he said. "Better than last time. I think with

more practice, you'll keep getting stronger."

I hadn't thought about practicing my new talent. The thought sent a tingle to my fingers. It was like the power inside me was asking to come out again.

Four hours. "That means it's dark. Is it safe to travel at night?"

Saffron handed Ashton his dagger from the table. "I don't think anything is safe for you anymore. The Reapers will keep hunting you until they finish the job. I don't know if that means death, or worse."

I bit the inside of my cheek as I imagined what could be worse. *Being undead is worse.* Saffron tossed me a pile of clothes. "Put these on. We'll see if a disguise helps at all."

Ashton's cheeks turned bright red. "Um…"

Saffron pointed to the door. "You can ready the horses."

I held back the smile as I realized that Ashton had probably pictured me in my underwear, or less.

Saffron gave me men's clothes. She tied my hair back and stuffed it into a hat to hide it. She was already dressed in trousers and armor, making her look like a man. She tucked her own hair into a hat.

"Hopefully we'll look like three men while we're riding. Much less likely to be bothered by anybody." She handed me my quiver and bow. "You'll want to wear these. In case we come across any human foes while we ride."

I stumbled as we made our way to the stable in the darkness of night. Clouds covered the stars and the moon, making it darker than usual. I saw a small light in what must be the stables and followed Saffron. Ashton was waiting for us when we arrived, horses ready.

"It's harder to ride at night," Saffron warned. "We'll go slower. Trust your horse and make sure you can always see me in front of you."

She looked at Ashton. "Do not let her out of your sight."

He nodded.

Saffron and I mounted our horses. Ashton extinguished the lantern before mounting his. We headed out at a steady canter.

We passed a few buildings of the very small town we were in. None of them had a light on. It must be really late. Or early. I searched for the moon to give me some sense of time but it was still obscured by the clouds.

We didn't talk as we rode. My mind wandered. I thought about these new powers I had and what they meant. I didn't know anything about sorcery. All I knew was that I had aligned with water. How did that result in the flames that I produced? They felt like ice when I made them. Maybe they weren't flames? But there was heat. Hopefully I could find somebody I could talk to about it at the trials.

We rode for a few hours in silence before the sky started to lighten. At first, I thought the moon had returned, then I realized it was the first watery light of the dawn. I could see the terrain we were crossing and realized we were going up. The trees had changed from the leafy ones we saw yesterday to the pine trees I'd grown used to at the Raven camp.

Saffron cut into the trees and led us to a stream. She broke the silence, "We need to rest the horses for a bit." She dismounted and guided her horse to the stream.

I climbed off of my horse onto shaky legs. I leaned against my horse for a moment until I regained my balance. My body still felt like it was in motion. I shook my legs, one at a time, then took my horse to the water.

"Are we in the mountains?" I asked.

"We are. Only a few hours more until we reach the check in point," Saffron said.

My shoulders relaxed. I'll be safe when we get to the trials. I sat down on a rock and rubbed my eyes with the palms of my hands.

"All right?" Ashton frowned.

"Yeah, just a little headache." I smiled at him. *Just another day of fighting for my life.* How strange my world had become. It was turning into one large blur of people trying to kill me. I looked down at my hands, recalling the magic that had come from them. *You're not as helpless as you used to be.*

"You sure?" Ashton's eyebrows were furrowed in concern.

I nodded. For the first time, I was starting to feel like I was gaining some control over myself. If I could learn how to master this magic, maybe I'd be able to prove myself useful enough to avoid marriage.

"Well, if we're all okay," Saffron interrupted, "We better get going." She looked up to the pink sky. "I'd like to get there before noon."

We rode for a while without incident. The trees around me had lulled me into a sense of security. Without warning, my fingers started to tingle and I straightened in my saddle. I gripped the reins tighter. Something was wrong.

"Don't worry," Ashton said from behind me. "You're feeling the magic."

I glanced behind me. "What do you mean?"

"That tingle? You feel it, right?"

"It's almost like the Reapers." I realized it was similar but not the same as what I felt with the Reapers.

"You'll get used to it." He laughed. "You're well on your way to being a sorcerer. It took me years before I started to feel magic. Your brother was right, it is strong in your family."

I focused on the tingling. Trying to isolate it, memorize it. It was as if I didn't even know my own body anymore. *Figures.* Literally everything in my whole life had been turned upside down. The landscape in front of me started to look fuzzy, like it was going in and out of focus. I squinted.

"You see that?" Ashton called up to me. "It's the ripple."

Saffron stopped riding. "Ashton, you'll need to go first. I can't see magic."

I stopped so he could get in front and she dropped behind me. The landscape in front of me was rippling as if it were covered by crystal clear water. It was hard to believe that Saffron couldn't see it.

A rush of cold, then warmth flowed through me as we crossed through the ripple. "What was that?"

"We passed through." Ashton explained. "Only those who are invited can enter."

"With guests?" How hard would it be for the Reapers to tag

along with somebody who had been invited here?

He looked back at me. "You and Saffron were added to the list yesterday. We sent a dove ahead."

We turned a bend on the trail and I saw a man standing off to the side. He smiled at us as we approached.

Ashton stopped his horse and dismounted. I climbed off my horse. The man in front of us was wearing burgundy robes and had long, black hair. He was probably only a few years older than Ashton.

"Welcome, friends." He bowed to the three of us. "Will the member taking the trial please state their name?"

Ashton stepped forward. "Ashton Robert White."

The man in the burgundy robes nodded at him. "Please tie your horses to the posts." He motioned across from him to three posts that had not been there before. "And drop all weapons in this box." A box materialized at his feet. My fingers tingled in what I now recognized as a response to his use of magic.

Ashton and Saffron placed their weapons in the box. I hesitated and tightened my grip on my bow.

"Excuse me," I began, "may I turn in my arrows and keep my bow on me? It was a gift and I don't want to part with it."

The man looked me up and down. "When are you taking your trials?"

My eyes grew wide. *How did he know I had magic?* "I don't think I'll be taking the trials."

"You eighteen yet?" he asked.

I shook my head. "Seventeen."

"Next trials, then." He nodded.

I opened my mouth to respond but closed it when I realized I didn't have anything to say.

"You may keep the bow," he said.

I let out a breath. "Thank you." I dropped my quiver into the box and took a step back from it. The box vanished. I gasped.

"It will be here when you leave," he said. "As will your horses."

I looked over to where Saffron had tied up our horses and found that they were gone. I blinked a few times to make sure I was seeing things clearly.

The man handed Ashton a coin. "This will take you where you need to go. Good luck to you, Ashton Robert White."

Ashton thanked him and gestured for us to follow him down the trail. We walked a few yards before he came to a stop. I saw the ripple clearly this time and recognized it for what it was. The tingle was no longer reliable because my hands had not stopped tingling. I wondered if it would go away or if it would last through the whole trials.

"Are we going through?" I asked.

Saffron turned to me. "Another ripple?"

I felt a pang of guilt that I was able to see the magic and she could not. I nodded at her.

Ashton pushed the coin through the ripple. It melted away before my eyes, revealing a sprawling meadow filled with colorful tents. People walked through the meadow and around the tents. All of this was hiding right in plain sight. I looked behind me. I saw the rocky mountain landscape filled with pine trees. In front of me, the gentle hills of the lush green meadow didn't match up. I followed Ashton onto the soft grass. It was like being in a dream.

Ashton smiled. "Bet you didn't see that coming."

My mouth was open. "It's amazing."

"It's a portal," he explained. "The coin is the only way in."

"Wow." I looked around the meadow. There were patches of yellow flowers scattered throughout and a blue butterfly flew in front of me. "It's beautiful."

I started to reach for Ashton's hand then remembered that Saffron was with us and pulled back. I bit the inside of my cheek. *I have to let him go. I can't keep doing this to myself.* My heart felt like it was being squeezed. *How do you let go of something that feels so right?*

Ashton pointed. "Our tent is over here."

We stopped in front of a purple tent. It had a sign posted outside of it with the number 47 written on it. Ashton pulled back the flap for us to enter. I followed Saffron inside.

There were three beds in the tent and on each bed were the supplies from our saddle bags. Everything we had on our horses was here.

"I don't think I'll ever get used to this." I shook my head.

"Just wait until you see the trials," Ashton said. "You haven't seen anything yet."

CHAPTER 18

After finally convincing Saffron to get some sleep, Ashton and I went to explore. I got used to the tingle of magic as we spent the afternoon getting to know the trial site. The meadow housed tents for all of the students who would be taking the trials, along with everything needed for the trials. He showed me the spaces they would use for the different tests he had to take. There were three public fields with stands set up for viewers and three large, closed in structures for private tests. Ashton would take his exhibition test first and then move on to the second round behind closed doors.

Where I grew up, there were no sorcerers. I had heard of them, but mostly in fairy tales or in whispered stories about the king. As I walked around the camp with Ashton, I studied all of the different people I saw. We passed a man wearing a purple scarf wrapped around his head, and a woman with a dress that looked as if it were made of feathers. I'd never seen such different clothing styles and the variety was overwhelming.

"Are all of these people sorcerers or apprentices?" I asked.

He shrugged. "Most of them are. Some are younger apprentices who are just observing. Some are family members who don't use magic."

My eyes darted from side to side, trying to take it all in. "There are so many of them."

"The Sorcerer's Guild is made up of three kingdoms. So these are sorcerers from Illaria, Gallia, and Sardinia."

Knowing they were here from other places made it seem a little less daunting.

"Ashton?"

I turned to see a petite girl with dark brown hair and tan skin running over to us. She threw her arms around Ashton.

My stomach clenched. I crossed my arms and glared at her. *Who is this girl? And why is she hugging Ashton?*

"I can't believe it's been a whole year since I saw you." She twisted a lock of hair between her fingers. "Last time we were here, we just watched. Now it's our turn." She slid her arm through his and guided him away, ignoring me completely. "Come on, I want to show you something."

Ashton took a step back. "Hold on, Celeste." He pulled his arm away from her. "I want you to meet my friend, Wilona."

Friend? Do you kiss all of your friends? I dropped my arms to my side but stood planted where I was. I forced a smile across my face. "Hello, Celeste."

He reached for my hand and tugged. Reluctantly, I stepped toward her. She was very pretty and I wondered what kind of friendship she had with Ashton.

"Oh, I'm sorry." She smiled at me. "I must not have seen you standing there."

Likely story. I held my smile.

"Are you training with Max, too?" she asked.

Before I could say anything, Ashton cut in. "Yes, she'll be testing at the next trials. She just missed the age cut off.."

Celeste raised an eyebrow and locked her green eyes on me. "First visit?"

I nodded, still holding my fake smile.

Celeste nodded her head in my direction but spoke to Ashton. "Can I trust her?"

Ashton didn't hesitate. "Absolutely."

"Well," Celeste tapped her fingers against her legs. "Why don't you come, too?" She glanced down at my hand, which was still clasped inside Ashton's.

"Great," he said, "lead the way."

Celeste took us into her tent. There was only one bed inside hers. For a moment I felt bad for taking away Ashton when she was clearly here alone. Ashton squeezed my hand, and the moment passed.

She lifted a small box that was sitting on the ground next to her bed and held it out to us. Her eyes flashed and her smile lit up her whole face. "I finished it."

Ashton let go of my hand and took the box from her. "You're kidding."

She shook her head. "See for yourself."

He opened the box and it emitted a purple glow. Ashton put his hand in and lifted the glowing purple orb. "It's amazing." He smiled at her. He set the box down on the bed and moved the orb from hand to hand. "I can't believe you did this yourself. I don't think anybody has made one in a hundred years."

I stared at the purple light in awe. It was beautiful. It was so bright, I thought it would hurt my eyes, but instead, it was calming. I wanted to ask what it was, but I didn't want to look stupid in front of Celeste, so I kept my mouth shut.

Ashton turned to me. "Here." He set the orb in my hand.

It was warm and smooth, how you would imagine a star might feel. It made me feel calm. Every muscle in my body relaxed and I decided that maybe Celeste wasn't so bad after all. I shook my head. What is this thing? I handed it back to Ashton and instantly, my tension returned.

"It's amazing, Celeste." Ashton placed it back in the box.

She smiled broadly. "And it's only the model. Once I'm officially a master, I can start working on the real one. Can you imagine how much more powerful it will be with a real dragon egg inside of it?"

"I still can't believe your uncle is letting you have that egg," he said.

"Dragon egg?" I knew there had been dragons in Illaria, but nobody had seen one in a thousand years. "I didn't know anybody still had them around."

Celeste closed up the box. "There are a few surviving eggs. Nobody was ever able to hatch a dragon, but they retained their healing properties. When I build the real orb, I'll be able to use it to heal people. It's a very ancient magic. I started studying it a few years ago. We'll have to talk some time. I'll tell you all about it."

A horn sounded from outside.

Thank the gods. I needed to get out of this tent and away from this girl. She was being nice to me, but I didn't want to like her. Not after how familiar she was with Ashton. Even though I knew it was ridiculous to be so protective of him, I couldn't let go. Not yet.

Celeste tucked the box under her bed. "Opening ceremonies." She walked toward the tent flap and held it open for us to walk through. We stopped in front of the tent, Ashton's hand still holding on to mine.

"I'll walk Wilona back and meet you there," Ashton said.

"Apprentice thing?" I asked.

"You'll get to go to the dinner," Ashton explained, "but everybody who is testing has to meet for a rules meeting and check in first."

"Go on," I said, "don't be late for me. I can find my way back."

"It won't take long," he said.

"Go," I said. "I'm fine."

He squeezed my hand. "I'll see you after the dinner."

A pulling sensation tugged inside my stomach as he headed away with Celeste. We hadn't ever discussed what that kiss meant or what we were to each other, but I felt connected to him in a way I'd never felt to anybody else. When we were together, I felt like I was home. It was a strange experience and it didn't make any sense. How had I gotten so wrapped up in him so quickly? My mind and my heart were at war with each other. It didn't seem possible to have these feelings for him so quickly, but they were there, impossible to ignore.

Ashton and Celeste disappeared through the crowds. Staring after him wasn't doing me any good. With a sigh, I went back to my tent where I found Saffron in the process of lacing up her boots. The armor was gone, replaced by a simple blue dress. Her curly blond hair hung loose. She looked rested.

"How was the tour?" she asked me.

I shrugged. "Alright. Mostly just tents and meadow."

She nodded. "Yes, that's true. It'll be more fun in the coming days."

I turned away from Saffron to hide a yawn.

"You need to get some rest," she put her arm around my shoulder, "but first, dinner and a show."

While I was in the tent with Saffron, a space in the meadow had been filled with large round tables. Each of the tables had baskets and platters of food. I searched the crowd of people for Ashton. Saffron guided me to an empty seat at a table near a raised platform. As soon as we sat, several other people joined us at the table. They were older and I wondered if they were parents of some of the apprentices who were testing.

The mood was jovial and I was soon surrounded by happy conversation. A white-haired man on my right introduced himself as a retired sorcerer. His first apprentice was now a master, here with his first apprentice. He laughed as he explained how he had grand-apprentices. For the first time, I realized how close the sorcery community was. Everybody seemed to know each other. As I participated in polite conversation, I stole glances around the meadow, trying to find the apprentices so I could catch a glimpse of Ashton.

Saffron leaned in to me. "He's fine. Eat."

I frowned, disappointed that I had been so obvious. Picking up a roll, I took a few bites. Chewing gave me an excuse to listen rather than speak so I made an effort to try some of everything on the table. The white-haired man was more than happy to tell me his entire life story, which was surprisingly interesting. Any time he'd ask me a question, I'd take another bite and limit myself to a word or two.

After a while, people began to stop reaching for food. Teapots and teacups appeared on all of the tables magically. I seemed to be the only person who was surprised. As the tea was poured, a murmur moved through the tables. Heads turned toward the sky where thousands of fireflies had appeared above us. The sun was nearly gone and the fireflies looked like glittering stars. The sound of applause rippled through the tables as a man walked across the platform.

He was small, probably about my height. He wore blue robes and a blue hat over his long gray hair. He spoke with a smooth, kind voice. "Welcome to the annual sorcery trials."

More applause.

He lifted his hands to silence the crowd. "This year we will be testing sixty-one students from three kingdoms. The next two days are set aside for practice, and you may ask judges questions. Then we will begin the testing. Tonight, we celebrate all of the hard work these young people have done to get here. If you'll turn your attention to the skies."

I looked up and my mouth fell open. The fireflies had positioned themselves into rows, then they began to ripple like waves. A group of fireflies shaped like a fish traveled through the waves. Other creatures I did not recognize began to swim through the waves. One had a large round head and eight arms wiggling under it. I saw a turtle and a star moving through the currents of light. Then the gold of the bugs began to melt into a bright green, then blue, then purple. They flashed through a series of colors all the while rippling and flowing like waves. It was the most beautiful sight I had ever seen. The ripples gave way to spirals of color that changed and flowed into one another. My neck was starting to get sore from looking up for so long. Just when I was going to give up and drop my head, the fireflies returned to their original color and spread out along the sky to look like stars.

CHAPTER 19

As much as I wanted to see Ashton after dinner, the exhaustion of the last few days won over and I was asleep before he returned. When I woke to birdsong the next morning, he was sound asleep in his bed. Part of me wanted to wake him and ask about his night. The more magic I saw, the more I wanted to start learning it for myself. Was it possible that I could take the trials on my own one day? Holding my hands above my face, I looked at my fingers. Somehow, I had made magic with my bare hands. If I had some real training, what would I be capable of doing?

Dropping my hands, I stared at the purple fabric of the tent. The sound of deep breathing mixed with the birdsong. *How can they sleep through all these birds?* Turning to my side, I tried to go back to sleep, but I knew it was useless. I surrendered to the morning and crawled out of bed. Since Ashton was still asleep, I quickly changed with my back to him before ducking out of the tent.

It was a beautiful sunny morning. I glanced back at the tent, half expecting somebody to tell me to turn around. I felt like the peasant girl sneaking to the woods. Nobody told me that I couldn't go out alone while I was here. Shaking the thought away, I moved forward, weaving in and out of tents. My breath came out in a cloud and I hugged my arms against my chest. It was quiet and peaceful. There weren't very many people walking around yet and the only sound I could hear was the music of the birds.

Despite the cold, I felt more at peace than I had in a long time. The tingle of magic in my hands had become comfortable and somehow made me feel safe. It was a different feeling than I got from the Reapers. I shivered. It was only a matter of time before I'd face off with them again. Pausing, I closed my eyes for a moment, breathing in the fresh air and the freedom. Once I left this place, who knew what I was in store for?

"Good morning, young miss."

With a start, I opened my eyes. The man who spoke at dinner last night was smiling at me. He was wearing the same blue robes. Gray hair hung loose around his shoulders. He was standing in the entrance of a tent and I realized I had stopped right in front of it.

"Good morning." I started to walk away, but doubled back to him. "The fireflies last night were really beautiful."

He inclined his head. "Thank you, I've been working on that for years." He sunk into a low bow. "Master Flanders at your service."

I dipped into a slight curtsy. "Wilona." I wasn't sure if I was supposed to be hiding who I was here. Ashton had introduced me as Wilona, but he always called me that.

Master Flanders stretched out his arms toward me, palms facing me. I flinched, unsure of what he was doing. I took a step backward and he lowered his hands.

"There is an ancient kind of magic in your veins," he said. "I haven't met anybody who aligned with water since the last Aqualine King."

My father aligned with water? The deeper I got into this new life, the more I learned about my family. Things I should have already known. *Does that mean he knows who I am?* If water is that rare, will this sorcerer guess that I'm a member of the royal family?

Wait. How does he know my alignment? Maybe he's just guessing, trying to get a reaction from me. I licked my lips and considered how I should answer. Was he testing me? Curiosity won and I lowered my voice. "How do you know that I align with water?"

He shrugged. "All sorcerers have unique gifts, though some are more impressive than others. For the most part, we are the same. We are trained in similar ways and learn similar skills. Our affinity with an element gives us an edge in any magic that uses that specific element. My special gift is that I can tell what other sorcerers' elements are."

"That would have been very helpful a few weeks ago." It would have been nice to avoid all of the misadventures I had encountered in the process of finding my element. But then, I don't think Ashton would have kissed me. *Which would have made my life much easier.*

I shifted my feet and looked away from Master Flanders. His unblinking expression made me feel like he knew what I was thinking. If he could read my element, what else could he do? He gave me the same feeling that Max had the night I snuck out with Ashton. Like he knew more about me than I knew about myself. The comparison sent a shiver down my spine. *No. Not quite like Max.* I took a small breath and looked up at him, trying to get a read on him. He wasn't like Max, *more like my grandmother.* She always seemed to know when I was holding something back.

"You misunderstand," he continued. "I can't read it until the magic has been unlocked within the person. You have to find it for yourself first. So, you see, it really is a silly gift. No real value other than helping me when I judge apprentices here at the trials. I have a feeling that your special gift is very unique."

I wrinkled my brow. *Those icy blue flames must be my gift.* If only I knew how to use them. Maybe this sorcerer was the one I had hoped for, the person who could help me. *Can I trust him?* I probably shouldn't tell him about the flames yet. Not knowing how far the king's reach extended, it was safer to keep details to myself.

"I haven't done any training yet." It was the truth.

"Now that is unusual at your age." He held his chin between his thumb and forefinger and seemed to be studying me.

Feeling self conscious, I worried I said too much. "I guess I should be going."

"Please, stay," he said, "I have a few hours and I haven't had the chance to teach new students since I started judging the trials. If you'd like, I can show you some basics."

I thought briefly about what Max would say. He'd say I had already said too much. Saffron would probably agree. What would Ashton say? I decided I didn't care. He'd spent the whole night out with Celeste. He didn't get a say. This man served on some sort of council and judged for the trials. He's probably harmless. "Okay. If it isn't an imposition."

He swept his hand out toward an area of the meadow where there weren't any tents. "Not at all. After you."

Master Flanders started me with learning how to stand to better channel magic. I stood with my legs apart, knees slightly bent and arms loose at my side. From this position, he encouraged the use of pivots, so you always kept one foot planted on solid ground at all times. Apparently, you could pull more source magic from the earth if you were always touching it. I greedily accepted every tip he offered me. Somehow, my blue flames sent the Reapers away but the trade off was that I spent the next several hours unconscious. I knew I needed to get stronger. If a stance would do it for me, I was willing to try.

"I'm guessing you already figured out what magic feels like?" he asked.

I nodded. "My hands and fingers tingle when I'm around it. Sometimes I feel it in the rest of my body, too. It feels cold, but sometimes it also feels hot."

He pressed his lips together. "You've used it. Your magic. You don't feel it internally unless you are in the act of using it."

I looked down, trying to hide the pink rising in my cheeks. I didn't want to explain about the blue fire or the Reapers.

"Did a friend teach you?" he asked.

I thought for a moment. "I guess so. I learned how to unlock an element box. Then I watched and did the same thing he did."

"What did you do, exactly?"

I hesitated, not sure if I should keep talking. He looked at me with kind, patient eyes. *My grandmother gave me that same look.*

He didn't seem like somebody who was going to harm me. Besides, the Reapers knew, so the king already knew what I could do. *Maybe he can help me.*

"I made blue fire." I watched his face carefully for his reaction to my words.

His mouth twitched and a half smile emerged. "Really? Why that is a rare talent, indeed. There's a reason why you said it felt hot and cold. That's because you are making arctic fire, though it's actually ice that looks like fire. It causes a freezing heat. Excellent defense against undead creatures. Especially strong against dark magic. That makes you very dangerous if you can learn how to control it."

Arctic fire. I wanted to know everything there was to know about this fire. "Is it only something that people who have a water affinity can do?"

He nodded. "Part of what makes it so rare. Most sorcerers are aligned to air or earth. Water and fire are rare, with water being the rarest of all elements. Magic is passed down in families. The Aqualine family had a water user in every generation." He winked at me.

He knows who I am. My heartbeat quickened. Should I stop talking? Maybe I should go find Saffron. My curiosity was stronger than my doubt, sending my mind reeling.

If this power was so useful, why was my family dead? Did they know how to use it? Could it have saved them when the duke attacked? Could it save me? "How does it help against dark magic and the undead?"

"The ice can penetrate deeper than other types of magic. The undead have to be killed from the inside out. So they can be killed with fire, but it has to reach the heart and too often, they put the flames out before it can burn through the body or the bones. The ice in the arctic fire can go right through the body. If you learn to control it, you'll be able to kill even the darkest creatures."

"Like Reapers?"

He nodded. "Yes, but you have to have perfect control and excellent aim. The Reapers have few weaknesses, so most think they cannot be killed. But if you can get that ice to penetrate to their hearts, you can kill them."

My heart swelled, filling me with hope. *The Reapers can be killed.* Being hunted by men, like the King's Guard, was not as scary as being hunted by the undead monsters that had been tracking me. *If I could learn to control my power, I could end them forever.* That would weaken the king and keep me safer.

I bounced up on my toes. "How do I learn to control that?"

He chuckled and looked to the sky. "I have about an hour left this morning. I can show you how to make a plant grow. It's usually the first skill we teach new students."

I crossed my arms over my chest. "I don't want to learn how to make a plant grow. I want to learn to control the arctic fire."

"Patience," he said, "You have to learn how to control your magic before you can harness something so powerful."

I dropped my hands to my side. "But I've used it twice already."

He lifted an eyebrow. "Did you stay conscious after you used it?"

I shook my head.

"Your body reacted in self-defense but it can't handle that amount of magic flowing through you, yet. You have to start at the beginning and learn to control it a little at a time."

It made sense that I'd need to build the skills to use magic. It had taken me years to develop my embroidery skills, but then I'd learned to use the bow so quickly. Massaging my temples, I wished I could just skip ahead. It would have been so much easier to learn this when I was a child. A wave of frustration filled me. There was so much I had missed out on while I had been hidden away.

He didn't wait for me to respond before dropping to the ground and resting his hand under a small flower.

I've got to start somewhere. I crouched down next to him, eyes glued to the little flower he was holding. Before I could even settle on the ground, vines began to spread from the flower. The tendrils expanded and stretched across the field, flower buds forming along the vines. My eyes widened. Bright yellow flowers, identical to the one he had his hand under, bloomed like magic. *It is magic.*

I gasped. "How did you do that?" How had this been kept from me all these years?

"Choose the plant you want to make grow and lightly rest your hand under the plant. You have to clear your mind of all thoughts except for those to make that plant grow. Imagine it sprouting, imagine the leaves filling out, imagine the blooms that will grow from your guidance. Will that thought into the plant. Help it grow."

It sounded too easy. After all of the trouble I went through to open the little box, how was I going to make a plant grow by thinking it? Feeling a little foolish, I took a deep breath and then rested my hand under a different yellow flower. *Grow.* Nothing happened. Dropping my hand, I pushed my hair away from my face. "Just imagine it growing?"

Master Flanders nodded. "Yes, but you have to believe it. Clear your mind of all else. Try to get inside the plant with your mind."

We were still alone in the field, though I could hear more activity in the distance as people started to walk around the camp. This was beginners magic and I was nearly the same age as the apprentices here who were ready to take their trials. *You've got to start somewhere.* Trying to ignore the sounds from the camp, I pushed up my sleeves and extended my arm toward the flower.

Cupping my hand under it, I closed my eyes. *Grow.* In my mind, I visualized the plant filling out with dark green leaves. I imagined it bursting with yellow flowers. The light tingling of magic in my fingers spread up my arm and intensified. Startled, I pulled my hand away and opened my eyes. *I did it.* Laughing, I stood up to stare at the plant. It had tripled in size while I had my eyes closed.

"This is amazing. I never knew I could do such incredible things." Who knew I'd be so proud of such simple magic. It wasn't making a fireball like Ashton, but it was magic. I controlled it and I was still conscious.

His knees cracked as he pushed himself up to standing. "I think you're just getting started, Wilona. I'm available after dinner this evening if you'd like another lesson."

"I'd like that very much," I said. "Thank you."

When we came to the trials, I figured I had found a safe place to hide for a week. I was weighed down by my impending marriage and the love of a man I could never be with. I was struggling to find that spark, that thing that made me unique, more than just a princess. I looked down at the flowers I had grown with my hand. With my magic. I found my spark. *Maybe there's hope for me after all.*

CHAPTER 20

The camp was busier after my impromptu lesson with Master Flanders. People smiled at me or inclined their heads as they walked by. More people in unusual clothing passed me. I hoped Saffron was awake so I could ask her to explain the cultural differences and customs of the kingdoms meeting here. I laughed at myself. *Those princess lessons really rubbed off on me.* I never would have wondered about the cultural differences of the people I saw before Sir Henry's lessons.

Ashton darted from around a tent, his face was white and his eyes wide. When he saw me his posture relaxed and the color started to seep back into his face. He pulled me into his arms. "Where have you been? I woke up and you were gone. I was so worried."

My body wanted to relax into his arms and enjoy the embrace, but I was hurt by being ignored all night. I pushed away and put my hands on my hips. "You were worried? How do you think I felt seeing that empty bed after dinner?"

His cheeks reddened. "You're right." He rested a hand on my waist.

I was suddenly aware of the people around us. I stepped back, away from his touch. "It doesn't matter, anyway," I said, turning my head away so I wouldn't have to look at him. "We can't do this. You know we can't."

He clasped his hand around my wrist and led me into the nearest tent. I let out a surprised gasp, worried that somebody would see us. Thankfully it was empty. He pulled me against his broad chest and brushed the hair away from my face. Butterflies filled my stomach. I stared up at him, my eyes locked on his. Something inside of me released and my body melted into his. *How does he do this to me?* Whenever we were alone, I felt like all of my willpower dissolved. Even if I knew it was a bad idea, even if I wanted to leave the tent, my mind couldn't make my body comply.

Lifting my chin with his fingers, he bent down to kiss me. A moment's anticipation caught inside me before his lips pressed into mine. Everything felt so right when we were together. I wrapped my arms around his waist and kissed him back with a fierceness I didn't know I had. A wave of heat traveled from his lips into mine. They burned and I almost pulled away. Then I felt the ice rising up inside me. It traveled through my body giving me a rush of cold that sent shivers through my entire body. The ice found its way to my mouth, mingling with his fire, sending a shock wave through me. I felt both hot and cold at the same time as I pressed deeper into the kiss and nearly lost the ability to breathe as our magic combined. There wasn't anybody else in the whole world. Just the two of us.

He broke off the kiss, pulling away gently. He let out a breath, a cloud escaping his mouth. "Whoa. That was intense." He brushed his fingers across my cheek. "I've heard of melding magic in a kiss, but that was incredible."

So that's what that was. I was still trying to catch my breath. I licked my lips then touched my fingers to my mouth. *Who knew magic had so many benefits?* There was no way kissing anybody else would ever feel like that. *How am I supposed to give this up?* I ran a hand through my hair and turned away from Ashton. This hadn't happened the first time we'd kissed. Something between us had changed. The longer we were together, the deeper our connection grew.

"We can't keep doing this." My voice cracked as a lump rose in my throat. "I can't keep getting closer to you. It's just going to make it more painful when I can't be near you anymore. The thought of you with somebody else is already killing me."

"What do you mean? Who else would I be with?"

I raised an eyebrow. "Come on, Celeste?"

"You're cute when you're jealous." He kissed me again, gently this time.

"You didn't deny it."

"You don't have to worry about Celeste." His hands moved to my waist. "You don't have to worry about anybody else. It's just you. Only you."

I broke out of his arms and walked to the other side of the tent. I started pacing. "That's what I'm talking about. This is getting too complicated. You know what my brother has planned for me. You know we can't be together." Imagining a life without Ashton was painful. *You've only known him for a little while. You're being foolish. Let it go.* Was this normal to feel? Would I feel this way about anybody else? What if I was giving away my only chance at happiness? I tried to hold back the tears, but they wouldn't stop.

Ashton grabbed my hand, stopping my pacing. He looked into my eyes. I turned away, afraid to face him. Gently, he drew my head around with his fingertips so I was looking at him again.

"Wilona, we will find a way. We have to."

I searched his eyes. He looked so sure of himself. A flicker of hope rose in my chest. Maybe it was possible. If I showed Max my powers, I'd be more important. Didn't he say sorcerers were the most important thing for our cause? *Not for you. You're worth an entire army in a marriage. That's much more valuable than a single sorcerer. You'll have to marry for an alliance.*

I shook my head. "It's not possible. Even if I get out of the marriage Max has planned, I'm still a princess."

"You can create a blue flame that sends Reapers away. That shouldn't be possible. You should have been killed when you were a baby. You shouldn't even be alive. I survived the loss of both of my parents. You and me, we've overcome so many more impossible things already. And the one that involves love is the one you are saying we can't do?"

Whatever I was going to say drifted from my mind, all focus lost. A grin spread across my face. "You love me?"

He pulled me in for a hug and rested his head on mine. "I thought that was obvious."

I pressed my head against his chest. I knew I shouldn't be feeling this way. Things had gone too far. I closed my eyes and realized it was too late. I had already reached the point of no return. There was no way I could marry somebody I didn't love. No way I could give up Ashton without a fight. Somehow, I'd have to figure out how to appease Max and get out of the marriage he had planned for me. Right now, I didn't want to think about it. I just wanted to enjoy the moment. Looking up at Ashton, I wiped happy tears off of my cheeks. "I love you, too."

*****

Saffron was playing cards alone on her bed when I went back to the tent. She didn't look up when I entered. "Ashton was looking for you."

I've always been a terrible liar and I hoped that Saffron wasn't seeing right through me. While I trust Saffron, I knew her heart belonged to Max and I had a hard time believing that she'd keep anything from him.

"I saw him before he went to his training session." I tried to keep my voice flat, disinterested.

She looked up at me. "You know, you're only making it harder on yourself by carrying on with him."

My mouth dropped open. *How does she always know?*

She piled the cards up into one stack in her hands and let out a sigh. "You're young. I get it. Just promise me something?"

I stared at her, still in shock over her last comment.

"Just promise me you won't take it too far? I mean, kissing is one thing, but there are certain lines that can't be crossed in order to secure a husband."

My cheeks turned burned. "Saffron!"

"Just keep your virtue intact, please."

I covered my face with my hands. *What kind of a girl does she think I am?* My face was probably bright red. Dropping my hands, I tried to send the embarrassment away. "I've had this talk with my grandmother. We can skip the rest."

She narrowed her eyes. "I'm serious, Wilona. I know you're trying to find a way out of this marriage thing, but it's going to happen anyway."

My chest was burning. For a moment, I was back in the tent with Ashton, the lingering heat of his kiss was still on my lips. Saffron should know better than anybody how hard it was to give up love. I was going to fight for it. I didn't ask to be a princess. I didn't want a throne. Max did. He was making a choice and expected me to follow in his lead. Maybe Max could give up love, but I wouldn't.

I am going to get out of this marriage thing. Just you wait. I almost told her as much, but it wasn't worth the argument. And I didn't want to bring it up until I had a plan. *Two weeks, six days.* I'll think of something. In the meantime, I needed to keep her happy. I cleared my throat. "You have a promise."

Saffron seemed satisfied with my answer and set the cards on a small table that had been added to the room while I was out this morning. I looked around the room. A dividing screen blocked Ashton's bed. I wondered for a moment where the new furniture came from but decided it wasn't important.

"We might not have weapons here, but I thought we could spend some time learning some hand to hand combat. Sound good?"

"Sounds like a great way to pass the day." I hesitated, then added. "I should probably tell you about how I spent the morning."

She put her hands up. "I don't want to hear about Ashton. Unless you're telling me you are no longer pure, in which case, I *really* don't want to hear it."

My cheeks burned and I shook my head. "No, no. I met a sorcerer." I told her about my lesson with Master Flanders and his promise to teach me again tonight.

She actually seemed pleased. "He's a friend to the Ravens. I'm glad you are learning how to wield your magic. It would be nice not to have to carry you while you're passed out."

Blinking, I stared at her in shock. "Why doesn't anybody ever tell me anything?"

She shrugged. "I didn't realize you wanted to learn. Why didn't you ask?"

Saffron had a point. I hadn't asked about learning magic. Maybe I should be talking to her more often. For a moment, I thought about telling her more about Ashton, but that was probably taking it too far. "I'd really like to learn more combat skills from you."

She smiled.

Saffron didn't let me change from the lightweight dress I was wearing into trousers for our combat training. Her argument that I would be wearing dresses more often so I needed to learn how to move in them. I kept tripping over the skirt as I tried to use the evasive moves she taught me.

"Do it again." She moved back to her starting position.

I sighed and moved back to where I had come from. *My bow would be really great right about now.* I ducked and twisted away as she came at me with a tall flower in her hand. It was hard to take her seriously when her sword was replaced by a flower.

The ringing of a bell offered a respite from the lesson. I wiped the sweat from my brow and put my hands on my side. "Time for a break?" *How was she never tired?*

Saffron tossed the flower on the ground. "I suppose it's a good time. You should get some rest before your lesson tonight. Magic uses a lot more energy than you think it does. Max is always so tired after he... never mind. Just get some rest. I'm going to say hello to some of the other Ravens who are here."

I headed back to the tent, grateful for the command to rest. My new life had not allowed for much in the way of down time so far. I wondered what it would be like if I couldn't think of a way out of this marriage. I'd be shipped off and married to some prince. My stomach clenched. Not a prince, a king. Since the first moment Saffron had told me of my lineage, I knew I didn't want to rule. Now I'd be forced to sit next to somebody while they did. I frowned. *That's probably even worse than ruling a kingdom in your own right.* I tossed and turned on the bed, worried my anxiety would keep me awake. Exhaustion won out and I drifted into sleep.

In my dream, I saw a throne emblazoned with the Ouroboros of my family's crest. Then I was sitting on it, looking out into a grand room full of people. I reached up and felt a heavy crown on my head. The room was filled with tapestries, the gold Ouroboros embroidered on them practically glowed. *Queen of Illaria.* Not some foreign kingdom. *My kingdom.* My pulse quickened. *I can't be queen. Max is supposed to be king.*

Saffron woke me with a gentle shake. I sat up, panting and sweaty. *What a strange dream.* It took a minute to realize where I was. *I'm in a tent at the Sorcery Trials.* I jumped out of the bed. "What time is it?" *Had I slept through my lesson?*

"It's okay," Saffron assured me. "Master Flanders is outside waiting for you. It's time for your lesson."

*****

"The second lesson we usually teach new sorcerers," Master Flanders began, "is to enchant objects so they can float. It's something that little kids really enjoy being able to do. However, I don't see it being much use to you. The objects have to be within your line of sight, so it's usually just as easy for somebody to take a few steps to retrieve the object."

I thought for a moment. "Unless you drop a weapon and you can't get to it."

He smiled. "You are the weapon when you master your sorcery. But for the sake of appearances, or in case you have your own apprentice someday, I suppose I can show you how to do it." He flicked his fingers up and a rock floated over to him. It landed at his feet with a thud.

I didn't wait for instructions. I copied his movements and called over a rock of my own.

A half smile reappeared on his face. "That usually takes a

week to teach a child. I expected you to be faster, but not that fast. How about this?" He lifted his hand and pointed his index finger. I watched the position of each finger on his hand to see how he lined them up. He drew a circle with the index finger and the noise from the people around us vanished. It got so quiet, I worried something was wrong with my ears.

Hesitantly, I started to speak. "What?" I jumped at the sound of my own voice. It was louder than I expected and came out in a sort of echo.

"It's a silence spell. Nobody outside of the spell's range can hear anything being said between us." He repeated the movement with his fingers and the sounds of the people around us flooded into me.

I took my stance and lifted my hand. I pointed my finger and was careful to place the rest of my fingers just right. I made the circle. The sounds vanished.

I jumped a little in my excitement. "This is amazing."

"The movements are important, as you have already figured out. But you can customize them to fit your own style. As long as the basic movement is there and you are concentrating hard enough, you will be able to complete the spell. He clasped his hands together in front of him and closed his eyes. The sounds came pouring back in.

I looked around. I must have lost my concentration. My shoulders sunk.

"That wasn't you," he said. "That was me."

"But you didn't even lift a finger. How?"

"Practice." We won't get there today. "But I want you to know that the highest levels of sorcerers don't have to use their hands. If you ever find yourself facing one, you won't have any hints as to what they are doing. Your brother, for example, rarely uses his hands."

I forgot that Master Flanders was a Raven, he must know my brother. "I've never seen Max use magic."

"Pray you never see him at his full power. I have never seen a sorcerer so young with power like his. In fact, I have seen very few who ever attain power like his."

A chill ran down my spine. *I thought Ashton was powerful and he's just an apprentice.* Being defenseless against Max scared me. He was my brother and we were supposed to be on the same side, but I didn't like feeling so helpless. *Don't trust anybody.* Was Max to be included in that warning? My bow would be no good against a sorcerer if I ever had to fight one. My jaw tightened. "Teach me more."

Master Flanders inclined his head then began a new spell. He pulled both hands up from his stomach to his chest, paused, and then raised them to the sky. He held them there a moment and then dropped his hands to his side.

I waited. Nothing happened. Then I felt a cold pinprick, a drop of rain. And another. And another. A light sprinkle rained down on us. Almost as quickly as it started, it stopped.

He raised his eyebrows. "Your turn."

I took a deep breath and closed my eyes. I centered my hands level with my midsection, and raised them to my chest. In my mind, I pictured thunderclouds, with lightning and pouring rain. I imagined wind blowing through the grassy meadow. I thought about the sound the rain would make as it pelted the canvas of the tents. Pushing my hands to the sky, I dropped them to my side so hard they slammed against my legs. I stood with my eyes closed, willing it to rain.

A thunderclap sounded from above. I opened my eyes and looked up as the first drops began falling on me. They were large drops and they were increasing in size. Thunder sounded again. Wind blew past me. The temperature cooled. I looked up at the gray clouds and laughed. *I made rain.* And not just rain, a thunderstorm.

Master Flanders put a hand on my shoulder. "Your brother can't do that." He looked up at the sky. "I don't know anybody who can do that."

My clothes were soaked and sticking to my skin. My hair was plastered against my face. I pushed it out of the way. "What does that mean?"

"It means that your brother should be the one who is afraid."

CHAPTER 21

Saffron and I made our way through the camp the next morning. It was more crowded as family and friends were arriving to watch the trials that started tomorrow. Most of the people around us were speculating about the thunderstorm last night. My cheeks hurt from smiling.

Saffron and I parted ways with quick goodbyes. She was attending to Raven business and I was headed to see Master Flanders. The only downside to my success with the thunderstorm was the fact that it had cut our lesson short. I hoped his schedule wasn't too full today. I knew it was my last chance to learn from him. Once the trials started, he'd be too busy. Then there was Max's impending visit hanging over me as it drew nearer. I rubbed the back of my neck. *What would I do when he got here? What would I say to him?*

Max was still so unfamiliar to me. He was my brother, but I knew nothing about him. All I knew was that he was completely absorbed by his ambition to become king and that he was a powerful sorcerer. I'd never seen him use his powers, but he was spoken of in high regard. Would he use his powers if he lost his temper? Should I be afraid of him? I thought back to the night in the tent after I unlocked my element. Max was furious, but he never acted like he would hurt me. *Maybe I'm overthinking this.* If I'm honest with Max about my powers, I might be surprised about his reaction.

While I knew I had to get out of the marriage he had arranged, I had yet to come up with a plan. So far, all I had was the hope that Max would be so impressed by my skills as a sorcerer, he'd find me valuable enough to keep with him. It didn't feel like enough to convince him, but it was the best I had. *I have to learn more.*

I found Master Flanders sitting in a chair outside his tent. A gray barn owl was perched on his shoulder and he was stroking her feathers. He smiled as he saw me approach.

"Good morning," I said. "Who's your friend?"

He stroked the bird again. "This is Juniper. She just returned from delivering a message for me." He held out a bit of food for the owl and she snapped it up. "I'm afraid she's a bit spoiled." He whispered to her and she flew away.

"She's a beautiful bird," I said.

"She is. Owls are faithful creatures. Less likely to allow interceptions of important messages. Not as pretty as doves, and not as frightening as ravens. Most loyal, though."

He grunted as he pushed himself to standing.

How old is he?

"I was hoping you'd return. I have some time this morning, and again this afternoon. After that, I'm afraid you'll be on your own." He pulled the flap of his tent back and I ducked inside.

His tent had two squishy chairs, a bookshelf filled with books, and a bed piled high with blankets. He sat in one of the chairs and waved me to the other. I sat, curious about what I was going to learn.

"You are headed into politics and court life. What I'm going to teach you today are perhaps some of the most important spells you can learn. I want you to keep the movements small. I'll exaggerate them when I do them so you can see, but the goal it that you could do these under a table or even while seated on a throne and nobody would be able to tell."

I nodded once. I tried to imagine what types of spells I would need to do from under a table and fell short.

He rubbed his thumb along the tips of his middle and index finger and then squeezed his hand into a fist. Then he released it. He looked at me. "Tell me your name, please."

I wrinkled my brow. *He knows my name.* As the word Wilona formed in my mind, my vision blurred and I felt a stabbing pain in my head. I squinted. I couldn't get the word out. *Etta.* I thought of the less familiar name and the pain ceased. I opened my mouth and tried to say Wilona. The pain returned. I couldn't do it. I tried the other name. "Etta."

The pain was gone. "What was that?"

"An honesty spell. Makes it painful for somebody to answer with anything other than the most true response to the question. And while you have known yourself as Wilona, it wasn't the truest answer for the question since it was not your given name."

My mind raced. This was a useful spell. There was only one problem. "If I use this, the person I've performed the spell on will know I did it."

He nodded. "That is correct. That's why it's not a party trick and is saved for the most dire circumstances."

"Go ahead and try it. I'll tell you if it works," he said.

I hesitated. I didn't want to make somebody else experience that kind of pain. "Are you sure?"

He nodded.

I copied the movements with my fingers, working to make them more subtle than he had done. Then I tried to think of a question. What could I ask? I went with something innocent enough. "How old are you?"

He laughed, then winced.

I wasn't happy to see the look of pain that crossed his face, but I felt a rush of pride. *I did it.*

"I'm 97 years old," he said.

I blinked a few times. I'd never met anybody that old. He didn't seem like he could possibly be over 70. Was he bypassing the spell?

"It's the truth," he said. "You look like you don't believe me. The spell holds up. Nobody can answer untruthfully once you've cast it on them. However, it only applies to a single question so you'll have to be very careful."

Don't trust anybody. Sir Henry's words had stayed with me

since I left his home. Master Flanders seemed to agree with him, otherwise he wouldn't be teaching me this spell. *What am I missing?* Something nagged at me, as if there were pieces of a puzzle waiting to be solved.

"Do you think I'll need this spell soon?" I asked.

Master Flanders steepled his fingers under his chin. "You might. We live in dangerous times and it's hard to know who to trust."

For a moment, I was the scared girl behind the aviary hearing the traitors talk about the letters. I felt safe when I was at the Raven camp, I trusted too many people. "Is there anybody specific you think I should be worried about? I mean, how do I know who I can trust?"

Master Flanders leaned back in his chair. "If it were me, I'd start out by not trusting anybody. Let them earn your trust."

Just like Sir Henry, Master Flanders was warning me against trusting anybody. Neither of the men even asked for my trust. In a way, that made me want to trust them. The only person who had asked for my trust so far had been Max. That same uncomfortable chill went through me again. Why was I feeling this way toward him? It had to be the lack of control. He wanted to control everything in my life. Of course that would make anybody unhappy. Trying to ignore the nagging feeling inside, I returned my attention to Master Flanders. "What else can you teach me?"

I spent the next several hours learning small tricks to help me to determine if there was anybody hiding in a room, if there was poison in my food, and how to keep somebody from speaking at all. I had a feeling these weren't spells that were taught to most new sorcery students.

After our session, I was exhausted. Saffron was right about the drain that magic could have. I collapsed into my bed for a nap.

I woke on my own to an empty tent. Saffron and Ashton were both still out. I stretched and peeked out of the tent flap to gauge the time. The sun was low enough that it might be time for dinner. Maybe I'd be able to meet up with Saffron or

Ashton.

There was an energy filling the camp that I hadn't felt before. The hair on my arms stood on end. *What is going on?* People were moving quickly, with purpose. The typical leisurely pace of the evening meal was gone. The expressions I caught on faces were tense, worried, and afraid. My heart pounded faster. I picked up my pace and searched for a familiar face.

Finally, I saw the back of a gray-haired man in blue robes. I hurried over to him. "What's going on?"

Master Flanders spun around to face me. His face was tight with worry. "Terrible news, I'm afraid. The king has declared war on Sardinia. He's gathering volunteers from all across the kingdom to join his army. We received word of a few towns who resisted his orders. They were burned to the ground. No survivors."

I couldn't breathe. Sardinia. *This is my fault.* I was supposed to marry the prince of Sardinia and the king must have found out. Now he was killing more innocent people because of me. How many more people were going to die while he hunted me?

Saffron came around a tent in front of me and she placed her hand over her heart when she saw me. She addressed Master Flanders first. "Did you hear?" Her voice was higher pitched than usual.

"Something new?" he asked.

She nodded then looked to me. She ran a hand through her hair and took a deep breath. Whatever she had to say looked to be causing her distress.

"What is it?" I asked.

She swallowed. "Your village was one of the villages that were destroyed."

No. I covered my mouth with my hand. *This can't be happening.* I'd been raised there. I knew those people. None of them did anything wrong. They didn't have anything to do with any of this. They just lived there, wanting to be left alone.

Saffron looked at me, brow creased in sympathy. "I'm so

sorry."

I stumbled backward toward the edge of a tent and crumbled to the ground. I held my knees to my chest and let the tears fall. How had my life gotten so bad so quickly? "I should have just let them kill me," I whispered.

"Why would you say that?" Saffron knelt down and smoothed my hair.

I sniffed and wiped my nose with my hand. "Too many people have died for me."

She narrowed her eyes. "You think this is about you? Why do you think he's acting like this? For the first time in fifteen years, the people have hope. You offer hope that things can start to change. You offer an alternative to his tyranny. He's been killing off our people for fifteen years already. He'll never stop. Even if he killed you, he'd never stop."

"I'm nothing." I wiped my tears on my sleeve. "I'm just some girl who had royal parents. Why isn't he going after Max?"

She shook her head. "I'm really not sure. Maybe he thinks you're the easier target."

"We can't fight back." My cheeks were burning with rage. "We can't beat him on a battlefield. This is never going to end."

Master Flanders' knees cracked as he knelt down next to me. "Why are you thinking of battle strategies that would involve an army when you don't have one?"

I stared at him in complete confusion.

"If you wanted to beat somebody who was great at chess, and they let you choose the game, would you choose chess? Or would you find a new game to play?"

He's right. We don't have an army. The king thinks he's invincible. He wouldn't even worry about a group of rebels attacking him. He prevented us from gaining an army, but we had other resources. A plan began to form in my mind. "We can't beat him at his own game. But we already know all of his plays. We know where he'll go and what he'll do. We know he wants to get to me and that he'll send men to destroy the places that help me. How many men does he send to these towns?"

Saffron's grim face started to lighten. "I'm not sure, we'd have to do some research, but I think it's a single company, around 100 men."

"We might not be able to take out an army, but can we take on 100?" I asked her. "Especially with a few sorcerers thrown into the mix."

"Master Flanders!" A heavyset man, face red with exertion, shouted as he came running toward us. He stopped in front of us and doubled over, panting. "Master. Flanders. They. Sent. Me. To…"

Master Flanders rested his hand on the man's back. "Easy there, Catch your breath, then talk."

The man nodded gratefully and took big gulps of air as he tried to steady his breathing. Finally able to speak, he began. "I was sent to find you. The other judges have requested an emergency session. They want to start the testing immediately so they can end the trials early. They need a vote by all of the judges."

"Thank you, Frederick." Master Flanders smiled at him. "I'll walk back with you so we can begin the vote."

Master Flanders and Frederick walked away. My knees were bouncing as strategies spun inside my head. For the first time, I started to believe we could win. *We could find a way to beat the king.*

"When does Max arrive?" I knew we couldn't make any decisions or do anything without his approval. *I'll convince him. We can take down the king together.*

"He is supposed to be here tomorrow. I imagine he'll be here sooner with the turn of events." She paused a moment. "I spoke with Master Flanders this afternoon." She gave me a nudge with her elbow. "He says you have some potential as a sorcerer. It's just too bad you're too old to go through formal training."

I lifted an eyebrow. "Too old?"

She nodded. "He told me about your talk with him. How he

was able to teach you a few skills but doesn't think you will have the time to really master the higher level magic."

I was completely confused. That was not what we talked about at all. I almost said something to object but caught myself. If Master Flanders was telling Saffron this, he had a purpose. For some reason, he didn't want her to know what I could do. He didn't trust her. I had put my trust so blindly in Saffron, I couldn't find any reason not to trust her. But maybe it wasn't Saffron he didn't trust. Maybe it was somebody Saffron talked to. She reported everything to Max. *It means that your brother should be the one who is afraid.* Things were getting very complicated. I had only known Master Flanders for two days, but he hadn't given me any reason to doubt him. Sir Henry's words constantly haunted me. How was I supposed to know who to trust?

CHAPTER 22

I was seated between Saffron and a thin woman with bright red hair in the spectator stands. For the first time in the history of the sorcery trials, they were beginning the testing in the evening. The upcoming war and the destruction of our own kingdom were weighing heavily on the crowd. Some visitors who had arrived only yesterday had already gone home. Those who remained behind were more somber than they had been on their arrival. Saffron assured me that there was nothing we could do in the two days it would take for the trials to wind down. I was thankful to be safe from the king's wrath for the moment, but felt guilty nonetheless.

To make up for the lack of sunlight, the judges created a series of glowing orbs of fire around the trial field. Now that I was learning sorcery myself, I was even more excited to see what the trials entailed. Ashton would be taking the field for his exhibition exam tonight. As far as I knew, the only thing he could do was to summon a wall of fire. I wondered what else I would see from him.

I fidgeted in my seat, impatient for it to start. I leaned in to Saffron and whispered. "How does this work?"

"Each candidate will have 10 minutes to show off their 4 best skills. Then the judges score them to determine if they pass."

"Do they have any rules or skills they have to show?" I wondered about the skills Master Flanders had told me were standard for beginning sorcerers. Were there standard test spells?

Saffron considered for a moment. "I don't think so."

I turned back to the empty field and the floating orbs of flames. *I need to ask Ashton how to do that.* Butterflies filled my stomach when I thought about him. I didn't get to wish him luck before the test. Everything happened so quickly.

Sir Henry's words echoed through my mind. For a brief moment, I wondered if I should worry about placing my trust in Ashton but shook it off. Sir Henry had also told me to trust my instincts and I didn't get any bad feelings about Ashton or Saffron. A nagging feeling inside me kept bringing up Max. *He's my brother. Just because he isn't the most friendly person doesn't mean I should be suspicious of him.* No matter what I told myself, the bad feelings kept returning. It must have been because of the marriage issue. *How could my brother be the one person in this whole mess that I don't trust?* I rubbed my eyes, trying to clear my head. Maybe Saffron could tell me some good things about Max to help these feelings go away. Just as I was building up the courage to ask some questions about Max, a girl walked into the meadow.

She had black hair that hung to her waist and tan skin. She wore a simple purple robe and walked with confidence. She stopped in the center of the field and turned to face the judges who were seated under the stands. We wouldn't be able to see any of the judges' actions or responses from our seats above them.

My eyes darted between the girl's face and her hands. I didn't want to miss any of her movements when she began her demonstration. She bowed low, then stood and placed her hands over her heart. She stood still for several long moments. I looked around at the people in the stands. Most of them had their eyes glued to her, so I trained my gaze on her again. Finally, she lifted her hands, palms flat, over her face and over her head. As they traveled over her face and hair, her appearance changed. Her skin tone was several shades lighter and her hair went from black to blonde.

My mouth dropped open. How was that possible? The

change only held briefly and her appearance reverted back to where it had started. She turned to the side and dropped to her knees. She rested her hands flat on the grass and then lowered her face until it was almost at the ground. She sat back up and waited. While I was staring at her, I noticed movement out of the corner of my eye. I glanced toward the movement and saw several rabbits headed toward her. They circled her before leaving again.

She raised her hands from a lowered position and the rocks on the ground around her began to hover in the air. She pointed in various directions and the rocks followed her finger to land softly where she indicated. A bell rang below me. A signal that she had time for only one more spell. She smiled and lifted the hood of her robes over her head, then she disappeared. I gasped. *How did she do that?*

A moment later, she reappeared, standing in the same place she had vanished from. I wondered if it was a spell like the silence spell where a field is placed around you.

After a bow, the girl walked off the field and a red-haired boy in the same purple robes entered. He hovered above the ground briefly and moved some rocks around. I didn't think he was as impressive as the girl. The only thing he did that stood out to me was that he was able to summon a huge gust of wind that blew the hats off of a few people seated near me.

As one candidate after another entered the space, my mind wandered. There wasn't much variety to the demonstrations so I started to think about what I would do if I were to take a trial. *What is Ashton going to do?* So far, none of the candidates had done anything with fire. Master Flanders told me fire was a rare element to identify with. Most of these apprentices would be aligned with earth or air. *That explains the rock trick.* Would Ashton be doing anything with his fire?

Saffron yawned next to me. It was getting late. I covered a yawn of my own. Some of the people had left the stands already. Movement in the center of the field caused me to glance over. A jolt went through me, it was Ashton. He was in the same purple robes that all of the other apprentices had been wearing. My heart picked up and I scooted to the edge of my seat.

Ashton bowed to the judges and his eyes flickered up to mine. He smiled. My cheeks felt hot. He turned his back on the judges so I couldn't see his hands. Then a circle of flames surrounded him, rising up until he was completely obscured by them. The crowd let out a gasp. My fingers tightened around the edge of the bench. The fire was being held a lot longer than most of the other spells I had seen performed. Ashton stepped into the flames. He walked right through them while they continued to burn, emerging unscathed. He made a low wave with his hands and the flames disappeared.

Then he cupped his hands in front of him. A small fireball appeared. He pulled his hands apart until the ball was the size of his head. He held it there for a moment. This would be impressive enough based on what the other candidates had done this evening, but he took it a step further. He spread his hands wide, shattering the fireball and causing it to rain down in thousands of little sparks. I reached my fingers to the sky, catching some of the falling embers. He was making all of the other apprentices look bad.

He bent down and placed his hands under a small flower. *This looks familiar.* The flower grew taller and larger than any flower I had ever seen before. It was quite beautiful. He took several steps away from the flower. With his hands at his side, I noticed only the most minute inclination of his head. The flower burst into flames. I could feel the heat from the fire all the way in the stands. My heartbeat quickened. With the smallest effort, Ashton could cause a lot of damage. I had a feeling I was only seeing a taste of his power as a sorcerer. Yet, his power didn't worry me. Somehow, I knew that he'd never harm me.

The bell rang, signaling he had time for only one more spell. Many of the candidates had saved the best for last, but everything Ashton had done had already been more impressive than the skills shown by the others. Ashton found me in the crowd again and winked at me. My heart fluttered. A cloud of gray smoke rose around him. When the smoke cleared, he was gone.

I waited, eyes wide, for him to reappear. Then I felt a tap on my shoulder. I turned. "Ashton?"

He grinned down at me.

The crowd around us noticed that he had materialized in the audience and they let out gasps and murmurs of surprise. Somebody started to clap and we were soon surrounded by applause.

"Show off." I smiled at him.

He squeezed my shoulder before walking down the stairs. He stood in front of the judges again, and bowed before walking off of the field. His magic was so different from the other apprentices who had been testing. He made all of them look like beginners. How did he get so good? Max. He learned from Max. I hadn't yet seen Max perform any magic but his skills must far surpass Ashton's.

"Saffron?" I whispered.

The next candidate had emerged and was calling bunnies around her. Saffron turned away from the field and raised an eyebrow.

"Have you seen Max's sorcery?" I asked.

"Not recently, but yes, I have in the past," she said, returning her gaze to the demonstration.

"How does it differ from Ashton's?"

She looked thoughtful for a moment. "Actually, I think Ashton's demonstration was almost identical to Max's when he had his trials. The audience was just as surprised then as they were today when he showed up in the stands."

"You were there?"

"Max and I were inseparable when we were younger." She sounded sad.

My stomach tightened. She has been trying to keep me from going through what she was going through. I thought of Ashton's smile, his touch, his kiss. *There is no way I'm giving him up. I won't end up like Saffron.*

The candidates filed out one at a time to show off their skills but I wasn't paying attention to them anymore. Focus gone, my gaze went right through them out to the field beyond. The darkness was peaceful and helped me to forget my worries. *A light.* I tensed and adjusted my gaze, searching. *Is it a shooting star? Please be a shooting star.* I saw it again. *Something is out there.* Then again. A brief flash of light appeared in the darkness beyond the testing field. I sat up straighter and fought to see into the darkness. The tingle of magic in my hands intensified. I nudged Saffron with my elbow. "Something's out there," I whispered. I didn't want to stir up fear from the people sitting around me.

She tensed and starred in the direction I indicated. The light flashed again. It was brighter this time. My heartbeat quickened.

She stood. "We need to go."

I followed her, looking back just in time to see the light flash again, brighter still. We headed down the stairs and Saffron knocked on the door under the stands where the judges were seated.

"It better be an emergency." A grumpy looking, angular woman said as she opened the door a crack. Her face tensed when she saw Saffron and me staring at her.

"What is it?"

"Something is going on outside the wards." Saffron told her about the flashing light.

The woman's face took on a greenish tint. She turned away from us. "Don't let the next candidate test. We're done for the night. Send everyone back to their tents."

She turned to us. "Saffron, head to the main tent and tell Mildred *Sfumato*. She'll get your weapons for you."

Saffron nodded.

"You," she said, staring at me. "Find Ashton. He should be at the candidate's tent. If they find a way to break the wards, we'll need his fire."

"Where is that?" I asked.

She pointed to a tent behind the stands then shut the door. I heard movement above us as people were preparing to leave.

They must have finished the last candidate.

"I'll meet you at our tent," Saffron said as she headed away.

I rushed to the candidate's tent and hesitated in front of it. You can't really knock on canvas. I pulled the flap back just enough to peek inside. The tent was full of apprentices who were sitting, pacing, or standing and talking with other people. They had no idea anything was going on.

An eye peeked back at me and I jumped.

The tent flap opened wide and a girl with wild, brown curly hair and bright green eyes stared at me. "What do you want?" she asked. "This tent is for candidates only. You won't get any clues about future trials from us."

I pulled my shoulders back and lifted my chin. "I'm here to get Ashton. It's important."

"Girlfriends can wait," she said.

"I'm not his -"

"What's going on out there? I heard my name," Ashton called from somewhere within the tent.

"Your girlfriend is trying to sneak you out," the girl said.

"You're an idiot." Ashton walked up to the girl. "Don't you know who that is?"

The girl's mouth went slack then she spoke again. "Um, some girl who isn't old enough to take the trials yet?"

Ashton laughed. "You might want to be a bit nicer to Max's sister."

Her jaw dropped and the color drained from her face. "I'm sorry I was rude. I - I didn't realize who you were." She lowered her head, then pulled back the curtain the rest of the way so Ashton could leave. "I'll see you later, Ashton."

"What was all that about?" I asked him.

"Let's just say, your brother has a reputation," he said. "Now, what's the big emergency - I'm guessing it isn't that you were dying to see me."

I touched his elbow. "This way. We're meeting Saffron in our tent." While we walked, I told him about the lights. When I was finished, I looked up at him. He was wearing a scowl.

His look said everything I needed to know. "So somebody is

trying to get in," I said.

He nodded. "It's never been done before, but it's always a possibility. The trials aren't exactly a secret even though we keep the location a secret. But there would be ways to find out where they were. Without a direct invitation by the Head of the Trials, you can't enter. There are too many protective spells and wards around the trials for easy access. It would take magic to get in. A lot of it."

"Like the kind of magic the king has?" I asked.

"Or his sorcerers," Ashton said.

"What do you mean?" I asked.

"The king has a following of at least eight sorcerers. We know the king himself can't get to you but since his Reapers keep failing, he must be trying something new." Ashton closed his hand around mine. "Don't worry. The council is made up of the most powerful sorcerers in the world. They'll be able to fight them off."

Cold ran through my body, filling my veins with ice. I was a fool to think I'd be safe here. I squeezed Ashton's hand. "I'm going to help them fight. I can't keep having others fight my battles for me."

CHAPTER 23

As we walked through the camp I noticed that the color of the tents around me was changing. The camp had once been dotted with all shades, colors, and patterns. Now, the tents were all turning an alarming shade of red one by one.

"Emergency signal." Ashton pointed to a tent that turned red. "Lets everybody know that they need to pack up and head to emergency exit portals. I've never seen them use it before."

Saffron was halfway through lacing up her leather armor when we entered the tent. Her sword and my quiver of arrows were sitting on the bed, along with a collection of daggers. I had a feeling there wasn't going to be much we could do with weapons like these if we were fighting against sorcerers. Ashton stepped behind the screen to change out of his purple robes. I looked around the room for a moment, feeling like I should be doing something but was unsure of where to start.

"You might want to change out of the dress," Saffron suggested. "Trousers are much easier to run in."

I quickly did as she suggested, attaching a dagger to my leg and tied on my leather wrist guard. Eyes closed, I silently went through all of the spells I had learned, trying to figure out if any of them would help me in this situation.

Saffron slid her sword into its sheath. "We're to meet back in the main tent. You two ready?"

I took a deep breath and let out a sigh. "It's been a few days since somebody threatened my life. I guess it's time again."

Saffron smiled at me. "You've come a long way from the

scared little village girl I rescued. You can do this."

If Saffron thought I could do this, I must be ready. *I have come a long way.* My grandmother would be proud of me. I tied the quiver of arrows at my waist and picked up my bow. "I can do this."

Ashton stepped out from behind the screen. He had shed the purple apprentice robes in favor of his usual tunic and trousers. Though he didn't look like a sorcerer, I now knew just how much power he could wield.

Saffron walked to the door. "I'll meet you two there."

She was giving us a moment and we didn't hesitate. I pressed myself against Ashton and buried my head in his chest. He wrapped his arms around me and kissed the top of my head.

"I don't know if you should go out there and fight," he said.

I pulled back and looked up at him. "I can make it rain."

"What are you talking about?" He brushed the hair away from my eyes.

"The thunderstorm yesterday. That was me."

He stared at me, unblinking. "You made that thunderstorm?"

I nodded. I couldn't read his reaction.

"Water and lightning," he whispered. He shook his head. "Who knew the most powerful sorcerer I've ever met would also be the most beautiful?" He kissed my forehead.

I grinned. "Master Flanders was sure surprised."

"It's not easy to surprise the Head of the Trials." He lifted an eyebrow. "I suppose I can't just keep you for myself. I can't wait to see what else you can do. You're going to surprise a lot of people."

I tensed. "You can't tell my brother. I don't know why, but Master Flanders wants me to keep it a secret."

"You're not doing a very good job," he teased.

I gave him a pleading look.

"Okay, okay," he said. He gave me a hard kiss on the mouth, then pulled away too quickly. "We better go."

Hand in hand, we left the tent. Ashton tried to pull his hand away, but I hung on. We were heading to battle and I didn't really care who knew about us.

The main tent was a buzz of activity when we arrived. Master Flanders was in the center of the tent assigning jobs to people. He glanced at our clasped hands when we walked up to him, but didn't say anything.

"Ashton, I need you at the emergency exit portal. It won't be activated until the camp is secured. People are already waiting to leave. Keep them calm and as soon as it opens, you send as many people out as you can. Don't hesitate to use your fire if you have to. Keep those people safe. If something comes in that isn't supposed to," he tossed a silver coin to Ashton, "this will close up the portal."

Ashton nodded. He started to head out of the tent. I pulled him back and gave him a quick kiss before letting go of his hand.

"Promise me you won't be too brave," Ashton said.

"You, too," I said. Ashton gave me one last glance as he left the tent. The back of my throat hurt and my mouth felt dry. *Please don't let anything bad happen to him.* I knew right then that I'd made the right decision to stay with him, no matter the cost. There was no way I could be without him.

Master Flanders approached with a tall, dark skinned man in black leather armor. It reminded me of the King's Guard. A chill ran through me. "James, this is Wilona. I need you to keep her safe, away from the fighting," he paused and lowered his voice, "James, on your life, keep her safe. You understand?"

James nodded then grasped my upper arm and started to drag me toward the door.

Using all of my weight, I pulled in the opposite direction. "You can't just hide me away." Yanking my arm out of his grasp, I turned to Master Flanders. "You know I can help. Let me fight."

Saffron shook her head. "You know we can't risk anything happening to you."

My nostrils flared. "I am not going to hide somewhere while

the king's sorcerers kill everybody. If they get in, I'm dead anyway. You might as well let me help."

Master Flanders' mouth twisted and he narrowed his eyes at me. "You sure you're ready for this? These are fully trained sorcerers."

"Are you crazy?" Saffron's voice cut through Master Flanders'. "She's not ready."

"I am ready. And I'm doing this." My knuckles were white from squeezing my bow so tight. "You can't stop me." Swallowing hard, I played the one card I had. "If Max isn't here, I'm second in command by birth. You have no choice."

"You have too much of your brother inside you." Saffron ran her fingers through her hair. "You do realize he'll kill me if I let you die."

"Then you better come with me and help me," I said.

Master Flanders wore the hint of a smile on his face. "James, take these ladies with you to the barrier. You'll all fight."

James nodded and led us away from the tent out toward the blackness where the wards ended. As we walked, the flashes of light were becoming brighter and more frequent than when I had first seen them.

A small band of older sorcerers, many in robes like Master Flanders, were already lined up in the middle of a field. Saffron and I stood behind them.

James had two swords strapped to his sides. Was he a sorcerer or a bodyguard? Whatever he was, he was apparently in charge.

"We have a few minutes before they break the wards. We are guessing it's about six sorcerers out there. Do not underestimate them. They have all been training alongside the king in dark magic and will be using ancient spells we're not familiar with. They are also trained as necromancers. If any of us fall, burn the body."

I swallowed. *Necromancers.* Forcing myself to breathe normally, I waited for more instructions. *You can do this. Nobody is going to have to burn your body.*

The tingle of magic spread up my arms and was tickling it

my neck. They were almost here. I pulled an arrow from my quiver and held it against my bow.

James pointed to a small woman in a flowing gray dress. "Britta, stand next to Wilona. Give her arrows an extra punch."

Britta nodded, then moved to stand next to me. Suddenly, my arrow felt like it was humming with energy. The tingle from the magic moved into my chest and was nearly running through my whole body.

"The wards are about to fall," I called out. Nobody questioned how I knew. They moved into their ready stances and Saffron lifted her sword. James unsheathed both of his swords and locked his gaze directly in front of him. I drew my arrow and waited.

A blinding light punctuated the darkness then vanished, leaving me momentary blinded. *The wards are down.* Blinking away the spots that danced in front of me, I focused on keeping my bow at the ready. It was too quiet. I could hear steady, quick breaths leaving my mouth. Squinting into the blackness, I waited.

A rush of wind hit me from the side, nearly knocking me down. I turned my arrow in the direction of the wind and peered into the darkness. Time seemed to have stopped moving as we waited. Out of the corner of my eye, another burst of light illuminated the darkness. Pivoting toward the light I caught sight of what must be a portal. My breath caught and my jaw dropped open. It looked like there was a tear in the sky and cloaked figures tumbled out in a cloud of dark smoke. The smoke filled the space around us, making it difficult to see. My hands began to tremble. *Maybe this wasn't such a good idea.* I let out a breath and tried to compose myself. Lifting my chin high, I focused on stilling my trembling hands. I needed to be steady to get a good shot.

The smoke began to clear and I searched for the figures. At first I didn't see them, then all at once they were on us. The battle didn't wait. It went from quiet to a roar in a heartbeat.

Flames whirled at me. I ducked, feeling heat pass over my

head. People moved all around me. Bodies slammed together. Screams filled the air. I scanned the scene, looking for a clear shot at one of the enemy sorcerers. My eyes locked on a man I had never seen before. He was launching fireballs into the fight. I drew my bow, aiming for his chest.

"As long as your arrow gets near him, I can help guide it in," Britta called out over the sound of the battle. She raised her hands in the air and stretched them toward the fire sorcerer.

Aiming at a moving target was something I hadn't practiced before and I was worried I would miss. Britta's words gave me confidence. With a deep breath in, I followed the man with my arrow. When I felt like I could get close, I released. The arrow flew through the air, moving slightly off the path I had sent it as Britta guided it. With her help, it struck with more force than I expected. It hit the man square in his chest. He fell backward, grasping at the arrow.

I pulled another arrow out of my quiver and looked for a target. Two bodies were nearby on the ground but I didn't have it in me to see who they belonged to. I caught sight of Saffron fighting with a short, white-haired sorcerer. James was pulling his sword out of somebody. A cry rang out from behind me.

I turned to see Britta collapse on the ground. *No!* A sorcerer in a dark hooded robe stood over her body. I couldn't make out the face in the shadow of the hood. He started to walk toward me. Fear gripped my chest but I pushed past it. Pulling out the dagger that was sheathed on my leg, I launched it at him. He caught the blade between his palms and didn't break his step. *Who is he?* His steps were slow and without urgency. My stomach twisted. I loaded an arrow in my bow and launched a quick shot at his chest. He glided away from my arrow and it flew past him.

I glanced around for help. He was getting closer. I took a deep breath and tried to clear my mind as much as I could with the battle raging around me. Magic was my only hope. I centered my hands level with my waist, and raised them to my chest. Instead of focusing on the entire storm, I thought only of lightning. My hair stood on end as electricity began to form around me. Pushing my hands to the sky, I dropped them to my side. I stared at the hood's shadow where his face should be and commanded the lightning to strike. I pulled in my anger, fear, and frustration. Everything I had and everything I was went into that summoning. Thunder sounded from above me. Smiling, I narrowed my eyes at the hooded figure.

A purple streak of lightning crashed into the ground, blinding me and sending me flying backward through the air. For a moment, all I could see was white light. Then my vision began to come back to me in spots. I scrambled to my feet shaking as I stood. All that remained of my attacker was a smoking crater. *How did I do that?* I killed a man with lightning. On purpose. This wasn't the first time I had killed somebody, but this time, I had set out to kill him with magic. Had anybody else seen me do that? What would they think of me? *You wanted to be here. You wanted to help.* This was the right thing, wasn't it?

Puffs of smoke began to appear around me. I coughed and waved my hand in front of my face to clear the air. It was dark again, the fire that had been lighting the fight was gone. Somebody sent up a fireball that glowed above us. There were less of us standing than we had started with. Britta, and two other sorcerers from our side were laying on the ground. One of the attacking sorcerers was laying on the ground coughing and wailing in pain. James and another man picked him up under his arms and dragged him away. A sorcerer I didn't know ignited his hands and walked toward the fallen. I turned around, not wanting to see their bodies go up in flames.

CHAPTER 24

As the adrenaline of the battle wore off, the fatigue of using so much magic rushed in. I knelt on the ground, taking a moment to regain my strength. People were flooding in from the camp toward the smoking battlefield. I recognized Master Flanders among them.

A weight lifted from me as I saw Ashton running toward the clearing. I stood and we met in an embrace. *Thank the gods.* He was covered in soot and smelled like a campfire. Whatever he had experienced on his end must have been pretty bad.

Ashton took my hand and pulled me away from the battle ground. "Everybody who is still here is meeting at the main tent. We have to get the directions to our emergency meeting location."

I stumbled as I walked.

He put his arm around me and helped steady me. "Are you cold?" Ashton pulled me closer to him.

"No." I sighed. I couldn't explain how I felt. *I could have died.* For some reason, that wasn't upsetting me the way it should have. Maybe I was getting too used to to the idea. I thought for a moment and realized the part that upset me the most was that I hadn't been able to save Britta.

"Britta," I said, "I didn't even know her, but I feel like it was my job to protect her."

Ashton looked at me with an intensity I hadn't seen before. "You almost died and your focus is on how you couldn't protect everybody." He shook his head. "I've never met anybody like you before. You care about other people more than your power. So different than your brother."

We were different. Piecing together what Max was really like was taking time but I was starting to get a clearer picture. I had a feeling he would sacrifice a hundred Brittas to gain the throne. Was he going to be any better than the king we had already? I felt sick to my stomach thinking of the number of people who had already died on my behalf. There had to be a way that I could help make this kingdom a better place. I stopped walking. "This has to stop."

"Are you hurt?" Ashton asked.

I shook my head. "No, not me. The killing. The death. All of these people died because of me. It has to stop. Maybe I should just turn myself over to the king and get it over with."

Ashton gripped me by my shoulders. "Are you insane? What good would that do? We need you."

My eyes narrowed. Was he speaking to me as a member of the White Ravens or as the girl he was in love with? I wasn't sure where I fit into anything. "The Ravens don't need me. They want to marry me off but I think I'd be better off dead than married to some prince I don't love."

"I'm not going to let that happen, and neither are you. You are too smart and too powerful to waste away as a figurehead somewhere. You need to help rule this kingdom." His tone was serious.

"Max is going to rule this kingdom."

"You should be there with him. When we meet up with him, we need to show him what you can do. There's no way he won't want you by his side. We can't take you away from Illaria." He wrapped his arm around my shoulder again and urged me forward.

Maybe telling Max was the right thing to do. Word of the battle would probably spread quickly. Soon enough everybody would know that I made lightning. I leaned into Ashton. I had never been so tired in my whole life. Creating magic was the most exhausting and exhilarating thing I had ever experienced. Every step caused my body to scream out in pain, but at the same time there was a sense of power I had never felt before.

Few people remained behind after the evacuation of the camp. Those that did were the members of the Trial Council and higher level sorcerers who held positions within the guild. Saffron and I were the only non-sorcerers in the group. I noticed several tattoos barely visible under torn and dirty sleeves. They reminded me that I would have to deal with Max soon and I wasn't sure what to expect. *I can't trust him.* It pained me to finally believe that truth. There was something inside telling me that I had to be very wary around my brother.

We all stood in a circle around Master Flanders so we could hear what was to come next. "We can't stay here. We are instituting Plan F to meet up at our secured location. Further instructions will be made there. Wilona, Saffron, you two are with me. Everybody else find a partner who can teleport. Did I miss anybody?" He looked around the room then he opened his hands to reveal bright green coins with the letter "F" printed on them. He handed one to each pair of sorcerers. "I'll see you all there."

Clouds of smoke began to form around me as sorcerers vanished to wherever we were all going. Ashton kissed me on the forehead. "See you soon." I smiled at him then he vanished in a cloud of smoke.

"Saffron, Wilona." Master Flanders reached his hands out to us. "Take a hand and don't let go."

I gripped his hand so hard I worried I was hurting him but the butterflies in my stomach wouldn't let me lessen my grip.

"Just hang on," he instructed, "it will be over quickly."

The smoke started to rise at my feet and then everything went black. Panic shot through me and my heart rate quickened. I couldn't see anything. I squeezed Master Flanders' hand tighter and he squeezed back. I focused on my breathing. Just as panic was starting to consume me, light returned. We were on solid ground surrounded by tall grass, next to a lake.

The first thing I did was look around for Ashton. I didn't see him or any of the other Sorcerers anywhere. *Oh no.* Something wasn't right.

Saffron removed her sword from her sheath and raised the point under Master Flanders' chin. "Where is everybody?" She pressed the point right against his skin. "Is this a trap?"

Master Flanders raised his hands in surrender. "Give me a minute to explain, please."

She narrowed her eyes and didn't lower the sword.

"Have I ever given you reason not to trust me?" he asked her.

She hesitated, then lowered the sword. "Explain, quickly."

He dropped his hands. "Something is coming, it's bigger than the battle for the throne. I am afraid Max isn't the best man for the job."

"Those are treasonous words, Master," Saffron warned.

He raised his hands again. "You know I have always and will always serve Illaria. I'm not saying Max can't be part of the solution. I'm telling you that Wilona is the one who should be on the throne."

"What?" I stepped back, hands in front of me, eyes wide. *Where is this coming from?* "I don't want to rule."

Saffron glared at me as if I had somehow planned this.

"I have nothing to do with this." My mind was racing, trying to figure out what was going on. "I don't want the throne. You know that."

Master Flanders placed his hand on Saffron's shoulders. "This is not Wilona's doing. It was ordained long before her birth. She is the only one who can prevent the Darkness that is coming to Illaria. You don't have to do anything right now other than keeping her here. Do not let her leave Illaria. I believe she is the key to our salvation."

A chill ran through me. My grandmother had read me stories about the Darkness. I never thought they were real. The stories told of thirst, starvation, a cursed land. A time when the barrier between the living and the dead was so thin, that some creatures could pass through. For most people, this would bring fear and terror. For a necromancer, it was a source for more power and more monsters to control. *The king would be unstoppable.*

"What could possibly be worse than the darkness we are already facing from the king?" Saffron asked.

"Before the Battle of the Dead, I was at the High Temple researching the cycles. The Darkness has not been in this land for a thousand years, but it's coming." He took a deep breath before continuing. "Yesterday I received word that the Ibearian River dried up overnight. The only other time that has happened was the year before the Darkness came."

"How do you know all of this? I've never heard of the Darkness," Saffron said.

"I have," my voice barely audible. I didn't think anything could scare me more than the king himself, but I was wrong. "My grandmother used to tell me the stories about it. During the Darkness, neighbors fought against neighbors, fathers against sons. It was a vicious time when everybody was afraid of everything. Even the dragons left. Illaria was almost wiped out by it until a sorceress trapped it in the sea."

Saffron pressed her eyebrows in. She didn't look like she believed me. "That sounds like a children's story."

"It was so long ago it doesn't seem real anymore," Master Flanders said, "but I assure you, it's true. I was studying it at the Royal Library before the duke burned it to the ground."

"Why her, then? Why not Max?" Saffron asked.

"There was a prophecy about a Sorcerer ruler who could stop the darkness. One of royal blood with power that hadn't been seen in generations. I thought Max was strong enough as a fire user, but now that I know Wilona's power, I think it has to be her."

"Max has made it very clear that he wants to get rid of me as quickly as possible. He won't let me stay here," I said.

Saffron frowned. "None of this makes sense. Why didn't you tell me this before?"

He shrugged. "I didn't know Wilona had the powers of the ancients in her blood. That changes everything."

Saffron stared at me. "You identified with water?"

I nodded slowly. Not sure of what any of this meant.

She sighed. "Okay. I'll try. We'll explain it to Max. He'll

want to know all of this."

Master Flanders nodded. "Thank you." He held out his hands again. "Let's go meet up with everybody else. I'm sure we've given them enough of a scare by now."

I gripped his hand and closed my eyes.

I opened my eyes when I felt solid ground under my feet. We were standing inside a large wooden structure that smelled faintly of animals. I think it was a barn at one point. We weren't alone this time. The other sorcerers were standing around waiting for us. I searched for Ashton, my heart skipping a beat when I saw that he was here safely. He strode over to me and stood next to me, brushing his fingertips against mine. Familiar and comforting warmth flooded my body. I moved closer to him so our shoulders were touching. All I wanted to was to be alone with him again. To feel his arms around me, his mouth on mine. I glanced up at him. The tops of his ears were pink. I wondered if he was thinking the same thing.

Master Flanders started speaking and the people in the room quieted to listen. "I'm afraid there are several items we must address. But first, a moment of silence for those friends who are no longer with us." He lowered his head.

The back of my throat burned as I recalled Britta's last moments. I lowered my head and reached my hand to clasp Ashton's. He gave it a squeeze. *What would I do without him?*

"You have all been through so much in the last fifteen years," Master Flanders began. "And I'm afraid to say that it isn't going to end any time soon. The destruction of the king is even more pressing than it was before. The Ibearian River dried up last night."

The older sorcerers in the room gasped. Ashton stiffened.

"Those of us who have been in the Guild for a long time know of The Darkness. We've been watching for the signs. If it follows the path it did last time, we have less than a year before it arrives. We cannot have King Osbert on the throne when the Darkness returns. It would mean the destruction of all of Illaria."

There were muffled conversations rolling through the room. A thin man with red hair stepped forward. "You know I've always tried to stay out of politics, never joined up with those Ravens. But I can't sit by and let Osbert channel the Darkness when it arrives. I'm with you, Flanders."

"Me, too," the pointy faced judge from the trials said. Then two more sorcerers stepped up to offer their support. "Gallia has a history of neutrality," one of them said. "But we all know that Osbert won't stop with Illaria. He'll move into our countries, too. We're with Illaria."

Some of the most powerful sorcerers in the world were stepping up to help us reclaim our home. Tears welled up in my eyes. After all of the terrible things I had seen lately, all of the killing, I was overwhelmed by the good in this room. These people who were willing to risk their own lives to save the lives of others. This was what it was supposed to be about. Helping people and putting an end to the atrocities committed by this evil king. It wasn't about power or the throne. Those things were secondary to the lives of the innocents who were being used in this deadly game. I never felt like that was the priority with the Ravens. But these sorcerers seemed to have the right idea. My powers were still new but I felt like I belonged with this group. Maybe being a sorceress was who I was supposed to be.

"Master Flanders?" A thin woman with hair so black it was almost purple stepped out of the crowd and approached the Master. "May I have a moment before you continue? I know it isn't really the time, but sometimes we need something good to come from something so dark."

He bowed his head and stepped aside for the woman.

"Most of you know me, but as we have some non-sorcerer guests," she nodded at Saffron. "I am Madame Lyndsey and I am the Head of the Apprentice program for the Guild. While Master Flanders is in charge of the Trials themselves, I make the final decision on who will earn the title of Master.

Tonight I watched three apprentices volunteer to fight against Sorcerers with decades more training than them. They did so with fortitude and grace beyond their years. Please step forward, apprentices."

Ashton let go of my hand and stepped to the center of the crowd. A boy I didn't recognize and another figure in a hood joined him. When the hood was removed I saw Celeste standing there. Her right eye was swollen shut and she had a scratch that tore across her jaw. Jealousy bloomed then faded as I softened toward her almost instantly. She was from Gallia. This wasn't her fight, yet she had been out there, defending strangers in a country that wasn't even her own.

"Ashton White, Bruce Cummings, and Celeste Moreau, you three have demonstrated beyond a shadow of a doubt that you possess the skills, dedication, and loyalty needed to be called Master Sorcerers. You are hereby no longer apprentices. You are inducted into the Guild with full status." She frowned. "I'm afraid we will have to complete the ceremony later. You are eligible to receive your marks and we will do so as soon as possible."

The handful of people standing around started to clap. Ashton, Bruce, and Celeste smiled in response.

A ripple of "Welcome, Master" rose through the circle as sorcerers stepped forward to shake the hands of the newest Master Sorcerers. Despite the danger on the horizon, I couldn't help but smile. Ashton deserved this. And from what I knew of Celeste, she deserved it, too. I didn't know Bruce at all, but he had been willing to stand up and defend the people of the camp, then I would treat him as a friend.

"Thank you for that, Madame Lyndsey," Master Flanders announced. "We do need to take the time to celebrate the things that make life worth living. This is a great reminder of how important our work is. With The Darkness on it's way, our mission to return the heir to the throne is more important than ever."

I looked around. There were twelve people here. Sorcerers who were going to help us take back the kingdom. For a moment, my dream resurfaced and I pictured myself on the throne. I could practically feel the weight of the crown. I shuddered. *I'm nobody special.* I wasn't ready to be a queen. Yet the dream tugged at me, begging me to face my fears. *No. You aren't going to be queen.* Who would want to be a ruler, anyway? The responsibility, the constant scrutiny, the threat of death hanging over you every second. I knew I wanted to help my kingdom, but I would happily hide away in a small village once the people were safe. Being queen wasn't something I wanted.

I looked around for a distraction. As my eyes wandered the space, I noticed smoke forming in the corner of the room. I shook Saffron and pointed. The people around me noticed my action and turned to look.

The smoke cleared and Max stood in the corner. He was wearing leather armor that was covered in blood. His dark curls were limp with sweat and his face was darkened with soot. "It was an ambush," he said. "They knew we were coming. We didn't stand a chance."

CHAPTER 25

A circle of chairs appeared and Master Flanders urged everybody to sit.

Saffron raced to Max's side. "Are you hurt?" She led him to a chair and sat down next to him. "What happened?" She spoke gently as she stroked the hair off of his brow.

He placed his hand on her shoulder. "I'm okay." He looked down at the blood covering him. He held up his arms as if holding an invisible person. "Master Edward died in my arms. There was so much blood. So much killing."

I gasped and collapsed in the chair across from Max. I covered my mouth with my hand and felt the burning of tears behind my eyes. *Master Edward is Dead.* My heart ached and my throat tightened, making it difficult to breathe. I stared at Max, trying to keep the tears at bay. He looked so fragile right now. Sympathy flooded me. Why had I been so angry with him? Saffron was right, he was under a lot of pressure. If he was this upset over the loss of his people, he couldn't be all bad. I gripped my chair with both hands and swallowed back the tears.

"What happened?" I breathed, the words barely audible.

He took a deep breath before speaking. "We got the camp packed up after you left and headed out to the new location we scouted. The first two days were without incident." He shook his head and lowered his eyes. "Last night as we slept, we were ambushed by a full battalion of the King's Guard. We fought as best we could but we didn't have the manpower and we weren't prepared. They outnumbered us. They knew exactly where we would be and when we would be there."

He looked away for a moment. "They didn't care who they killed. Even the children weren't spared. They slaughtered everybody they could." All color drained from his face as he told the story. He held up his hands, palms facing me. "My fire is the only reason why I'm alive. The only reason I was able to save anybody at all. They weren't prepared for a sorcerer. They didn't have any with them."

"That's because they were all at the trials, trying to kill Etta," Saffron said.

He looked at Saffron next to him, then to Ashton and me across from him. "All of his sorcerers were there?"

Saffron sucked in a breath. "They must have timed it so that they hit everybody at the same time. It wasn't just about Etta. It was about taking us all out."

Max's curls slipped back onto his forehead. Just like mine did. He pushed them away. His brows were pressed together and his mouth twisted in pain. I wanted to give him a hug. He looked back up, jaw clenched, eyes flashing. There's the Max I know. I couldn't help the smile that spread across my face. I might not like the tough, leader of the Ravens Max, but he's the Max I know and I was happy to see him return.

"That's exactly what they did. I checked in with the other camps before I came here. I wanted to warn them. It was too late. Most of the Ravens are gone. There's only about a hundred of us left."

"No," I whispered. How could this be happening? So much death. It was never ending. Tears rolled down my face. Everything they had worked so hard for all this time was gone.

"How'd they know?" Saffron asked.

Max's voice was steady. "Micah and Jasper. They were the ones feeding information to the king. He knew everything."

Saffron's eyes flashed with rage. "Did you get them?"

Max cracked his knuckles. "I got Jasper but Micah took off with the few guards who got away. I'll get him soon enough, and I won't be quick to kill him." The look in Max's eyes was pure hatred. I remembered the stocky man who joked with me in the Raven camp. Despite his kindness, he made me feel uncomfortable. *Trust your instincts. Trust nobody.* Sir Henry was right. I clenched my fists. It must have been Micah behind the aviary. I should have listened to my gut. I wouldn't make that mistake again. I had no doubt that Max would take care of him. *Unless I find him first.* The thought startled me and a chill ran down my spine. Maybe I wasn't so different from Max, after all. Maybe that wasn't such a bad thing. *This has to end. The king has to be stopped.*

Nobody spoke. I looked around at the brave people who fought for my life alongside me. We knew going into that battle that we might not make it out alive. Yet we did it anyway. Because this was too important. Somehow, somebody had to put an end to the king's tyranny.

"It's never going to end, is it?" I asked. "He's never going to stop."

Thirteen faces looked at me. All of them wore a mask of sorrow. All of them looked tired and defeated. We were practically strangers, but I felt a connection to all of them. We forged a bond that most people wouldn't understand. I thought of the Ravens. The people who joined knowing it might cost their life. The people who watched loved ones die and families torn apart. Master Edward. His whole family had fallen at the hands of the king. And now he had joined them.

"We have to fight back." I stood, jaw set and fists clenched. My sorrow was replaced by anger and it burned like heat through my veins. "We can't let this keep happening. Something has to be done."

"I'm not sure we have the resources," Saffron said softly. "We'll have to regroup."

I shook my head. "That's what he's counting on. He won't expect us to strike now."

"You're right from a strategy point of view," Max said. "But Saffron is also right. We don't have the resources."

I stared at Max. Had he agreed with me? A defiant smile crossed my face. I was feeling bold. *I'm not the scared little village girl. I am powerful.* "How many King's Guards can you take on alone?"

He thought for a moment. "Ten probably, maybe more."

"We have eleven sorcerers in this room. We don't need an army. We just need to set a trap for them to come to us." I saw the flicker of understanding flashing in the eyes around me.

"We just need some bait." I put my hand on my chest. "And you happen to be in possession of the one thing the king wants."

Ashton jumped in front of me. "No. You can't be serious. It's too dangerous."

Madame Lyndsey stood and signaled for Ashton to sit. He obeyed her silent motion.

"It will be dangerous, but nothing we can't handle," she said. "So far, the king has only sent his guard and his sorcerers to capture her or to punish any town that aids her. We know the protection spell on her is holding. We can limit the danger by having her visit a village that supports our cause. Then we can hide her in a secure location. When the king sends his guards in to punish the village, we'll be waiting."

Saffron stood. "We can't have all of you fighting. If the king hears that there were eleven sorcerers waiting in the woods, he'd stop sending his guards in. It would have to look like we just left one or two of you behind after Etta passed through. We don't want the king to know how many sorcerers we have on our side."

"What about the Reapers?" Ashton asked. Everybody turned to look at him. "Are we prepared for them?"

Conversation and shouting erupted around me and I turned my head back and forth trying to follow all of the ideas. Everybody seemed to be on board with some version of the plan. While none of the plans allowed me to participate in the fight, at least I could be of some help by being the bait.

Max stood again and waited silently in the center of the circle of chairs. As people noticed him, they began to quiet down. He lifted his hand toward me. "While my sister is making a brave gesture here, it might not be necessary. We have a tentative alliance with Sardinia. The king has declared war on them, likely because he found out that Etta was engaged to marry their prince."

My cheeks flushed and I turned my head away from Ashton. We both knew I wasn't planning to honor the engagement.

"Before Etta left for the trials, we scheduled a rendezvous with the Sardinian ambassador in Luxor. I think that we need to consider this meeting before we start using my sister as a sacrificial lamb."

Murmurs rose around me and my heart sunk. My choices were marriage to a stranger or bait for a Necromancer. While I should have considered one to be a better choice, they both felt like a death sentence. *I'm pretty sure I'm the sacrificial lamb in either situation.*

Master Flanders stepped to the center of the room and raised his hands. The chatter quieted down. "There are a lot of good ideas here. But I suggest we take a break and get some rest. It has been a very long day. I will take first watch. Wilona, you'll sit with me to keep me company. Saffron and James, you'll be second. Max and Madame Lyndsey, you'll be last watch."

He waved his hands and a pile of blankets appeared in the center of the room. Nobody argued with him. As people spread out around the barn to find quiet corners for sleep, Master Flanders and I climbed to the roof to keep watch.

The stars were sparkling in the inky cloudless sky. My eyes felt heavy and stung from the tears. I focused on the cool breeze to help keep myself alert. Shivering, I hugged my knees to my chest. Looking out into the clearing I noticed that the barn was the only thing for miles. There weren't even any trees to give us cover.

"Where are we?" I asked.

"Farmlands west of Yorkton."

I pictured the map of Illaria in my head and tried to place Yorkton. I shook my head. I didn't remember. If I survived all of this, I was going to ask for a map.

"I have something for you." Master Flanders held out a

small parchment scroll.

I reached for it and untied the ribbon that held it closed. I squinted at it in the moonlight but couldn't make out the words. "What is it?"

"It's an apprentice scroll," he said. "It shows that you are an apprentice sorcerer and that you have permission to use magic for training or in times of need. It's a helpful little piece of paper."

"But I'm not an apprentice."

"How do you figure?" he asked me. "What does an apprentice do?"

I thought for a moment. "I guess they learn magic from a master."

"Is that not what you have been doing for the last few days with me?"

I nodded.

"Well then, I suppose that makes you my apprentice." He pointed to the bottom of the scroll. "It has my seal on it. Lets everybody know you are training with me." He shrugged. "Might be helpful in the future to have the seal of the Master of the Sorcerer's Guild."

"But I thought you couldn't take on an apprentice?" I thought back to the day we met.

"I couldn't if I was still a trial judge, but I resigned my position last night when the wards fell."

"You didn't have to do that for me."

"Yes, I did." The intensity of his gaze was visible despite the low light. "I believe in you. And you are going to need my help in the months to come. Finding a way to take down the king is just the beginning."

I rolled the scroll back up and tied the ribbon around it. An apprentice. Was I actually going to learn to control my magic? Become a fully trained sorcerer? I tried to picture myself in the middle of the trial stadium, showing off what I knew. Would I even make it that far? My life was so uncertain and while I tried not to think of it, I knew there was a possibility I'd be facing my own death sooner than I'd like. And if we did somehow manage to take down the king, there was the Darkness to consider. Some good news would be very welcome right now. "Can we focus on one problem at a time?"

He chuckled. "For now. Yes, let's focus on one problem at a time." He stared off into the distance.

I sat next to him, listening to the crickets and feeling the breeze on my cheeks. Somehow I had just become an apprentice sorcerer. I tried to picture my life in the village. Living with my grandmother and dreaming of a simple life. I had no idea how big the world was. I pulled the necklace out from under my tunic and rubbed the familiar piece of metal between my finger and thumb. Who was I? I no longer felt like the scared girl from a small village. But I didn't feel like a princess, either. Now I was adding sorcerer's apprentice to the list. Is it possible that I'm all of those things?

I miss you grandmother. What I wouldn't give to talk to her again, just one last time. I wiped a tear from my cheek, hoping that Master Flanders couldn't see it in the darkness. Looking up into the stars I could almost feel her looking down on me. *Are you proud of me, grandmother? Am I doing the right thing?*

When the watch was over and I finally pulled a blanket over myself, I was too tired to think anymore. I slipped into a deep, dreamless sleep.

*****

I sat outside the barn listening to the wind blow through the grass. If I closed my eyes, I could pretend I was back at home in my forest. I concentrated on breathing deep and slow. Plans were being made to meet up with the Sardinian ambassador tomorrow. An argument had broken out between the sorcerers and my brother over my impending marriage.

Max didn't believe in the warnings of Master Flanders that The Darkness was headed to our land. I didn't want to sit there and listen while other people worked to dictate my future. Especially when I had no intention of going through with any marriage arranged for me. I held my palm out in front of me and concentrated, copying the movements I saw Ashton make to create the flaming orb. A small ball of icy fire rose up from my hand. I closed my hand around it and tried it again. I alternated between making and quenching the flame for several long minutes. *Why do they have the right to decide my fate, anyway?*

I had spent my whole life doing what I was told, with the exception of my few trips to the woods. Until I got involved with the Ravens, I had been happy with the path I was told to take so I never questioned it. I didn't know of any other options. Now I knew how large the world was and how many possibilities there were. How could they expect me to throw away those possibilities to marry somebody I didn't know? Possibilities like Ashton. My stomach tightened. What was I going to do when they realized that I wouldn't go through with the marriage?

It didn't matter. One way or another, I was going to start making my own choices. So far, I'd had no control over anything in my life. Everything had been planned for me since the beginning. Any control I thought I had was an illusion. *Two can play that game.* Max could plan a marriage for me, but it didn't mean I had to go through with it. In the end, how bad could it be to walk away from a marriage? There were worse things coming.

My mind shifted to the Darkness. Growing up I always thought it was just a story. Now I knew that what I had learned as a child was probably carefully considered to prepare me for my future. Why else teach a peasant girl to read, write, speak Gallic, and ride a horse? If I am somehow part of a prophecy to save my kingdom, I have to stay here.

I lost everything a few weeks ago. Losing my home and my village didn't hurt the way that losing my grandmother had. I felt so alone. Ashton, Saffron, Master Flanders, and even Max made it so I had something to lose again. *I'm not going to lose them. I'm not leaving Illaria. If they try to send me away, I'll run.*

Light footsteps approached and Ashton appeared from behind the corner of the barn. He sat down next to me. "You okay?"

"I'm not marrying some guy from Sardinia. No matter what they come up with in there."

He smirked. "Well hello to you, too."

I wasn't in the smirking mood. "You know that anything I say is just to keep Max happy, right?"

Ashton's pressed his mouth into a line. "You really going to give up being a queen for me?"

"Happily," I said.

"Okay." He turned and stared into the grass, a smile spreading across his face. We sat next to each other in comfortable silence as the sun dipped low in the horizon. I could have sat there with him for hours. All too soon, we were interrupted by Saffron calling to us.

I sighed and stood, brushing the grass off of my trousers. I offered my hand to Ashton and helped him up. Our walk back into the barn was slow. I wanted to drag out this moment as long as possible. I knew that once I entered that barn, nothing would ever be the same.

I realized I was holding my breath so I tried to focus on maintaining steady breathing. Ashton's fingers brushed against mine and I ached to clasp his hand. Instead, I pulled away. He clenched his hand into a fist and put some space between us. My chest felt tight. Denying what I felt with him was like denying a part of myself. My life had become very complicated in a very short time. I paused in front of the closed doors. Please be done fighting. I didn't want to hear any more arguments about my life. I didn't think I could keep playing nice. As we crossed the threshold tension still hung in the air.

Master Flanders and my brother were seated in front of everybody else, clearly the highest ranking people in the room. There was an empty chair directly across from them waiting for me. My heart was pounding. I didn't want to do this anymore. I didn't want to be their puppet. I knew I'd have to listen but they couldn't make me stay. I faced them with my chin held high.

"I'm sorry you had to hear all of the disagreements earlier, Wilona," Master Flanders began. "Your brother and I have been working together for years and we have a plan we believe is best for everybody." He winked at me. I flinched, trying to figure out what he was silently telling me.

Max took over the conversation. "Etta, you are new to the Ravens and to being royalty. Your duty is first and foremost to your kingdom. You will be marrying the prince of Sardinia, but we will be asking for a year-long engagement, citing your lack of experience with royal protocol so that you can have time to learn before you are married."

A year. I fought back the urge to scream at my brother and bit the inside of my cheek.

I looked from Max to Master Flanders. He gave me a subtle nod. Like he was telling me to go along with it. I narrowed my eyes at him, then caught myself and worked to make my face impassive. I knew Master Flanders had no intention of sending me away from Illaria. Something else was going on here. For some reason, he was pacifying Max, playing politics. I was only just beginning to get a taste of how politics worked. *Another reason I don't want to rule. Too many games.* I lowered my head in a bow and raised it. I wanted nothing more than to look to Ashton, but I kept my gaze locked in front of me, chin held high.

"Thank you, Max." I inclined my head. Even as the words came out, I was thinking of ways to get out of the marriage. A lot could happen in a year.

CHAPTER 26

I sat quietly at the back table of the tavern where we were waiting to meet the Sardinian ambassador. Max and Saffron were seated on either side of me. Ashton and Celeste were seated at an adjacent table. The selected tavern was crowded with people who were enjoying the evening with their friends. Our stoic faces didn't blend in with the smiles emanating from most of the people around us.

I straightened my skirt and fidgeted with a button on my cloak while I waited. I didn't touch the ale that was sitting in front of me. After the last experience I had with alcohol, I promised myself I would avoid the stuff at all costs. I didn't like the giggly, wobbly creature I had become after consuming the beverage. It was important to maintain control over myself so I simply stared into the amber liquid.

Max and Saffron flinched at every sound. A crash in the kitchen, the tapping of another patron's boot on the floor, the opening and closing of the door, or a loud laugh.

"How much longer should we wait?" I asked. I had no idea if it was customary for an ambassador to keep people waiting.

Max set down his cup. "We'll give them a few more minutes."

I ran my finger around the rim of my cup, trying to keep myself busy. Every time the door opened, I'd lift my eyes from the cup, and hold my breath, worried that the ambassador had arrived. If he didn't show up, the marriage couldn't be finalized.

Then the door opened again. When I glanced up, a figure wearing a long brown cloak and faded clothing looked toward us. His clothing didn't seem to match my vision of what an ambassador should look like. He glanced around the room nervously before walking over to our table. Pulling down his hood, he settled into a chair across from me. Max cleared his throat and nodded to the newcomer. I stiffened in my chair, hands gripping my cup too tightly. *So close to getting out of here. Why did you have to show up?*

He inclined his head toward me. "My lady."

I returned the gesture and gave what I hoped was a friendly smile, forced as it was.

He moved his gaze to Max and inclined his head slightly toward him. Max returned the greeting with the same gesture.

A barmaid noticed the addition to our table and walked over. "Can I get you an ale?"

He nodded, a smile filling his face. "Yes, thank you."

After she strode away the smile faded. "I'm afraid I have bad news. King Osbert has promised invasion if we continue with our current agreement."

Max leaned across the table. "You know we have to fight him eventually to secure the throne."

The man nodded in agreement. "Yes, but we aren't ready. We won't be able to keep the alliance without risking too many Sardinian lives."

I bit the inside of my cheek to keep the smile from betraying me. *He's calling off the engagement.*

Max's eyes shone with anger. "This isn't part of the deal. You told me this was done. You told me your country was ready to fight."

The man lowered his eyes. "I'm sorry. The king is not well. He's afraid of going into war with a brand new king on the throne. He thinks it will make us too vulnerable to inside attacks. We can't appear weak as we transition to a new king."

"And how will it look to have a king with no queen? No way of producing heirs to secure the future?" Max hissed.

"I'm afraid that's already been addressed." The man

swallowed. "The prince married in secret two days ago. Apparently he was in love with one of the queen's ladies. A duchess. The deed is done."

Max slammed his fist on the table and ale splashed out of my glass. A few heads turned to look at us, but they didn't linger. I held my breath, afraid of what Max might do. I'd seen him upset, but never seen him lose his temper and the look on his face was terrifying.

"You are throwing away a great alliance here. When we take back the throne you'll find no friend in Illaria."

The ambassador's eyes darted around the room. Sweat beaded on his forehead. He moved his face closer to Max. "We've already found a friend in Illaria." He backed away and let his words sink in.

Max stood. "The king? You betray me for the usurper?"

My breathing quickened as I watched the scene unfolding in front of me. *Sardinia made an alliance with the king?* Would Sardinia be coming after the Ravens? My chest tightened at the thought of more guards pursuing me. The king had sent his own guards and his Reapers after me already. How was I supposed to survive if he started sending more people after me?

The ambassador stood as well, shaking his head. "They don't know I'm here. I came out of respect for your cause. To warn you that you are not safe. The king will not stop until she is dead." He nodded his head in my direction. "Word got out about her little lightning trick. He'll send an entire army after her if he has to."

I felt the color drain from my face as panic gripped me. *A whole army?* All of my fears were coming true. My pulse quickened but a tiny flicker of pride registered inside of me. *A whole army because of my lightning. They're afraid of me.*

Max ignored the lightning comment and turned to me. "Have Ashton take you back. Go now."

Feeling numb, I made my way over to Ashton's table. He rose when he saw me walking over and we quickly made our way out the back door of the tavern, Celeste at our heels.

"It's over," I said. "The alliance is gone." I didn't have it in me to say any more and I couldn't help but wonder if Master Flanders saw this coming.

I thought I saw a faint flicker of a smile cross Ashton's face in the dim evening light. He clasped my hand and Celeste's hand and in a cloud of smoke, we disappeared.

*****

I woke with a start to a crashing noise and jumped out from under my blanket. My eyes darted around the barn, hunting for the source of the sound. My heart was pounding and it quickened as I realized I was alone inside the vast space. Realizing I was safe, I took a few steadying breaths. My head was pounding. I rubbed my temples but the throbbing continued. *Probably just hungry.*

I listened carefully and looked around the room to make sure I wasn't missing anything. There was muffled conversation outside the barn. When I opened a door, I discovered a rush of activity. People were darting around making a lot of noise. I winced. *What I wouldn't give for one of grandmother's headache teas right now.*

With all of the noise, I was amazed I slept so long. I walked out into the grass and saw a few familiar faces. It was the Ravens. At least what was left of them. There were faces I didn't recognize as well. Either survivors from the other camps or new recruits. Though what would bring people to the Ravens after the slaughter, I could not imagine.

Hammers slammed against structures being built and a blacksmith clanged against swords and armor. Voices in conversations carried through the space. The smell of cooking meat mingled with fresh bread. A series of ovens had been constructed and a woman was pulling loaves of bread out. *Where did they all come from?* I felt like I was in a dream. *A very loud dream.*

I shielded my eyes against the sun with my hand as I looked around for one of my friends. I cringed. *Celeste.* She waved to me and I forced a smile. I still wasn't completely comfortable around her. She ran over to me. *Great.*

"Isn't this amazing?" She was breathless in her excitement. "They all came back. All of the Ravens that survived came back. And they brought friends. The word is out. People know about you and that the king is hunting you. They want to help."

Without thinking, I grabbed for my pendant and slid it back and forth along the chain. "They can't stay here."

She frowned. "Why can't they stay here?"

I looked around at all of the people gathered. They were in danger, all of them. "It's not safe. I won't have more innocent people dying for me."

She put her arm around my shoulder as if we were childhood friends. I tried to subtly shrug it off but she either didn't notice or didn't care.

"That's what's so great about you." She flashed a smile at me. "You care so much about all of your people. But don't worry. They've got wards up. Nobody can find us here. They took extra precautions this time. Only 3 people can even give the location to the camp. It's all very advanced magic."

I wasn't sure if she was being condescending or kind. It was probably best if I just got away from her. Her high, sweet voice was making the throbbing in my head more intense. "Have you seen my brother?"

She shook her head. "Not since last night. Boy was he mad that he can't marry you off! Serves him right if you ask me. He should be listening to Master Flanders and to you." She took her arm off of my shoulder and lowered her voice. "If it were up to me," she stepped closer to me so I could hear her whisper. "I'd be pushing for a new queen instead of a king." She winked at me.

My mouth dropped. Celeste *was* being nice. Maybe even too nice. I swallowed. "Thank you, that's kind of you to say, but I don't think I'm the right person for the job."

Her face turned serious and she locked her eyes on mine. "That's exactly what makes you the best person for the job, the fact that you don't want it. It isn't about power for you."

I didn't know how to respond so I just gave her a polite smile.

"You're awake."

I spun around to see Ashton walking toward me. Butterflies filled my insides at the sight of him.

"Celeste explaining things to you?" he asked.

"A bit. Seems we have a new camp," I winced.

"What's wrong?" he asked, eyebrows creased in concern.

"Just a headache," I said, "I could really go for a good cup of tea right now."

Celeste's eyes widened and she grabbed my hand, pulling me with her before I could object. "Come on."

I stumbled after her. "What are you doing?" Just when I was starting to warm up to Celeste she decided to act like a crazy person.

She led me to a small tent barely large enough to fit a single person and pulled me inside.

"I'll wait out here," Ashton said before the flap closed behind us.

I narrowed my eyes at her. "What are we doing here?"

She rolled her eyes at me. "I know you don't like me, but have a little faith. Sit down." She pointed to a bed roll on the ground that took up most of the space inside. I wasn't even sure how we both fit in here. I pressed my lips together and considered walking out. With a sigh, I decided to humor her. She was one of Ashton's closest friends, after all. I probably needed to get used to having her around.

Celeste's back was to me, digging through something. When she turned to face me she was holding the small box I had seen at the trials. She handed it to me, smiling. "Go ahead."

I accepted the box from her and lifted an eyebrow in silent question.

"Open it, take the orb out, hold it for a minute. See if it helps." She mimed the process with her hands as she spoke.

I recalled the calm feeling the orb created last time I held it and curiosity led me to open the box. I held the warm, glowing purple orb in my hands and all of the tension in my hands melted away. The warmth spread up my arms to my shoulders, relaxing them, into my neck, my jaw, my head. Soon, my whole body felt relaxed and recovered. "This is amazing."

She inclined her head. "Thank you."

I placed the orb back into the box. My headache was completely gone. "Thank you, Celeste." I felt like I should say more, apologize even, but I wasn't sure where to go from here. I didn't have a lot of experience making friends.

"You two doing okay?" Ashton popped his head in the tent.

"Great," Celeste said, offering her hand to me. "The orb works, got rid of her headache."

"That's great!" Ashton held open the flap so Celeste and I could exit.

We walked back toward the heart of the new camp, back into the noise. This time, none of it bothered my head.

"We just have to get you going on that full size one, soon. We could sure use it," Ashton said. A shadow crossed his face and the humor left his eyes.

"What's wrong?" I reached my hand out to him, then pulled back.

His eyes flicked down to my hand for a moment, then back up at me. "They're planning an offensive attack. They want to try to take out the king before the Sardinian army can get here. And they still want to use you as the bait."

"It can't be that much worse than what we've already faced then, right? I mean, if it helps us bring him down sooner, it's worth it," I said.

He shook his head. "You know how I feel about you risking your life."

I reached my hand for his again and this time I grasped it in mine. "Then you're going to have to stick with me and help keep me alive."

Celeste cleared her throat and I felt my cheeks get hot. I dropped Ashton's hand and crossed my arms over my chest. Ashton took a step back from me and brushed a hand through his hair. Thanks to Celeste's warning, we appeared almost normal when Max reached us.

"You're awake," Max said. "Good. We have things to do." He paused in his step and looked at the three of us. His eyes narrowed for just a moment before going back to normal. "Ashton and Celeste, they need you with the other sorcerers. Etta, follow me."

I glanced back at Ashton as we were forced in opposite directions once again. The weight of marriage had been lifted, but it felt like they were purposefully keeping us apart. Max would never approve of the two of us. I sighed and picked up my pace to keep up with Max. *Never a dull moment.*

"We received some information this morning," Max said as we walked. "There is speculation that the king will be overseeing any action against you. That likely means Reapers."

"He's never done that before," I said. "He's just sent others. What about the protection on me?"

"My guess is that he's upset that the other attempts on your life have been unsuccessful. He probably wants to be the one in charge, even if he can't touch you."

My hands felt clammy. I knew the king couldn't touch me, but having him show up in the same place I was terrified me. So far, I'd faced Reapers and the King's Guards, but never at the same time. Would we be able to fight them all?

I followed Max to table outside the barn. A fabric covering shaded the table and those who stood around it. Seven men in armor surrounded the table, heads bowed as they studied a large map. When they heard me approach, all eyes lifted to focus on me.

Saffron was the only woman in the group. She smiled when I arrived. It made me feel better knowing that she was part of the group planning this offensive. When I offered to be the bait so we could take down some of the King's Guard, we didn't think the king would be participating. Now there was the real threat of the king himself showing up at any place he thought I might be. And he'd probably bring his Reapers. My fingers busied themselves with a fraying piece of fabric at my waist. I took a deep breath and tried to think of something more pleasant than undead monsters.

"Everybody, this is my sister, Etta." Max rested his hand on my shoulder and pushed me toward the table.

The men standing around the table bowed at me.

Dropping my hands to my side, I inclined my head to them but didn't speak. Max's heavy hand resting on my shoulder was a silent cue for me to stand there without comment.

He stood next to me against the table and began to share the plan. The fact that the king was going to take the lead in my destruction was apparently bringing joy to the group.

"We thought it would take years to get him out on a battlefield without his undead army. He won't think to prepare more than just some King's Guards and his sorcerers to take out a little girl," one of the armor clad men explained.

"We have to strike now while he thinks she's without the Ravens for support," said another.

"But they'll know she has sorcerer support. I'm sure he had loyalists at the Trials. And he'll know about the lightning. Everybody does. They're singing songs about her."

Max's grip on my shoulder tightened. I stepped away. *Songs about me?*

Max lifted his hands in the air to pause the conversation. "Then we need to get the word out there that it wasn't her. That she can't do magic. It was a set up to make her look more powerful."

Several of the men around the table nodded. Saffron narrowed her eyes. "I don't think that's necessary," she said. "The whole reason the king is going to oversee this is because he thinks she has power. He probably wants to be there to instruct his sorcerers on counter-spells since he can't cast against her himself. We need to show her as unafraid. Maybe even play up the princess thing. Make her look like she thinks she can get away with anything. Put her out in plain sight, without any fear."

I bit down on my lip and looked from Max to Saffron. He was actually going along with this? I wasn't sure if I should be happy or worried. How long had I waited to help? My stomach knotted. While I wanted the king gone, the thought of being out in the open, surrounded by sorcerers, was terrifying.

Max steepled his fingers under his chin, then nodded. "Saffron's right." He gestured to her. "Lay out your plan for us."

A half smile flickered on her face for a moment before she got serious again. She began to explain the plan while the men listened with rapt attention. I tried to focus as much as I could on the different parts but my mind kept replaying my interactions with the Reapers. Max still didn't know about the arctic fire. They wanted to keep me hidden, but I could help.

"And this is where you will be." He pointed to Luxor, the town we had been in last night. "You will be stopping in several shops and making it very clear you are there. We need a lot of witnesses. The people of Luxor are supportive of the Ravens and have an exit strategy for when the king and his guards arrive."

Max continued to explain the plan. "Meanwhile, we'll be drawing guards to the cities of Marina and Taurin while we set up our traps at Luxor. It should help us to disable the King's Guard enough to bring them down."

"What about the Reapers?" I asked.

Max raised an eyebrow. He set down the stick he had been using as a pointer. "We anticipate they'll be with the king."

"And where will I be?" I looked to the map, wondering if any of the small stones or blocks were supposed to represent me.

"We'll have you back here where it's safe after you've made your appearance." Max smiled at me. I didn't like it when he tried to play the part of the concerned big brother. It wasn't natural for him.

Nobody else is going to die for me. I took a deep breath. *Time to reveal my secret.* "I'm the only one who can take down the Reapers," I said.

I heard a few murmurs as people realized what I had said.

Max smiled at me indulgently. "I heard about your lightning and while that is an impressive trick, it was probably beginner's luck. Besides, it won't work on Reapers."

I shook my head. "You don't know everything about me."

Saffron locked eyes with me, then turned to Max. "It's true. She can take down the Reapers. I've seen it."

I could feel the weight of everybody's eyes on me. I looked down, feeling overwhelmed by the pressure and expectation.

"And you didn't feel the need to tell this to me sooner?" Max said through clenched teeth.

"We haven't had a chance to talk since the attack on the Ravens," she said calmly.

Max placed his hand on my shoulder, using a gentler voice. "How do you get rid of them?"

I looked up, reluctantly and blew out a breath. *Here goes nothing.* "I can make arctic fire."

Max's mouth pulled into a tight line and he stared at me for a long moment.

"She is the daughter of the king," somebody across from me said.

CHAPTER 27

Fire flashed in Max's eyes. He was furious with me. "Why didn't you tell me you found your element?"

"I'm sorry," I whispered.

Max stared at me for a moment. His eyes softened and he took a deep breath. He turned to address the group. "Clearly in our efforts to stay alive the last few weeks, we had some communication issues. If Etta does indeed have the ability to create arctic fire, and control it, we may have to revise our plans."

I looked at each man around the table. Their attention seemed more focused on me now than on my brother. I could feel something shifting but I wasn't sure what it was.

"Etta, you'll need to go to Master Flanders. See if he can help you to wield and control this *special* talent of yours," Max said.

I flinched at the word special. There was still anger, or maybe envy in his voice, and it made me uncomfortable. I was so excited to have found a family when I discovered I had a brother. But so far, it hadn't turned out the way I'd hoped it might. My shoulders dropped. I felt like I'd let him down somehow. Or like I had hurt his feelings. Maybe I was wrong to keep it from him for so long. Before Max could say anything else, I walked away from the table.

I found Master Flanders sitting alone on the roof of the barn. From this vantage, he could see the whole camp and all of its busy, chaotic progress. He didn't even turn to look at me as I approached. I sat next to him and embraced the relative silence of the rooftop. I took a deep breath and looked down at the pendant around my neck.

Closing my eyes, I allowed myself a few minutes to consider what my life might be like if I didn't wear this necklace. If I was just a peasant girl living with her grandmother. I'd have woken up this morning and eaten breakfast with my grandmother. We would have harvested vegetables from our garden and maybe gone into town to trade for some other goods. Maybe I'd flirt with one of the boys in town or gossip with some of the girls.

I sighed. My life had never been like that. I'd never had any friends until Saffron found me. My thoughts flashed to Saffron, then to Ashton. Now that they were a part of my life, could I ever go back to a time without them? Was it worth having the quiet, peaceful life of peasant in order to be safe from harm? Would I trade the few precious kisses from Ashton for a life of vegetable gardens and embroidery by candlelight?

I shook my head. *No.* I couldn't go back to that life, even if it was a choice. I had come too far. I could shoot a bow and I could make a plant grow with my hands. I could call on a thunderstorm and make somebody tell the truth. I had Ashton, however brief our time might be, those kisses, it was worth it. And I was going to keep fighting for more.

Steeling myself, I opened my eyes. I dropped my legs to the ground and sat up straight. When I turned to look at Master Flanders he was already looking at me with a smile on his face.

"Looks like you've figured something out," he said.

I nodded. "Yes, I have. I need to learn how to control my arctic fire."

He smiled. "I've been waiting for you to ask for a while. I'm glad you're finally ready."

A crowd gathered around me as I stood behind the barn with Master Flanders. I tried to hide the self-conscious feeling sweeping through me at having an audience watch me learn how to use my magic. So far, all of my training had been done privately. It was a big change to have everybody standing around and whispering about the girl who could make Reapers go away.

I took a deep breath in and bent my knees to sink into my stance. I raised my hands and concentrated. I felt the heat well up inside me, felt the tingle of magic, but the cold was missing. I released my stance and dropped my arms to my side. The people around me groaned. They wanted a show.

"I can't feel it." I rubbed my eyes with my palms. "I feel the heat, but not the cold."

"It's okay," Master Flanders assured me. "It's a very complicated bit of magic. When you did it before, your life was in danger. You had adrenaline to push you."

I shook my hands out and paced in a circle. "It's so frustrating." I had been working on this for an hour already. A few of the people in the crowd gave up and walked away. It was a relief to see them go.

"Maybe I can't do it in front of people yet," I mused.

"We can go." A man in the crowd offered but made no movement to actually leave.

Master Flanders lifted his hand. "No, that's not necessary. If you can bring this about with the pressure of a crowd and control it, we can get you to stop passing out after you use it."

"I need a minute." I sat down on the ground and cradled my face in my hands. *Think. How can you make this happen?*

A gentle hand on my shoulder brought me out of my head. I looked up to see Ashton. He reached a hand down to help me stand. "Not going so well?"

I laughed. "That's an understatement." I lowered my voice, "I'm starting to worry that maybe I never even did it in the first place. Like maybe I imagined it."

He laughed back. "You did it. Twice. I was there, I can tell you that you did it."

The crowd had thinned while I sat in the grass. I was grateful. *Maybe if I wait a bit longer the rest of them will leave.*

Ashton leaned in so he could whisper in my ear. "You can do this. I know you can." He walked away to give me some space.

His confidence stirred something inside me. I took a deep breath and turned away from Ashton and the other observers. I closed my eyes and visualized myself creating the arctic fire. What if I couldn't ever do it again? I shook my head, trying to dispel my doubts. My heartbeat quickened. What if the Reapers came back and I couldn't save anybody? I pictured the first time they came. Ashton trying to face them alone. If I hadn't stepped in, he wouldn't be here. Fear and anger welled up inside me and I felt an icy chill run through my veins. The corner of my mouth turned up in a smile. *The ice has returned.*

I took a step back and lifted my hands. I could feel the ice running through my veins. Then the heat came, it stung but I powered through. I imagined that I was the only thing between my friends and the Reapers. I wasn't going to let anybody else die for me. I thought of Master Edward and the feeling intensified.

I pushed the icy heat through my hands and the blue flames erupted. I formed the flames into a ball and lifted it above me before letting it come crashing down. Then I closed my hands, extinguishing the flames. I collapsed on the ground, exhausted, but conscious.

Ashton ran to me and wrapped his arms around me. "Stay with me."

My breathing was heavy and the world spun. I was fighting to stay conscious. "I did it."

He hugged me tight.

I was so excited I planted a kiss on his cheek. I didn't really care who was watching. *I can create arctic fire whenever I want. I can control the fire. Now I just need to get stronger.*

*****

The attack would take place in a few days. We planned to strike against the two guard stations nearest Luxor shortly after I started making my presence obvious in town. The hope was that the guard stations would not be able to send reinforcements. Dealing with the king, whatever army he brought, his sorcerers and Reapers was enough.

Ashton still wasn't pleased with the plan, but I doubted he would be happy with any plan that involved using me as bait.

"It's going to be fine, Ashton." I was in my now regular place behind the barn working on managing my fire. In the last couple of days, the crowd of people watching me had disappeared as everybody prepared for the upcoming attack. Most of the time I practiced alone. Today's practice time with Ashton was a rare gift. Making arctic fire was getting easier every time I worked on it. I was able to create it faster and recover faster after each use.

Ashton frowned and crossed his arms. "I'd feel better if I was going with you."

I let go of the arctic fireball I was holding in my hands and dropped my hands to my side. "You know you can't do that. Micah knows who you are, and he knows what kind of power you have. Besides, Celeste can handle it."

Celeste and I had spent some time together over the last couple of days, and we were surprisingly forming a friendship. It was helped by the stories she told me about the sorcerer she trained with growing up. She was so clearly in love with him, that I no longer felt jealous of her spending time with Ashton.

"Ashton." I put my hands on his shoulders. "You have to let me do this and you have to support me." I dropped my hands. "I can't do this without your support."

He sighed. "Fine. I know you can do this. I just didn't want you to." One side of his mouth lifted in a sideways smile. "I have a feeling I'll never be able to keep you from doing anything."

"I think you're starting to learn," I teased him.

Celeste called out to us. I turned to see her rounding the corner of the barn.

"How's it coming?" she asked.

"I'm getting better," I said. "Faster."

"That's great." She smiled at me. "You're going to need the speed this time, I imagine. Plus, I don't want to die so it's in my interest for you to get it right."

I laughed at her. "I see where your concern comes from."

Celeste radiated an optimism that I hadn't seen much of lately. She was also a very powerful sorceress. She squeezed in a few lessons with me, teaching me spells that she thought I might be able to use if I happened to be captured or cornered.

"I'll take over, Ashton." She nodded to him. "Max asked for you."

Ashton nodded back and glanced around. Seeing that we were still alone, he gave me a soft kiss on my cheek before he walked away. We hadn't had any real privacy since the trials but I cherished even the slightest reminder of how he felt about me. I watched him walk around the barn, out of sight.

Celeste clapped her hands together. "Now where did we leave off?"

I pursed my lips and thought back to our stolen hour of practice time yesterday. "Shield spells."

"That's right. We learned how to make a shield around just you. Today I want to show you how to expand the shield so you can protect people around you. You know, just in case."

"That's perfect." The one thing that kept driving me in my practice with the arctic fire was my desire to protect my friends. It was the only way I found the strength to offer myself as bait.

I got into my sorcerer stance and held out my arms, palms pushing outward. Celeste stood next to me.

"Okay, now just like yesterday but you need to add me to your shield. Picture it expanding, picture both of us in the bubble of protection."

I concentrated and felt the tingle of magic move from my fingers and down my arms. I could feel the shield spreading from my hands and encasing me. I pushed it further and felt it expanding.

"You've got it," Celeste encouraged. "Keep pushing."

I closed my eyes and focused.

"There." Celeste reached out her hand, her fingers brushed against the shimmery shield I created. "Great job. I hope you never need to use this, but you never know."

I smiled and released the shield. It was hard to hold it. I was breathing heavily. When Celeste showed me how to do this, she held it for a really long time. "How did you hold that so long yesterday?"

"It's all about practice. Remember, I've been training with magic since I was four years old. You just started."

"You knew you wanted to be a sorceress at four?" I asked.

She shrugged. "I didn't really have a choice. Where I grew up, if you had magical ability, you started training with a tutor at four. When I was six, I was sent to the Sorcery Academy. It was nearly full time training until I was old enough to take the trials."

"Did you ever go home and see your family?" I wondered what it would be like to have a family you never saw.

"They visited me for holidays. It's just how it is." She shrugged again. "I didn't know anything else."

"Are there a lot of sorcerers in Gallia?" Maybe we should be focusing on forging a stronger alliance with them.

"Not any more than other kingdoms. But we train anybody with magical ability in the schools, not just nobility. So maybe we have more trained sorcerers." She looked a little sad.

"I'm sorry." I looked down briefly. "I keep asking you questions about your home while you are stuck here with us. You must miss it."

She shook her head. "I'm here because I want to be here. Ashton is my oldest friend, which means you're my friend, too. For years, I've been hearing from Ashton what it's like for your people. My country is peaceful. I can't imagine living in fear of your own king. It needs to change and I want to help."

"Thank you," I said. I didn't have words strong enough to express how I felt.

"Besides," she added. "You're half Gallic."

My brow creased and I stared at her. I'd never thought of that before. Most of the conversation around my family was centered on my father. My mother was rarely mentioned. Maybe people here didn't know as much about her since she was from Gallia. "Do you know anything about my mother?"

Celeste pursed her lips and looked up, thinking. "Not really. I was very young when she became Illaria's queen."

"Do all children in Gallia get tested for magic, even royals?" I asked.

"Yes, they are. It's a big part of our culture," she said.

The thought of my mother training in sorcery warmed my heart. *Maybe I'm following in her footsteps.*

CHAPTER 28

I took a deep breath. *Today's the day.* Saffron pulled the ribbon on my corset tighter and I gasped.

"Sorry, but we need you to look the part today." She let out some slack and then tied it up.

"How am I supposed to fight in this thing?" I tried to wiggle a little and struggled to move.

"You don't." She brushed my long hair away from my face and pulled it into a gold net at the base of my head. "You'll be able to change after you've caused enough gossip."

"What if the king just shows up?" I swallowed. I had seen my fair share of sorcerers teleporting from one location to another with no effort.

"He won't right away. There aren't any sorcerers in that town to get information to him quickly. It's a half day's ride to the nearest guard station, which will be under our control. And it's a full day's ride to the castle from there. You'll have at least a day and a half before he arrives."

My stomach had been in knots all morning, making me feel nauseous. I closed my eyes and went over the plan in my head again. I was to act the part of a noble lady out with a friend for a day in town. The fact that two women were on their own in town without male escorts would draw enough suspicion that people would start to talk. After letting my pendant slip a few times, people would figure out who I was. We didn't want the king to know we were drawing him in, but we had to get people to discover me. A lot of people. The more people who knew, the greater the chance that somebody loyal to the king would go to tell him.

I touched my hair and frowned. I didn't enjoy having my hair pinned up on my head. I knew I'd end up with a headache before the day's end.

An entire corner of the small tent we were sitting in was taken up by the dress and cloak I had to wear. I sighed as I glared at it. "Let's get this over with."

Saffron helped me into the gown. "Don't you think this is a bit excessive?" I lifted a sleeve and ran my finger over the pearls sewn around the cuff.

"We want you to stand out," she reminded me.

"That won't be a problem," I said under my breath.

Somebody outside of the tent cleared their throat. "You dressed?"

My heart jumped. It was Ashton.

"Come on in." Saffron pulled open the tent flap.

There was barely enough room for the three of us to stand in the tent.

Ashton's eyes traveled from my head to my feet. He lifted his eyebrows. "You look like a princess."

Saffron placed a hand on each of our shoulders. "You have two minutes. That's all I can do. Do not mess up the dress or her hair." She left us alone in the tent.

Ashton stared at me for a moment. "You look beautiful, but I think I prefer the real you."

That was probably the best thing he could have said. I smiled at him. "I'm nervous."

"You'll be great." He tilted my chin up to him and lowered his face to mine. The kiss was hard, hungry, intense. It was like a floodgate had been opened and everything we wanted to do over the last few days was suddenly possible. His hands roamed my body, exploring places they had never been. I ran my fingers through his hair and wrapped my arms him around him.

He moved his mouth down to my neck, kissing me on the sensitive skin. He kissed the exposed skin of my shoulder, under my chin, my collar bone. Shivers ran through my body and I pulled him in tight, resting my head on his strong chest.

"You'll be there, right?" The brave facade I had been putting on for everybody else was collapsing around me. He was the only person I could show my fear to.

He took hold of my hands and stared deep into my eyes. "I"ll be watching every step you take. I promise." He pulled me in for another tight hug.

I closed my eyes and breathed him in. I wanted to carry this memory with me, no matter what happened after I left this tent. "Our time is probably up." I felt a lump rising in my throat. *If something goes wrong.* I couldn't think like that. *It's going to be fine.* "I'll see you soon." I couldn't handle saying goodbye. That seemed too final.

He kissed me again. This time, it was softer, his mouth barely touching mine. He lingered, his mouth less than an inch from mine, warm breath against my skin. I didn't want it to end. Finally, he pulled away and I sighed, every inch of my body aching for more.

"See you soon," he said. He squeezed my hand then left the tent.

I swallowed back the tears that were threatening to rise up. If everything went according to plan I wouldn't see him again for two days. If things didn't go according to plan, I might never see him again. I cursed silently. *Where were these thoughts coming from?* As we drew nearer to the moment of truth, my confidence was waning. I needed to fight the dark thoughts, keep them away. I squared my shoulders and lifted my chin. *I can do this.* I walked out of the tent into the sunshine. Saffron was waiting for me.

"I'm ready," I said.

She nodded. "Good. There are only a few hours of daylight left. It's time."

Celeste was dressed in a gown only slightly less ornate than my own. Master Flanders gripped our hands and I closed my eyes as the familiar darkness of teleportation descended. I clenched my jaw and before I could take a breath, we were outside of Luxor.

"Good luck, ladies." Master Flanders squeezed my hand.

"You won't be alone. Our eyes are already in town."

"Thank you, for everything," I said.

"Don't get sentimental on me now." He smiled. "You are the strongest sorceress I have ever met. You'll be just fine."

I nodded.

"Take care of each other," he said as the gray smoke enveloped him.

We were alone. Celeste pulled her hood up over her head. "Ready?"

I pulled up my hood. "Now or never." I closed my fingers around the pendant clearly prominent against my chest. I dropped it, feeling a rush of butterflies in my stomach at the thought of leaving it exposed. If only my grandmother could see me now.

Our first stop was the nicest inn, The Tiger Lily. We entered and Celeste set an elegant, blue silk coin purse on the counter. The woman behind the counter looked up, eyebrows raised at the sight of the bulging purse.

"How can I help you, ladies?" she asked.

"We would like your best room for the evening." Celeste allowed her Gallic accent to come out as she spoke. I bit down on my lower lip to keep from laughing at the scene. Most of the time Celeste spoke Illarian with no trace of her Gallic tongue. She sounded like a different person.

The woman raised an eyebrow. "Just the two of you? No escorts?"

Celeste lifted the purse. "We'd appreciate your discretion." She lowered her voice. "Sometimes us ladies just need a break from all of the expectations," she glanced at me, "and pressure of everyday life."

The woman looked from Celeste to her purse. "Of course, my lady." She inclined her head in a slight bow.

Celeste pulled out a gold coin. Probably enough money to cover a week's stay at the inn. She passed the coin to the woman. "For your kindness."

The woman's cheeks flushed and she covered the coin with her hand. Her eyes traveled around the room, then she tucked it in her bodice. I caught her gaze fall on my pendant, she flinched, then looked back at Celeste. She cleared her throat. "I'm Bethany. If there is anything I can do to make your stay more comfortable, please let me know."

"Thank you, Bethany," Celeste said. "We have some business in town. Will you have our room ready for us when we return?"

Bethany inclined her head. "Of course."

Was she reacting to my pendant or the gold? I kept my face expressionless and followed Celeste out of the inn.

"That went well," Celeste said. "We might not need to go anywhere else. She might be turning you in right now."

"Probably not after that coin you gave her," I said.

"Did I give her too much?" Celeste asked. "The money in Gallia is different."

I laughed. "Maybe I should take over the purse. You gave her enough for her to buy food for a month."

We stopped in front of a dressmaker's shop. I eyed the simple dresses in the window with envy. "Let's go buy something more comfortable."

When we entered the shop, all three of the seamstresses froze. I knew what they were staring at. The dresses we were wearing would have taken a team of seamstresses months to construct. Even one dress of this quality would keep a shop like this running for a whole year.

One of the women came to her senses. "Good morning, ladies." She dipped into a curtsy.

"Good morning." I inclined my head toward her. "My sister and I are visiting your town for the day and found that we didn't pack anything for travel. Do you have anything ready we could purchase?"

"I'm afraid we don't have anything as grand as you might want." She lowered her eyes.

Celeste waved her hand dismissively. "We don't want grand. We want comfortable. These dresses draw too much attention."

The woman nodded and gestured for us to stand on the

raised platforms in the corner for measurements. She called her ladies over and they brought measuring tapes. A mousy woman with light brown hair started to take my measurements. She froze when she came face to face with my pendant. Her breath caught. I looked away, pretending not to notice her gaze locked on my family's crest.

This close to the king's castle, the people of Luxor had been in the path of the Battle of the Dead. They knew the history even if it wasn't supposed to be talked about. They would know the crest of the old king.

I risked a look down and noticed that the other two women were now staring at my pendant. I cleared my throat and she went back to taking measurements. *I think we found the right place.*

We left the seamstress with a couple of boxes of simple skirts and blouses that were already prepared. Probably for somebody else who had ordered them. The generous payment we left would make up for the unhappy customers.

We dropped the packages off at the inn with Bethany. Having packages to return to made our stay more believable. I longed to change into the more comfortable clothes, but it wasn't time yet. We had to wait for the signal.

As much as I was dreading the king and his Reapers, I was hoping that the seamstress or one of her ladies was on their way to him now. The longer we waited, the more time I had to imagine all of the terrible possibilities ahead.

Celeste seemed to be just as restless as I was so we decided that going to a busy tavern for dinner would be one of our best ways to get noticed while not having to keep smiles plastered on our faces. Bethany provided the name of a location and we found our way there.

"This corset is stabbing me," I whispered to Celeste.

"I know." She rubbed her side. "Mine too."

As we walked, my fingers began to tingle. I stopped mid-stride.

"I feel it, too," Celeste said.

I reached for her hand and pulled her into an alley. We cut through the alleyway and the tingle in my fingers started spreading to my arms.

"It's getting stronger," I said.

We exited the alley onto a busy street lined with vendors selling from tables and tents.

"This way." Celeste threaded her arm through mine and we walked into the crowd, arms linked.

My eyes darted from side to side as we cut our way through the crowd. I searched the faces we passed for familiar ones or for anybody who looked too interested in us.

Out of the corner of my eye, I saw pink sparks fly up in the sky. My heart rate quickened. *The seamstresses sent word to the king.*

"It's time." I lifted my chin toward the sparks.

Celeste nodded.

We turned into another alley and tried a door. It was unlocked. Celeste peeked behind the door then stepped inside. I followed her.

We were in a back storage room. The room was small and dark. A strong, spicy scent filled my nose. A curtain separated the space we were occupying from the rest of the building. I pulled back the curtain and peered beyond. It was a small store with shelves full of bags of powder. Spices. As my eyes adjusted to the dim light I saw that the room we were in contained large barrels, boxes, and bags of spices.

We started to peel off the dresses and I breathed a sigh of relief as I untied the corset. The tunic and pants under the dress gave me a feeling of freedom. I roughly pulled the netting out of my hair and tucked my hair into the cap that had been hidden in my skirts. Though my face was too feminine to allow me to pass as a man, I would be far less conspicuous in this clothing. I helped Celeste with her own cap and we looked around for somewhere to hide the gowns.

I pulled the lid off of a barrel and found that it was nearly empty. I shoved the gowns inside. *The merchant is sure going to have a surprise when he opens that.*

We snuck back into the alleyway and headed for our meeting point at the far end of town. Word was out and if all went as planned, the king would be here tomorrow.

CHAPTER 29

Celeste and I reached our destination, an old pottery mill on the edge of town, without incident. The tingle of magic never left my fingers and occasionally flared up my arms. My stomach twisted. It wouldn't be long before we'd be facing the Reapers. I swallowed back the nausea threatening to surface.

Madame Lyndsey was waiting for us at the mill. Her face was dark, eyes grim as we approached.

Something is wrong.

She stretched her hands out to us. "Quickly, take my hands. We're going back."

"This isn't the plan." My eyes darted around for some reason for the change.

"No time to explain. Hold on." It was an order.

We grabbed for her hands and before I could imagine why we would leave, my feet touched down on soft grass.

I pulled my hand out and rounded on her. "What happened? Why did you change the plan?"

"You didn't feel it?" She narrowed her eyes at me, knowing the answer already.

My shoulders dropped. We were so close.

"We didn't know that one of his sorcerers was in town. They put out a tracing spell. It would have led them right to you. All element of surprise gone. The king could have just sent his Reapers right to you." Her eyes softened. "I'm sorry."

I pushed my hair out of my eyes and dropped my hands at my side. This was so frustrating. Then my breath caught in my chest. The people of Luxor.

I gripped Madame Lindsey's arm. "What are we doing to help the people of Luxor? If the king arrives with his Reapers, they won't stand a chance."

She looked down. "I don't know yet. We might not be able to do anything. We can't risk putting you in mortal danger."

"This is not what I agreed to." I glared at her. After everything I've done, how could they do this to me? Nobody else can take out the Reapers. They need me. *Max*. This was all Max.

I could hardly get the words out though my clenched jaw. "I never would have agreed to put all of those lives in danger. We have to help. You have to take us back there. The king is probably already there."

Madame Lyndsey put her hands up to stop me. "You know I can't do that. I'm afraid they want to keep you here."

I looked at Celeste. "I'm right, aren't I? We have to get back there."

She clenched her fists at her side and lifted her chin. "Whatever you want to do, I'm with you."

If Madame Lyndsey wasn't going to help me, I'd find somebody who would. I broke into a run, heading for the barn. It was empty so I kept running. *There has to be somebody here who can help us get back to town.* I went from tent to tent and couldn't find anybody. The place was a ghost town. *Where is everybody?*

Panting, I stopped running. Celeste by my side, just as winded.

"Nobody's here." Panic spread through me. *They lied to me.* "Celeste, do you have anything to do with this?"

She shook her head. "I have no idea what's going on."

"They lied to me. *To us.* They never planned on having me help. They're going to try to take on the king without us." Heat burned in my chest. Fists clenched, I let out a scream. *How dare they.* I wasn't the same weak girl that Saffron saved from the King's Guard. I was tired of being treated like a child.

"Why would they do this to me?" I asked. I turned on Celeste and grabbed her arms, squeezing too tightly. "What's happening there without us? Nobody can stop the Reapers. We have to get back."

"They know that I can't teleport yet. We have to convince Madame Lyndsey." Celeste took off at a sprint and I followed her.

Madame Lyndsey was gone. I cursed.

"Celeste." I grabbed her hand. "You have to get us there. You can do this. I know you can."

Her eyes widened. "I've only done it once before. And never with another person."

"That doesn't matter. There's always a first for everything." I squeezed her hand. "Take us to the Inn. They'll never expect us to go there. They'll assume it was a set up."

She swallowed hard and closed her eyes. "Here goes. Hold on tight." She crushed my fingers in her grip.

Gray smoke rose up around us and I held my breath. The world went dark and I felt that familiar nausea that came with teleporting. I let out a sigh of relief when my feet hit solid ground. We were both standing at the entryway of the inn. I took a deep breath.

"You did it." I covered my mouth to keep a laugh from escaping.

"I did it." Celeste let out a breath and took a moment to compose herself.

Bethany was still manning the front desk. She stared at us, jaw dropped open in surprise. I put my finger to my mouth to tell her to stay quiet. Closing her mouth, she nodded.

"Go and hide, Bethany. Get somewhere safe," I whispered.

She pulled a key from a wall of hooks behind her and tossed it to me. "In case you need somewhere to go."

I caught the key and closed my fingers around it. "Thank you."

"Good luck, your highness," she whispered.

Celeste and I headed up the stairs toward the room. Inside, we found the packages that we had purchased. Digging through them we found what we were looking for, two simple brown cloaks. We put them on and pulled up our hoods.

Despite the fact that I knew we couldn't hide from the king's magic, the cloaks made me feel better. They might be enough to buy us a little bit of cover.

"You ready?" I asked.

"Let's go."

As soon as we opened the door to the room, I was hit by a wave of magic. My entire body tingled. The king was here, somehow I could feel him. Then the cold hit me, making me gasp.

"What's wrong?" Celeste whispered.

"The Reapers. They're close by." My stomach tightened and I swallowed hard. I focused on the thoughts I needed to make the arctic fire. I needed to protect my friends. Celeste, Ashton, Saffron, Max. I couldn't let anything happen to them. My body was vibrating with energy and the cold intensified. I knew it was my own ice building up inside me rather than a response to the Reapers.

The tingle of magic was more intense than I had ever felt. Long shadows filled the alleyway as we walked noiselessly toward the edge of town. Every so often I got a peek at the main streets and shops. They were empty. We were told that the town was made up of many who were loyal to the Ravens and they would get to safe places. I didn't realize how effective the hiding would be.

Being alone in the silence of a town the size of Luxor was unsettling. Eerie quiet had replaced the usual sounds of the town. I expected to see Reapers at every corner. The alleyway dead-ended as we neared the edge of town. We were forced onto the main roads. I pulled the cloak up around me tighter as we walked along the abandoned street.

The twilight ahead of us was glowing and it wasn't from the last bits of daylight. Flames illuminated the sky in bursts. As we put the town behind us, the flames grew stronger. It wasn't a natural fire, it was sorcerer fire. The scent of smoke filled my nostrils and my whole body tensed.

The sound of yelling traveled through the still evening air. From where we stood, it was impossible to tell who was making the sound. *The attack is happening right now.* All I could think of was my friends facing off against the king's sorcerers. Or worse, his Reapers. I didn't wait for Celeste, I ran, focused on getting to my friends as quickly as possible.

The sky was darkening quickly, but the illumination from the sorcerer fire flying back and forth cast shadows over the figures engaged in battle. Pausing to catch my breath, I squinted into the smoky air, trying to find somebody I recognized. People were running from place to place and it was difficult to concentrate with the noise of the battle.

Celeste caught up to me, just as breathless as me. She leaned over and put her hands on her knees, taking deep breaths. "What's happening?"

I was still trying to make out where my friends were in the chaos in front of me. Golden curls caught my eye, and I stood on my tip-toes, straining to make out the figures in-between the flashes of firelight. *Saffron.* She was engaged in a sword fight with a tall man wearing the armor of the King's Guard.

I shouted to Celeste over the din of the battle, "There's Saffron."

Following Saffron, I was able to locate a crude line being held by the Ravens and the few sorcerers who had come with them. Saffron and the Ravens were out front, Max and the other sorcerers were behind them. The Ravens attacked the King's Guard while the sorcerers threw whatever element they favored at the opposing sorcerers. For now, the sorcerers seemed to be focused on one another rather than the other people who were present in the battle.

Scanning the line, I searched for Ashton. A lump rose in my throat. *He's not there. Where is he?* My heart pounded in my chest. *He has to be here.*

"There's Ashton," Celeste yelled, pointing to a tall man with honey-blonde hair.

I let out a sigh of relief, then instantly tensed up again. The tingle from the Reapers was still lingering. We weren't close enough to the battle to see all of the details. I needed to get closer yet, but I didn't want to draw the Reapers out to my friends.

A cheer rose up from our line and I narrowed my eyes on the scene in front of me. It looked like one of the king's sorcerers went down along with several of his guards. From our vantage point, it looked like we were winning. *It seemed too easy.*

"I'm going to help," Celeste called to me.

I nodded. "I'm looking for the Reapers. Promise me, if you see them, you run."

"I will." She ran toward the front line and positioned herself near Madame Lyndsey.

I searched the sky, the space around me, and behind me. I knew they had to be here, waiting.

The chill of the Reapers crashed through me like a wave, pulling me toward the battle. My breath caught in my chest, as if I had been drenched with cold water. They were close, I could feel them. Gray smoke from across the field spread o'er the ground toward my friends. *Time to go.* No more waiting, I had to get there. I pushed my way to the front line. My breathing was coming fast and shallow.

As I reached the line, the sky darkened. All the fire was gone. In the faint light of the moon, the remaining King's Guard ran from us, toward the king's sorcerers. The Ravens were left there, standing in the dark. The attacks ceased. I found Max staring at his hands in bewilderment.

"What's happening?" I asked. I took a few deep breaths, steadying myself. *Something isn't right.* My eyes darted around in the darkness, trying to make sense of what was happening. Somebody stepped on a twig near me, the noise sounding too loud. My heart felt as if it were trying to break out of my chest. I spun around, then let out a sigh. It was just Madame Lyndsey. I tried to calm myself down. All of my senses were overloaded as I prepared for something to jump out of the darkness.

Max looked at his hands then looked at me. "You're not supposed to be here."

"Well, I am so tell me what's going on," I yelled.

"Something's wrong," he started, "my magic's gone." He

lifted his hands like he was trying to call his fire. Nothing happened.

A chill deeper than I had ever experienced before came over me. Four hooded figures glided across the field. The Reapers.

I looked at the helpless sorcerers around me and anger burned inside me. I knew it was probably pointless, but I reached inside myself to feel for that fire. My insides burned with heat and the ice flooded my veins. *My magic is still here.* I stepped in front of Max, ignoring him calling out to me. The blue flames started to crackle in my hands as I walked toward the hooded figures.

I could smell the death they carried with them and concentrated on breathing through my mouth. *You are not going to hurt my friends.* I took a few more steps toward them, then slowly raised my hands. The flames shot from my palms, freezing the Reapers in their path. I started to feel light headed, but pushed through it, reaching to my toes to find any power that had not been used. The light was so bright it illuminated the entire field as if it were daylight.

Consciousness was slipping from me and I knew I had reached my limit. Releasing the flame, I collapsed to my knees, fighting to remain alert. My eyes took a moment to adjust to the darkness now that the flames were gone. I didn't see the Reapers anywhere in sight. I pushed the sweat tinged hair from my face and sucked in breaths in rapid succession.

The sound of a single person clapping echoed through the wide open space. A dark hooded figure slowly walked toward me. I tried to push myself to standing but collapsed back onto my knees. I wasn't strong enough yet. It was taking everything I had to stay conscious.

I glanced behind me but all I could see was darkness. My friends were gone. My heart was pounding in my ears. *This is it. This is how I die.* I lifted my chin, at least I'd die with some dignity.

The hooded figure was only steps away from me now. When the hood was pushed back I could make out the dark features of a bearded man in the dim light. He knelt down next to me.

The king.

"I must say, Etta, you have been exceedingly difficult to kill. Now that I've seen your power, I understand why that is. You are everything I hoped you would be."

His words didn't make sense, but in my state I didn't know if I could even trust my own ears. All I knew was that he'd been trying to kill me for weeks. He was probably here to finish the job. I kept my jaw set in defiant silence. I wasn't about to beg for my life. Though, I wasn't above begging for the lives of my friends.

I swallowed. "Be done with it then, just let my friends live."

His mouth turned upward and a row of perfectly white teeth showed in his smile. I shuddered. There was something so unnatural about his smile.

"You know I can't touch you, Etta," he said.

"You had no problems sending in your guards and your Reapers to finish me." I didn't recognize my voice. It was defiant, I sounded *brave*. My fingernails dug into my palms and I forced my mouth into a tight line. I might have sounded brave, but inside, I was screaming.

"Not today, Etta. You've earned at least that much. But I will expect you at my castle for dinner tomorrow. I assume you got my invitation?" He turned his hand in the air and produced a scroll just like the one I found on the raven's leg. I pulled away from it as if it were poisonous.

"Why would I come to dinner at your castle? So you can kill me there?" I said.

"I can guarantee your safety at dinner. However, I cannot guarantee the safety of your friends if you do not show." The smile turned to an exaggerated frown.

I looked away from him. *He knows exactly how to hurt me.* I was willing to die for my friends. Not wanting to show weakness, I locked my eyes on his. "I'll be there."

He stood. "Good. You may bring a guest, but not that meddlesome brother of yours." He dissolved in a cloud of gray smoke.

"Etta!"

"Wilona!"

I turned around to see a large group of people running toward me, crying out frantically. In front on me, the king and his sorcerers were gone. Only the Ravens remained in the field. I tried to push myself up to standing again and instantly felt dizzy. Staying seated was probably my only option right now. They could come to me.

Ashton was the first to reach me. He dropped down next to me and lightly touched my arm. It was as if he was afraid he'd break me. "Are you hurt? What were you thinking?" His voice was high pitched with panic.

I took hold of one of his hands in mine, giving it a squeeze. It was all I had the energy to do. "I'm fine. Just tired." I sighed. "I'll need help getting back."

"What happened?" he asked me quietly as people circled around us.

"I'll tell you later." I locked my eyes on his. He didn't press the issue.

Max knelt down next to me and Ashton moved away from me. I wanted to tell him to stay. I didn't want him out of my sight. But Max was in charge. He set his hand on my shoulder. "How did you do that?"

"I'm not sure," I said.

"You made them all go away," he said.

He hadn't seen the king.

CHAPTER 30

My head was throbbing and each step I took felt like I was carrying a hundred pound sack on my back. I winced every time I moved. I was grateful to Saffron, who had convinced Max to let me rest before he began interrogating me.

I turned over on the blanket, trying to find a comfortable position. It wasn't happening. Despite my exhaustion, my mind wouldn't let go of my conversation with the king. He was expecting me tomorrow. I turned again, unable to make the king's face leave my mind. How was I going to explain this to Max? He would never agree to let me go. *But if I don't go, the king will keep killing the people I care about.* I pressed my palms into my temples hoping for some relief from the pain. Using the arctic fire made my entire body hurt. I wondered if Celeste was still awake. *I could use that orb right about now.* I sighed. *If she's asleep, I don't want to wake her.*

None of this had gone the way we hoped. I laid back down on the blanket. There wasn't anything I could do about it tonight. *Tomorrow I'll tell Max the truth. And then I'll go to the castle. There is no way around it. I won't let him stop me.*

Somehow, my body finally beat out my mind and I sunk into sleep. It was a restless sleep. In my dreams, the king appeared and turned into a dragon that swallowed up all of my friends one at a time before finally turning his massive jaws on me. I woke up drenched in sweat.

The sun had already broken through the horizon and the sky was a warm orange color. I half expected it to be a gray, colorless day. It didn't seem right to have such a cheerful sky when my insides were churning with fear and anxiety.

The Ravens were already awake and in the process of serving breakfast. Over the last couple of days several large wooden tables had been constructed. The camp now looked very similar to the old Raven camp. When I made my way toward the tables, a hush fell across the space. My heart picked up. Everybody was staring at me.

I swallowed hard and pushed my hair out of my face, self-conscious. The hush remained for what felt like several long minutes. A man I didn't know walked up to me.

"Thank you, your highness," he said.

"Please, that's not necessary." I waved him away. "I didn't do anything special. I just did what was right. Anybody else would do the same."

"No," he said, "most people do what is easy."

I bit my lip. Being unused to recognition, I wasn't sure how to react to this. So I smiled at him and nodded once. He seemed satisfied with my reaction and returned to the people who had gathered around to watch.

Out of the corner of my eye I saw a group of people walking toward me. Turning, I saw Max and several sorcerers trailing behind him. My heart leapt at the prospect of seeing Ashton, but he was missing from the group. Saffron and Celeste were not among the entourage either. *That's strange.* Since I met her, Saffron had almost always been with me or Max. *I'm sure I'll see them soon.*

Max paused his progress but didn't really stop walking. "Did you eat yet?"

I shook my head.

"Have some breakfast then join us in the barn." He walked away without waiting for a response.

The circle of chairs had returned to the barn and were occupied by the sorcerers that had stayed to help the Ravens. There was only one empty chair, directly across from Max. The conversation broke as I took the empty chair in the circle.

Max lifted his chin in greeting, then addressed the sorcerers sitting around us. "We'll continue that conversation later. For now, let's hear Etta's report from the incident last night."

I glanced around the room and clenched the sides of my chair with my fingers. Where were Saffron, Ashton, and Celeste? They were usually at these meetings. "Where is everybody?"

Max looked around the room. "This is the senior council for sorcery. Everybody's here who needs to be here."

I noticed Master Flanders smiling at me and I loosened the grip on my chair a bit. "Where should I start?"

Max rested his chin on his fist. "Start at the point where you disobeyed me and came to the fight."

I pressed my lips together. "You mean the part where you lied to me?"

He narrowed his eyes. "Plans changed. You disobeyed. Continue."

I wanted to yell at him. He was the one who changed the plans, not me. After everything we'd been through, how could he still treat me like I couldn't take care of myself? *Fighting with him now isn't going to fix anything.* I pulled my shoulders back, sitting straight up in the chair. "After I realized that I was missing the battle, I asked Celeste to teleport us to the inn. She was able to get us there and then we joined you."

Max nodded. "Go on."

I looked around the circle. The faces of the sorcerers around me were impassive. Master Flanders offered me a small smile and nod. I swallowed then continued. "Celeste went to join the line and I looked for the Reapers. I could feel them, so I knew they were close."

"You could feel them?" Madame Lyndsey asked.

"Yes," I shrugged, "can't you?"

She lifted her eyebrows. "No, Etta."

I looked up and my eyes met Max. He eyed me suspiciously. My palms started to feel sweaty.

"When I finally saw them, none of you could use your magic. I could still feel mine so I went out to meet them. To try to protect everybody."

Max leaned forward in his chair. "What happened after the Reapers? We couldn't see you for a few minutes."

I glanced at Master Flanders. He nodded at me. I took a deep breath. "That's when the king came to me."

Gasps filled the room around me and I winced. *They really hadn't seen it.*

"That's not possible," Max said. "The wards should keep him from you."

"They only prevent the king from touching her. Not from speaking to her," Master Flanders said.

I hesitated a moment before saying the next part. The part I knew would cause the most controversy. "He told me he'd kill everybody if I didn't agree to meet him for dinner at his castle tonight."

Max slammed his fist on the arm of the chair and shot up to standing. "Absolutely not."

I stood up across from him, fists clenched. "You know I have to do this."

"It's a trap," Madame Lyndsey said. "You have to know that. He might not be able to touch you, but he could have the Reapers waiting for you."

I shook my head. "I don't think it is. You weren't there. He was right next to me and I couldn't move. I was too worn out from using magic. If he wanted me dead, I'd be dead right now."

Max started pacing inside the circle of chairs.

"Max, I have to do this." I was surprised how strong my voice sounded. "Besides, he said I could bring a guest - it just can't be you."

Max paused and glared at me. I took a step back.

"You know she's right. The king clearly wants something from her or he would have had her killed last night." Master Flanders stood next to Max. "I think you need to let her do this. She's proven she can defend herself."

Max sank back into his chair and rubbed his eyes with his thumb and index finger. "This is not going as we planned."

"It's a war, Max," Master Flanders said. "Last night was a battle. A battle that we can claim a tentative victory thanks to her."

Max ran his hands through his hair and settled his gaze on me. It had softened at Master Flanders' words. He nodded. "Okay. You can go."

A wave of both relief and horror flooded me. I lifted my chin. "I'm taking Ashton." My eyes held Max's and I didn't blink.

"You two work well together," he said. "You can go find him and let him know." He waved a hand at me.

I took one last look at the sorcerers sitting around the circle then inclined my head toward Max and left the barn.

*****

"Are you sure you want to do this?" Ashton asked for the third time.

Every time he asked me, my resolve crumbled a little. "Please stop asking that. You know I have to do this."

He sighed and stretched his hand out to mine. I took hold.

"Be careful. Get out of there right away if you sense anything is off," Max called.

A small crowd had gathered to see us off to our meeting with the king.

I smiled at them. "We'll be fine." I squeezed Ashton's hand. "Let's go."

He squeezed my hand in return and gray smoke started to circle my feet. I felt my feet leaving the ground as I hovered in nothingness. Next time I set them down, we'd be standing in front of the king's castle. I tried not to think about the knots in my stomach as my feet found solid ground.

As the smoke cleared I saw the domineering fortress that was the king's home. It was a massive stone structure. At the top of the castle, I saw small dots that must be archers guarding the entryway. The tingle of magic flowed through my entire body. This place was overflowing with magic. I let out a breath as I failed to feel the coldness of the Reapers. They weren't here.

Ashton's hand was still in mine. A shiver moved through him, though he faced forward without a glimmer of fear in his eyes. I let go of his hand, took a deep breath, and forced a half smile. It was the best I could do. His mouth was set in a line of repressed worry.

"It's going to be fine," I said. What had I done by bringing Ashton here? I'd never forgive myself if something happened to him. Then again, I doubt he would have wanted me to bring anybody else.

We stared at the castle for several minutes, unmoving. A loud clicking noise punctuated the silence and I flinched. The drawbridge started to descend. *He must know we're here.* I took a tentative step forward. When Ashton followed me, I picked up my pace.

The bridge was lined with armed guards. A chill ran through me as I walked through the line of guards. Their eyes followed us as we walked but they didn't advance.

A young woman with bright red hair waited at the end of the drawbridge. She wore a long flowing black gown and stood with her hands clasped in front of her. She curtsied low to us as we approached. "Welcome, your highness." She drew out the words as she spoke.

I didn't attempt to smile at her and did not return the greeting.

When she realized that I wasn't going to speak, she spread her arms wide. "We are so pleased to have you in our home."

She wasn't much older than me and I wondered if she was the king's wife. I wasn't sure if I felt bad for her or if I hated her.

"Please, follow me. The king has set up dining in the great hall." She walked toward a massive archway, her long dress flowing over the cobblestones.

The archway led into a large, dark stone hallway. There were no windows so the only light came from the sconces on the wall. I hugged my arms across my chest. The temperature dropped inside these thick walls, it was freezing. Ashton walked right next to me. His fingers brushed against my hip every so often. I was grateful for his closeness as we strode further inside the king's fortress.

We made several turns and passed closed doors before finally reaching another massive archway. When we crossed through, the temperature rose and I was no longer cold. This room was lined with windows, making it almost cheerful. Four large fireplaces, one on each wall, roared with bright flames.

The king was seated at a long table but rose when he saw us enter. He smiled at me as if we were old friends and spread his arms wide. "Etta, so nice of you to join me."

In the darkness of our meeting last night, I couldn't make out the details of his face. He was younger than I expected him to be. He had brown hair with no signs of gray and a full brown beard. He was about the same height as Max, making him on the tall side of average. He was likely muscular under the leather armor he wore. His face was surprisingly friendly, with warm brown eyes and a full mouth. *This is the man who killed my whole family.* I clenched my fists at my sides.

Forcing myself to be civil, I inclined my head slightly in the faintest of bows.

He extended his hand, palm up. I hesitated before extending my own. He took hold of my hand and lowered his face, giving me a soft kiss. A wave of nausea rolled through me from his touch. All of this pretending and formality was making me uncomfortable. It took every bit of my willpower not to pull away. *I'm in his home surrounded by his guards. Now is not the time to upset him.*

I risked a quick glance at Ashton. His face was red, his mouth pulled into a tight line.

The king noticed the shift in my gaze and looked at Ashton for the first time. "Who is your friend?"

Trying not to show my repulsion, I pulled my hand back as slowly as I could. I gestured to Ashton. "This is my friend, Ashton White."

The king smiled. "Welcome to my home, Ashton. Won't

you please, both of you, join me for dinner?"

We followed him to the grand table, covered in food. Cautiously, I sat in the chair he indicated for me to sit at. I was seated at his right, with Ashton on my right.

Servants arrived and they silently filled goblets with wine and piled our plates with food. I stared at the meal in front of me and kept my hands in my lap.

"Please, eat." The king took a sip of his wine. "I promise if I wanted you dead, you'd be dead already."

Hesitantly, I took a sip and nibbled on some of the food. The king smiled and ate his own food.

We sat there in awkward silence for a long time, the king happily eating, while I tried to look like I was eating. Ashton's hands remained in his lap.

Finally, the king set down his fork and waved his plate away. A servant came and collected it. Then they retrieved mine and Ashton's plates. I was grateful that the farce of dinner was over.

"Etta, I can see that you are a woman who wants to get straight to the heart of the matter." The king folded his hands on the table in front of him. "As I'm sure you realized, I do have ulterior motives for asking you here today."

My pulse quickened. *Of course you do.* What could he want from me? He's been trying to kill me since I was a baby. Other than my death, what could he want? My hands were sweaty and I tucked them on my lap under the table.

"I have to admit, I didn't think you'd have such control over your power so quickly. I suppose that goes to show that one of your talents can excel even without formal training." He laughed to himself, a low rumbling noise. "While I have been trying to kill you, you have developed quite the following. There are songs about you spreading across all of Illaria."

My brow furrowed. *What does that have to do with anything?* Max seemed just as irritated about this as the king. Who cared if a few peasants were singing songs about a girl who made lightning?

He laughed again. "Why, you've become rather popular with

the people in the last few weeks. So if I were to kill you, imagine how bad that would make me look." He took a long draw from his goblet.

"When it was just your brother, I didn't care about those pesky Ravens. They didn't stand a chance, but you..." He set down his goblet.

"Why me?" I asked. "Why didn't you try to kill my brother? You had people on the inside the whole time, it would have been so easy."

He narrowed his eyes. "He didn't tell you, did he?"

"Didn't tell me what?" I asked.

The king's smile almost looked sympathetic. "I didn't do anything about the Ravens because they were harmless with him in charge. They gave people false hope, kept them occupied. When they found you, the hope became real."

"I don't understand."

"You are the heir to the Aqualine throne. If people didn't believe it before, once you started using water elements, they couldn't deny it. Your brother only has a small claim on the throne, which is really only valid if you were to give up your claim."

"Just because our parents weren't married when he was born?" My voice was high. Was the king playing tricks on me? Trying to confuse me?

"That's what he told you? I wondered what lies he had been sharing to gain his followers." The king shook his head. "No, my dear. Your brother has no right to the throne at all. Unless you offer it to him." He paused for a moment.

What is he talking about?

"While it's true that you share the same father, you do not share the same mother. His mother was a childhood romance your father had years before he even met your mother. Max was raised by his mother away from the throne. Hidden so as to not ruin your father's reputation. So, no, my dear, I never needed to seek out your brother. He was never a threat to my throne. You, on the other hand. You are the real thing."

I stared at the king, wide-eyed.

A grin spread across the king's face. "How mad was your brother when I ended your engagement to the Sardinian prince? You do realize, that under Illarian law, you'd be giving up your claim on the throne if you married a foreign prince. Why do you think your brother wanted you married so badly?"

I felt like the wind had just been knocked from my lungs. The pieces to the puzzle were sliding into place. *How had I not seen this before?* In my mind, it all made sense, but I didn't want to believe it. I turned to Ashton. "Is this true?"

Ashton's eyes were just as wide as mine. "I don't know."

The king's smile was poisonous. "I have no reason to lie to you. You know it's the truth."

I swallowed. My eyes searched the room for something to take my mind off of what the king told me. *Max has been lying to me.* I didn't want to believe it.

"Go ahead," the king said. "You know the spell to see if I'm being truthful, don't you? My old teacher would have taught you that right away. Master Flanders has always been the paranoid type."

My breath hitched. *Master Flanders taught the king how to use magic?* How was it possible that I was learning magic from the same man that taught such a monster?

"I take it from your expression that I was correct in my assumption. I'll wait." He leaned back in his chair. "Unless you need a review on the spell."

My chest tightened and I crossed my arms over my chest. *I didn't need his help.* I inhaled and moved my fingers in my lap to cast the truth spell. I thought about how to phrase my question carefully. I'd only get one. "Do Max and I share the same mother and father?"

The king locked his eyes on mine. "No."

Is he lying? Maybe he knew some way around this spell. *But if he's telling the truth will it matter anyway? Who would believe me? I need something that I can take back with me.* Some type of common knowledge information that would prove this was true. My leg brushed against Ashton's as I fidgeted in my chair. A momentary flicker of heat transferred to my leg. Ashton felt like he was on fire. Was he holding it inside him waiting, just in case? *That's it.*

"Water." I stared at the king. "Everybody said my father aligned with water. What was my mother?"

"She never told me specifically, but I believe it was air," the king said.

"It can't be," I said. "She must have been fire."

The king shook his head. "My poor girl, they really have kept things from you, haven't they? The entire royal family in Gallia aligns with Air. They've never had a fire sorcerer in their line. You can ask your Gallic friend. She'll tell you."

My eyes widened for a moment. "How do you know about my friends?"

"You were in town with a Gallic girl. I assume she's a friend." He interlaced his fingers and rested his hands on the table.

I slumped back in the chair. *Of course he knew about Celeste. He's had people watching me whenever possible.*

"I still don't understand what I'm doing here," I said.

He leaned forward. "Don't you see? They're lying to you. They want to keep you from reaching your true potential. Your half-brother, he's a fire sorcerer. While that is rare, it's not as special as the power you wield."

If the king was telling me the truth about my mother, there was no way Max could be my brother. Why had they been keeping so much from me? I would have supported his claim on the throne even if he had told me he had a different mother. I never wanted to rule. "Who was his mother?"

The king gave me a bored look. "Her name was Lady Gracelyn. She was a frequent visitor to the castle. Your father and she grew up together and they fell in love. They hoped to marry one day. But Lady Gracelyn was already spoken for. When she fell pregnant, she refused to say who the baby belonged to. Your father arranged for her to hold titles and land in her own name. It was clear who the father was and her newfound wealth made it so her betrothed could overlook her pregnancy."

"Why are you telling me all of this?" I asked.

"Because I want to end this rebellion that is starting in my kingdom. To do that, I'll need your help."

My eyes narrowed and I scoffed. "Why would I ever help you? You killed my family. You've been trying to kill me."

The king pushed his chair back from the table and stood in a single fluid motion. "Can you imagine how much power we would have together? How much power our children could have?"

My blood went cold, and it wasn't from Reapers. *How dare he.* "Do you seriously think I'd help you?" I was yelling now. "You're the last person I would ever help. The day you die, I'll celebrate."

He leaned across the table toward me, unflinching at my words. "We'd be unstoppable together. You could rule, as is your birthright, at my side."

I pressed myself back against my chair, trying to get further away from him. *How could he even suggest such a thing?* "I never even wanted to rule. I didn't want any of this."

"You were born to rule, Etta. Power like yours does not belong to the masses. It belongs on the throne." He held his hand out to me.

My lip curled and I turned away from him. The thought of helping him was nauseating.

"Etta, my patience won't last forever." His voice was stern. "Your place is here, as my queen."

I pushed my chair back and stood. "I'd never marry you." My words came out through clenched teeth. *I have to get out of here.* If I gave in to him, every sacrifice ever made for me was worthless. All of those deaths meant nothing. I thought of my grandmother, of my parents and all the others who gave their lives to see the end of his reign.

"You will." He snapped his fingers.

A guard came through the archway with a frail woman in his arms. I gasped. *Grandmother.*

"If you ever want to see your grandmother again, you'll be my bride."

I looked at the woman who had raised me. A lump rose in the back of my throat and my eyes burned with tears. How many times had I imagined this? The chance to have just one more conversation with her? The chance to tell her goodbye.

"Wilona?" she coughed. "Is that you?"

I couldn't speak, my throat was too tight.

"Wilona, I hear you are getting married. I'm so happy for you." The small figure clasped her hands together.

I froze. My grandmother was dead. I watched her die. *This isn't my grandmother.* I glared at the king, my eyes locked on his. I watched as the triumphant smile from his mouth spread to his eyes. Without breaking eye contact, I reached my hand behind me and found Ashton's hand. I squeezed hard three times in a row.

The king's eyes flashed and he yelled out to me as the gray smoke consumed us.

CHAPTER 31

When my feet touched solid ground I collapsed into a fit of sobbing. *He is using my grandmother's body.* All of the pain, anger and fear of the last few days consumed me and I shook with tears.

Ashton wrapped his arms around me and held me, stroking my hair. How did this happen? How did I end up as the pawn in Max's plan for the throne? How did I end up facing the same problem with the king? Why did everybody want to marry me off for their own power? Wasn't I good enough on my own?

When I finally ran out of tears I pushed the damp hair away from my face and wiped my eyes. "I'm sorry," I said.

He smoothed back my hair and pulled me in for a hug. "Don't be. You have nothing to be sorry for. You are the strongest, bravest person I know."

I wiped away a few stray tears on my cheeks and took a deep breath. *I am strong.* It was time to start making my own decisions. How did I go about doing that? I pulled out of the hug and looked around. We weren't at the barn. It was dark but in the dim moonlight I noticed that we were surrounded by trees. "Where are we?"

Ashton smiled. "Back at the old Raven camp. I thought you could use a moment to breathe before we face Max."

The tension fell from my shoulders and I exhaled. "Thank you." I closed my eyes and focused on the sound of the wind in the trees. I missed that sound.

"Come on." Ashton took my hand and led me through the trees. I stumbled in the darkness but he seemed to have every step memorized. Sadness washed over me when I remembered that this place had been his home. Now it was a ghost town, just like my village.

In the shadows and shifting light of the moon I started to make out a small structure. A roof on stilts. We were at the archery training area. My heart sank. *Master Edward won't be here. He'll never be here again.*

Ashton made a tiny fireball in his palm, illuminating the space. My unfinished bow was still in the vise. In the center of the bow, Master Edwards had carved a delicate Ouroboros with waves that spread to the ends. I put my hand over my mouth and choked back tears. Once I pulled myself together, I traced the intricate carvings with my finger tips.

"I was hoping he'd left it for you," Ashton said. "I didn't know he added the carving. It's perfect."

I nodded and loosened the vise to remove the curved wood. I held it to my chest, hugging it. *Thank you.* It was like Master Edward was still looking out for me. I thought about his lessons, how he demonstrated such faith in me. I smiled. "Remember when he caught us kissing in here?" *Had that really only been a week ago?* So much had happened since then. My relationship with Ashton was so new, but it was as if we had always been together.

Ashton smiled. "I feel like we've climbed a mountain since then."

"And we have more to climb," I said.

Ashton reached out for the half finished bow in my hand. He held it, running his fingers along the carving. "You know, Master Edward was one of the few people that always spoke his mind. Used to drive Max crazy." Ashton paused. "He never called Max by a formal title."

I looked up at Ashton. "Really? He was the only one who ever used a formal title on me. Called me *Your Highness.* Said it was the same thing he called my father." A shiver ran through me. *He knew all along.* "He was trying to help me figure it out.

The title, the bits of information about my father. He was trying to help me."

Ashton passed the bow back to me and started walking around the archery shed. He lifted and lowered the flame in his hand as he inspected every inch of the space. *He's looking for something.*

I carefully propped the bow against the workbench and started looking as best I could, though I had no idea what for.

"When I was a kid," Ashton said, "Master Edward used to make scavenger hunts for us. Gave us clues that took us from one place to another all around the camp. Maybe he left you something before they packed up the camp."

I straightened. *A clue.* Picking up the bow, I ran my fingers along the carving again. This time taking in the details better. Ashton noticed what I was doing and walked over to offer more light. With the flame right over the bow, I could now make out a few subtle details in the wave design that I had missed. There was a tiny owl carved into the waves at the top of the bow. I smiled, remembering when I told him about the little owl I liked to visit. Maybe this was more than just a decoration. "It's at the aviary."

Ashton extinguished his flame. "I'm hoping we're the only ones here but it's better to be careful." He offered his hand and we headed for the aviary.

As we walked, the voices of the men who had been plotting against me replayed in my mind. My stomach twisted and I gripped Ashton's hand tighter. They weren't here now, but it was hard to shake that feeling of being so vulnerable. *You're not that girl anymore. You won't have to run away and hope somebody else can save you. You can solve your own problems now.*

My meeting with the king increased my problems. I knew what I should do, what I was born to do, but how was I supposed to become a leader? I wasn't prepared. We reached the aviary without incident, the only noises coming from the wind in the trees.

Ashton closed the door behind us and ignited a small fireball. The light flooded the room, casting strange shadows.

The feather covered floor and lingering smell were all that remained of the birds who had called this place home. Ashton started to shift the feathers around with his feet.

"Don't bother," I said. "If he left us something, I know where it will be." There's only one place he would have hidden something. The top corner, where my favorite owl had sat. "Give me a boost?"

Ashton released his fireball into the center of the room where it floated on its own. Then he interlaced his fingers and I used the makeshift stirrup to climb to the middle shelf. I balanced on the shelf, Ashton supporting me from behind while I felt around on the top corner. My fingers brushed against what felt like a thick branch. Grabbing it in my hand, I hopped down.

The branch was a cleverly carved cylinder that opened to reveal a rolled up piece of parchment. It said: *Annalise Sutton, Greenville.*

My shoulders sunk. *Another clue.* "Do you know what this means?"

Ashton read the scroll and frowned. "No, and it's going to have to wait. We can't head out to Greenville right now. It's too dangerous and we have other things we have to take care of first. They'll be waiting for us at the barn." He handed me back the scroll.

I inserted it into the cylinder and closed it up, clasping it tightly in my fist. "Now what?"

"Time to go back and tell them the truth," Ashton said.

"And what about Max?" I asked.

He shrugged his shoulders. "He's your brother. That's up to you, but you should be queen."

"I know." I looked at the feathers on the ground and pushed them around with my foot for a moment. "I don't want to send him away. He's the only family I have."

"Then don't," Ashton said.

"Do you think he'd agree to help me? If I tell him I want to rule?" I asked.

"I don't know," he said flatly.

My shoulders dropped. "I don't know if I can do this." My voice was tight, barely audible.

He tilted my chin up and stared into my eyes. "You can do this."

"I never wanted this, you know," I said.

"I know. But this is bigger than you. This is about the people of this kingdom. *Your* people. You were born for this. You can do this."

I swallowed. "I can't do this without you."

He smiled at me. "You won't have to. I'm not going anywhere. I'll follow you anywhere."

I ran my thumb over the bow I was holding. Master Edward believed in me. Ashton believed in me. Even the king himself saw me as a threat. *Ashton's right.* This wasn't just about me. This was bigger than. While I stood here in safety, more and more people were dying. *My* people. "Do you think the people will follow me?"

He raised his eyebrows. "Without a doubt. I wasn't even looking for you and you won me over, how difficult can it be to win over people who are searching for hope?"

I smiled. "You make it sound like it's going to be easy."

"Nothing worth doing is easy," he said. "But it can be done. You are the rightful queen of Illaria and you belong on the throne. I believe that. This is just the beginning."

I reached deep down inside of myself to pull out any strength I could find. I was going to need it when I faced Max. He wasn't going to step aside gracefully. "I'm ready. Let's go reclaim my throne."

"One last thing." He smiled then pulled me in for a kiss.

*****

A large fire burned in the center of the camp. Nobody was asleep despite the late hour. I walked in behind Ashton. People stood when they saw us and watched us silently. I tried to smile but struggled to hold any expression on my face for too long.

In the barn, sorcerers paced or stood in clusters around the room. Max was sitting in a chair next to Saffron. Both of them stood when they saw us. My stomach clenched as I realized what I was going to have to say.

Saffron ran to hug me. "Thank the gods. Are you alright?"

I nodded. "I'm not hurt, but the king isn't happy with me."

Max scowled at me, his face was dark. *He knows what the king told me.*

The other sorcerers in the room surrounded me, eyes wide in anticipation.

I tried to stand tall despite my shaking hands. "The king told me something I never knew. Something that was hidden from me." I locked my blue eyes on Max's dark ones. *How had I never seen it before?* The signs were there. I took a deep breath and let it out slowly. Every eye in the room was on me. "Max isn't the rightful king. He's my half brother. I am the only true heir to the throne."

"No," Saffron called out. "He was born out of wedlock, but you have the same parents. Don't you, Max?" She stared at him.

Everybody turned their gaze on Max. He laughed. "Can you imagine her as our queen? Can you imagine what it would be like to have a girl on the throne?"

Saffron took a step back from him. "You lied to me?" Her voice broke.

"I did what I had to for Illaria. My father was the king. Why does it matter who my mother was? I am the one who can bring back the greatness of this land."

I took a step toward him, my cheeks felt like they were on fire. "No. You can't. You don't care about the people of Illaria. You only care about yourself. Your reign is over."

He moved until his face was inches from mine. "You aren't going to take this away from me."

My fingers tingled and magic shot through my body. My hands felt hot. I looked down to see small orange flames kissing my hands. The fire played in my palms. How was I doing that? Max looked down and backed away.

I forced myself to take deep breaths and called the magic

back, closing my hands around the flames. "Help me, Max. We can do this together."

He shook his head. "I should have let the king kill you when he found you."

The sorcerers in the room started to shuffle around, moving away from a possible battle.

My eyes stung. *How could he say that to me?* "We're still family." I sounded like a little girl. I cleared my throat, forcing myself to find the voice that Lady Genevieve would want me to use. "You're the only family I have and I want you by my side, but this is my path, my throne."

He glared at me and looked around the room. Nobody said a word. He balled his hands into fists. "You can't do this. You'll fail as a queen. You won't even make it past the king."

Master Flanders stepped in between us. "She did tonight."

"That's only because of the protection she has." His upper lip was raised in a snarl. "Without that, she's nothing."

"I don't think she's nothing. She will be a wise and compassionate ruler. You'd do well to heed her request to join her," Master Flanders said. Then he walked around me and stood behind me. Madame Lyndsey and Celeste crossed the room to stand by my side.

A rush of gratitude filled me. I felt stronger with them behind me. "We can still do this together, Max." My voice was clear and calm.

"I won't be second to you again. My mother raised me to be king. You weren't supposed to be born. Your mother was barren. For all I know, you're a bastard just like me."

His words felt like a hand squeezing my heart. "How can you say such things? You know all I want is what is best for the kingdom."

"You don't know the first thing about ruling." He laughed, a cold high sound. "I'll go for now, but you'll be begging me to come back before you know it. Or you'll be dead and they'll come to find me." He looked around the room again. "Ashton, let's go."

Ashton had been silently standing behind me the whole

time. He stepped in front of me and faced Max. "No, Max. You've lost. It's time to do the right thing."

"You're choosing her over me?" Max spat. "I taught you everything. And you give it all up for a pretty face." Max shook his head. "You know she'll drop you as soon as she gets what she wants. You can't trust women."

"Is that how you feel? What about me? Our 15 years together?" Saffron said. Her eyes were red and her cheeks blotchy from tears. "This is everything we could have hoped for. You don't have to be king. You can still help the kingdom and we can be together. Wouldn't that be enough? Aren't I enough?" She placed a hand on his shoulder. "Why don't we go to your tent. We can talk about it more tomorrow."

Max pushed her hand away. His gaze didn't even soften at the sight of her tears. "That might have been enough once. I'm not a love sick teenager, anymore. I've outgrown you. I moved on."

He shook his head and turned to Ashton. "Just looking at you makes me sick. I thought you were smart enough to learn from my mistakes, but you fell into the same trap I did."

He spun around and took a few steps. "Anybody who wants to be on the side of the future king is welcome to join me." Three sorcerers dressed in black robes followed behind him.

Max turned and stared right into my eyes. "She'll be dead in a week. When the king is done with her, and you're begging me to return, maybe I'll come back." He pointed to Ashton. "When you've had your fill of her, you know where to find me."

In a cloud of smoke, Max and his followers were gone.

My heart was breaking. He was my brother. He betrayed me, but he was the only family I had. I felt like I was moving in slow motion. I blinked back a few tears, trying to hide my emotions from the room full of sorcerers. Everybody was watching me. I bit the inside of my cheek to keep the tears back. *Be strong. Say something.* I was trying to gather my thoughts when I heard commotion outside of the barn. The Ravens camped outside were making a lot of noise. My whole body tensed. *Has the king found us?*

I searched for Ashton as I made my way toward the barn doors. He wasn't standing behind me anymore. *He must already be outside.* I broke into a run, the other sorcerers at my heels. When I pushed open the doors, I was greeting by a hundred people who had formed a semicircle in front of the barn. Ashton was standing in the center. He dropped into a kneel and lowered his head "Your Highness," he said.

The people standing around him all dropped to one knee. I could hear the rustle of robes behind me and turned to see that all of the sorcerers had done the same.

My throat burned as the tears rose to my eyes. I swallowed and found my voice. "Please rise."

They stood and two hundred eyes watched me. Gratitude flooded me and I placed my hand over my heart. "Thank you, thank you all," I said.

Ashton lifted his fist in the air and shouted. "Long live the queen!" A chorus of voices called out in unison, "Long live the queen."

ABOUT THE AUTHOR

Dyan Chick is a high school teacher who lives in Colorado with her family. As a child, she spent many days reading, writing her own stories, and living in make-believe worlds. In seventh grade, she was given an award for most likely to publish a book. With this novel, she has fulfilled that prediction.

To find out about future books, sign up for the mailing list at
www.dyanchick.com

This book was published independently. One of the best ways to help support independent publishing is to leave an honest review. Please take a few minutes to share what you thought about this book by reviewing it on Amazon and Goodreads.

ACKNOWLEDGMENTS

Thank you to my family, friends, and everybody who helped me take this book from dream to reality. I would not have completed it without the support of so many. To my husband, who listened to me talk about nothing but writing for months - and put up with me spending most of my free time alone, writing. To my family who acted as cheerleaders and early readers, especially Danielle, who is now my number one fan. To my mom, who likes to brag about me to everybody she meets. To the fabulous Nathan Lowell, who was one of my first readers - he helped me to get over the fear of putting my work out there for others to read. Thank you for that boost of confidence, Nathan.

Thank you to my incredible cover artist, Clarissa Yeo. Her work helped give life to the world I created. My editor, Laura Kingsley, did a fantastic job of pushing me to give depth to my story. Thank you to my proofreaders, Betty, Sarah, and Madi (my accidental proofreader).

Of course, I would not be here without my critique group. From that first meeting where Wiley circled all of my adverbs, to the day I finished my first draft they have been nothing but supportive. My Dragons, who let me lean on them when I'm having a bad day and put up with all of my big goals (2,000 words a day for 2017). I can't tell you how much you have helped me with this process. I am eagerly awaiting the day I get to read this page in your books.

Finally, thank you to my students, past, present, and future. There are pieces of you in my characters. You all have helped to shape the world I created. A place where women are strong. A place where creativity is valued. My characters are inspired by the strength you all have shown while facing things that would cause many adults to crumble. Know that you are valued and you deserve all of the wonderful things that life can offer you, even if you have to walk through fire to reach it.

Made in the USA
San Bernardino, CA
09 June 2017